By JOHN R. PETRIE

The Quarterback's Crush

TIMOTHY AND WYATT MYSTERIES
Buried Secrets

Published by HARMONY INK PRESS
www.harmonyinkpress.com

BURIED SECRETS

JOHN R. PETRIE

Harmony Ink

Published by

HARMONY INK PRESS

5032 Capital Circle SW, Suite 2, PMB# 279, Tallahassee, FL 32305-7886 USA
publisher@harmonyinkpress.com • harmonyinkpress.com

Buried Secrets

Cover Art
http://www.tiferetdesign.com/
Cover content is for illustrative purposes only and any person depicted on the cover is a model.

Trade Paperback ISBN: 978-1-64405-304-1
Digital ISBN: 978-1-64405-303-4
Library of Congress Control Number: 2019903342
Trade Paperback published October 2019
v. 1.0

Printed in the United States of America
∞
This paper meets the requirements of
ANSI/NISO Z39.48-1992 (Permanence of Paper).

To my dad. Thank you for everything. You're my hero.
To Maria and Cara for always being there.

ACKNOWLEDGMENTS

THANKS TO Alisha Klauger and Christine DeLuna for reading early drafts and letting me know when I was on the right track and on the wrong one.

Thanks to the real Julia Madden for being my sister.

As always thanks to Danny, Drew, Justin, Matthew, Vita, Emma, and Carson, just because.

Many, many thanks to everyone at Harmony Ink and Dreamspinner: Anne, Dawn, Jaime, Janet, and everyone there. Thank you. Thank you. Thank you.

PROLOGUE

WYATT CORTLAND was sweating in the stifling heat, swinging the sledgehammer into the wall, working out his anger with every impact. His shirt was soaked, and he could hear the other two guys on the crew upstairs taking out the bathroom and the bedroom walls. They put him down in the living room because he was the new guy and there was only one window, meaning by the time they ended the workday, he'd be covered in sweat, dust, and grime. He didn't care, and he wiped his sweaty forehead with a sweaty forearm. Wyatt dropped the hammer on the floor and grabbed a piece of the wall.

Something square and dusty caught his eye. Leaning against a beam, it was covered in dirt and grime, and he stared at it for a moment. Wyatt bent down and pulled it out of the wall. It was a metal box, not too heavy, still locked and covered in dust. The hinges weren't rusted, just dirty. Wyatt could hear something moving around inside the box when he carefully shook it. More than one something. He'd heard stories about people finding hidden fortunes in walls. Money. Jewelry. He listened to the guys banging away upstairs and quietly left the house. He slipped the box underneath the passenger seat of his pickup truck. Wyatt took a minute to light up a quick cigarette and take a few drags before he went back in, picked up the hammer, and swung again.

CHAPTER ONE

SHERIFF BENJAMIN Mitchell picked up the smaller coffee cup from the holder and handed it to his son, who slouched in the passenger seat.

"Timmy, hold your coffee, please."

"Timothy." His son looked up and smiled at his dad. "If you don't call me by my name, how am I supposed to get anyone else to?"

"That's on you, kiddo. And sit up straight. You'll ruin your posture."

Timothy gulped from his coffee. "You have anything outstanding tonight, or are you actually coming home for dinner?"

"Ha. Ha. I love the fact that you're acting as if I'm an absentee father." The sheriff pulled over to the corner and put the car in Park. He waved at Lacey, Timothy's friend, and held out his fist for his son to bump. "I'll see you tonight. Are you getting a ride home?"

Timothy smiled. "Not sure. I'll see if I can get one of the track team guys to give me a lift."

His father shook his head and grunted. "Incorrigible." He sighed heavily. "I guess anyone's better than *Ethan*."

"Ethan wasn't too bad, Dad. Heh. Bad Dad."

"Laugh it up, Timmy." He reached into the back seat and handed Timothy a bag lunch. "He was a dick."

"Dad! Seriously, you're the worst."

"Yep," his father said as Timothy pushed the door open. He leaned over and raised his voice. "I'm the worst dad ever!"

Timothy laughed and waved as he headed toward his friend, Lacey Cutler. Lacey wore a pair of white shoes with red shoelaces and black pants. Her T-shirt was tie-dyed red and black, and she had red and black streaks in her brown hair to match. She was smiling and stayed sitting on the ledge of the steps as she waited for him.

"Hey, babe!" Timothy smiled at her and dropped his bag on the ground. "Nice look today, Little Edie." He'd named her after Edie Beale from the movie *Grey Gardens* shortly after they'd become friends because she always wore whatever she wanted, regardless of weather or fashion. They weren't exactly best friends, but he liked the fact that she didn't expect him to be the stereotype of a Gay Best Friend. Plus her aunt was gay, and they visited her over in Greenville as often as they could.

"Thanks," Lacey said as she pulled a bottle of water out of her bag. "My aunt did the streaks last night." She sipped from her bottle and pointed at his coffee cup. "You're going to kill yourself with that stuff, especially at this stage of your development. Boys your age are in special need of the proper nutrition."

"Nope," Timothy replied, downing his remaining coffee. "Not becoming a vegetarian."

"Do you have my stuff, Tim?" The new voice was deep and thick with a Southern accent.

"Timothy, Bo," he replied without looking around. "Not Tim. Not Timmy. Timothy. And yeah, I have your stuff."

"You're not in California anymore, Tim. You're in South Carolina, so now you're Tim." Bo Watterley crossed his arms over his chest and stared at Timothy. He was trying to be intimidating, but he wasn't any bigger than Timothy, so the sheriff's son simply smiled.

"I have it." He reached into his bag and pulled out a manila folder. "Here you go. You have my money?"

Bo grabbed the folder and sneered, a quick snort of air coming out of his mouth. "I'm getting this for free, faggot."

"Look, Bo. You hired me to run a background check on your parents. I did it. We agreed on seventy-five bucks. Pay me."

"Fuck off." Bo looked down at the file and started walking into the school.

"You can have that one for free, but the juicy stuff is in the second file." That sentence stopped Bo, like Timothy knew it would.

Bo walked back to Timothy and Lacey. "Yeah, right."

"Seriously. It's good stuff. You'll love it."

"You're lying." Bo dropped the folder he had on the ground and threw a punch at Timothy, who grabbed the hand long before it reached him. Timothy wrapped his own arm around Bo's elbow. He brought his leg behind Bo's and swept him down to the ground, bouncing his head on the dirt. Timothy shot his own fist forward, stopping barely an inch from Bo's nose.

"Nope. Not lying. Also, a brown belt in Goju karate. You want the new file. Pay me. I take a risk every time I run one of these reports and I don't like taking risks." He twisted Bo's arm slightly and heard a couple of girls snicker as they walked by the scene while Lacey calmly sipped from her water. "The price has gone up to one hundred. Due by tomorrow, at which time I will give you the rest of the report. Got it?"

"Shit. Shit. Shit. Yeah. Yeah. Fuck, man, you're gonna break my arm."

Timothy dropped Bo's arm and took a step back and away from him. "Good." He bent down and picked up his bag. "And don't use the word *faggot* again. It's rude and hateful. And, next time you do, I *will* break it."

Lacey jumped down off the ledge, and they walked into the school. "Rough."

"I know, but he's been on my case since day one. And I didn't really hurt him. Besides, I don't mind a little rough." He reached the door and held it open for her.

"Is there really a second file?"

"Of course." He didn't tell her that he still planned to hold back some information. There wasn't any need for Bo to know that his dad had an outstanding warrant in Alabama. Bo didn't need to know that his dad was a deadbeat who owed money to his first wife, who he never actually divorced and with whom he'd had a daughter. Timothy didn't like Bo, but he wasn't cruel. And even though he wasn't doing anything technically illegal, Timothy knew doing background checks on his schoolmate's parents wouldn't be looked upon kindly by his dad.

"You're strangely hard-core for a California gay dude," Lacey said as she stopped at the fountain by her locker and refilled her water bottle. "Sure you don't want to hydrate with the good stuff?"

"I'm sure. Coffee is sent from the heavens and water simply comes from the earth."

"You do realize coffee couldn't be made without water, right?"

"Don't ruin it for me." He walked with her to biochemistry and they sat down in the second row. "Hey, can you give me a ride home after school? My car's in the shop and Dad's going to be at work."

Lacey nodded, and they both looked up as Mr. Ridley walked into class, talking before he put his grade book and coat down. Lacey and Timothy had begun their bonding by being science nerds together, and both looked forward to science class and school in general. The day passed quickly, and by the time they walked into the cafeteria for lunch, the two of them were joined by a few other friends.

For being both the sheriff's son as well as openly gay, Timothy was actually mildly popular. He wasn't a bad looking guy. He had dark hair, short on the side and longer on the top. He also had a side business with a few of the girls at school, occasionally hacking into social media accounts to look for cheating boyfriends. The popular girls liked him and kept their boyfriends in check, making sure they didn't pick on the gay kid. The brown belt in karate he used on a couple of football players when they came after him earned him a grudging respect from the other boys. Mostly he and Lacey hung out and studied and sometimes drove the forty-five minutes to visit her aunt in the nearest "city" of Greenville. And Lacey wasn't like most of the other girls in school who thought having a gay friend was cool. She liked him for what he was and didn't expect gossip and clothing advice.

When the final bell rang and students practically ran for the doors, Timothy and Lacey took their time, not wanting to get caught in the small traffic jam as the cars all struggled to go home. By the time they got out to the parking lot, there were the teachers' cars and a few others, mostly belonging to the students in detention.

As they were walking toward Lacey's car, a door slammed and a deep voice called out.

"Hey!"

Pulling in a deep breath, Timmy turned around, thinking Bo was coming after them. He didn't see Bo. Instead he saw a big guy, someone who'd been in his homeroom class. When was it? Maybe two years ago, his first year here.

"Hey, you're Tim, right?"

"Timothy. Not Tim. Not Timmy."

"You remember me?" The guy's voice was deep, sort of raspy, and Timothy could smell the cigarette smoke from his clothes. He towered over Timothy and Lacey, at least six feet two to Timothy's five feet nine. And worse he had to outweigh Timothy by at least forty pounds. Timothy might be able to take him if he started a fight, but it wouldn't be easy, and if the guy got in too close, Timothy wouldn't stand a chance. "I'm Wyatt—"

"Right," Timothy interrupted, taking as much charge of the conversation as he could. "Wyatt Courtland, right? You were in my homeroom a few years ago."

"Yep. I gotta talk to you," Wyatt rumbled. He pushed the brim of his baseball cap back slightly, turned to Lacey, and shrugged. "Private like. Sorry."

Timothy's brow furrowed. Polite. How cynical was Timothy that this guy's being nice was setting off alarm bells? "About?"

"It's private. C'mon, Timothy. I gotta show you something, and then I'll drive you back here to pick up your car."

"I don't—"

"Please."

Timothy sighed. He turned to Lacey with a smile. "If my body turns up, remember that this guy"—he jerked his thumb at Wyatt—"was the last one to see me alive."

Lacey rolled her eyes. "Not funny."

Timothy turned to Wyatt. "Let's go. You can drive me home. My parents won't be back from work and my car's in the shop, so you don't have to drive me back here."

Timothy hoisted himself up into Wyatt's truck. Wyatt climbed into the driver seat and turned the key.

Wyatt looked over at Timothy, almost apologetically. "Sorry, I don't have AC." He leaned his arm on the doorframe and put the truck in drive.

"Um, Wyatt," Timothy said, trying not to stare at Wyatt's thick arm. "Seat belt."

"What?" Wyatt looked at Timothy as he stopped at the school's parking lot exit.

"Put your seat belt on, please. My dad's made me watch about a million car accident videos about people who don't wear their seat belts."

Wyatt sighed and half took his foot off the brake while he wrestled the seat belt into its lock. "Happy?" Wyatt had a half smile on his face.

"Ecstatic," Timothy replied. He looked over at Wyatt's big shoulder. "Nice tattoo." Timothy nodded at the yin-yang symbol he'd noticed on Wyatt's right arm.

"My dad was in the Navy after he dropped out of school. He went over to China for a little bit. Said it was all about balancing and stuff. I got it the day I turned eighteen. Seemed like something to do. Honor my dad and all that, right?"

"Right. Sure." They rode the rest of the way in silence.

TIMOTHY'S HOUSE was a small two-story red- and white-sided structure near enough to the center of town that his dad could get to work quickly and easily. The front yard was small but well kept. In the summer, his mom and dad sat on the porch with a beer or a glass of lemonade and waved at the people walking by. That was a little too small-town America for Timothy, so he generally stayed inside on hot summer nights, watching crime shows on TV and practicing his karate forms.

Timothy breathed a little sigh of relief when Wyatt pulled his truck into the driveway and turned it off. He wasn't too worried about Bo trying to get back at him, but he was always aware that even though the girls of small-town South Carolina might be fine with a gay friend, their parents and brothers weren't always as open-minded. Instead of leading Wyatt into the house, Timothy unlocked the gate in the fence and brought him out back. The backyard was barely bigger than the front, but it had a picnic table, and Timothy plopped down with his back to the house and dropped his bag on top of the table.

"So, Wyatt, what's going on?"

Wyatt set his backpack on the ground and looked around the yard. He put his hands on the table and then raised them and wiped them on his shirt. Timothy waited, impatient. He took in Wyatt's thick arms and broad shoulders coming out of a T-shirt, which had once had sleeves but were now cut off, maybe to allow more room. Timothy sighed. He was not going to fall for a pair of pretty eyes and big biceps again. Wyatt took his baseball cap off and ran a big hand through his too-long dirty blond hair, then put the hat back on.

"Can you help me?" Wyatt didn't look directly at Timothy as he was speaking. "I think I did something wrong."

"I can't fix a traffic ticket, Wyatt."

Wyatt reached down and grabbed his bag. He hoisted it up, and it clunked heavily on the table. He unzipped it and pulled out a dusty metal box. Wyatt put it in front of Timothy. "I found this."

Timothy looked at the lock and saw it was broken off. He frowned and looked up at Wyatt. "Did you do this?"

Wyatt shrugged. "It was locked."

Rolling his eyes, Timothy shook his head. He lifted the lid and carefully flipped it back. Inside the box Timothy saw a pile of papers and photographs. He picked up a few and looked at them. The top one was a photograph of a young teen, maybe thirteen or fourteen. Dark hair and eyes, thin, looking sad and a little scared. Next in the pile was a newspaper article. The date and the name of the newspaper were trimmed off the top, but the article had a slightly grainy black-and-white photo of the boy from the first photograph. The headline above the photo said: Bobby LaFleur, 14, Missing Since Tuesday.

Timothy frowned and looked at Wyatt. "Where did you find this?"

"Do I have to say?" Wyatt looked away, and his jaw clenched.

"If you want me to help you out, the first rule is: don't lie to me. The second is: don't hide anything from me. The third is: don't lie to me or hide anything from me."

"I found it in a wall."

"What?"

Wyatt finally looked up at Timothy's eyes. "Sometimes I do demolition for a friend's dad. If we find something in the house, he lets us keep it. As long as it's not a big pile of cash or drugs, he's cool with it." Wyatt scratched the back of his neck. "We're not all gonna get to go to a big, fancy college." His voice was defensive, and he cut off whatever he was going to say next. He paused and took a deep breath. "I know this kid. He's my age. Our age, Tim."

"Timothy."

"Right. Sorry. Timothy."

Timothy flipped through the rest of the pages. A few more photographs. One of the boy with no shirt on at a pool. A couple more articles, each one shorter than the one before. The last item sent a strange chill up Timothy's back. It was a poem written in a swirling, expressive, but precise cursive.

He keeps me safe at night and day
He keeps the cruel, cruel world at bay
He is strong and gentle and lovely and kind
He is always on my mind
But he hides
From himself
From me
From the world both here

And the world to be
Will he ever
Just be here?

"I knew him." Wyatt's voice was quiet.

Timothy looked up from the poem, across the top of which was written *I like your subject matter. Poetry should be personal, but the structure needs some more work. Extra credit if you rework it. TM.*

"Sorry, what?"

Wyatt nodded to the photos. "I knew him. Him and me, we're the same age. The last time I saw him was four years ago." Wyatt kept an eye on the photos and brought a hand down on top of the pile. "I knew him." He stood up and rubbed his face. "You mind if I smoke?"

Timothy shook his head, seeing Wyatt was close to anger. No, not anger. More of an overwhelming something else. He opened his mouth to say something sarcastic but decided against it and went to the steps to pull out the small bucket of dirt his parents kept for the cigarette and cigar smokers who came by. So far, it was only Wyatt and Deputy Mike. He crossed the small yard to where Wyatt was standing, flicking his lighter until the cigarette caught. Wyatt took a deep drag and exhaled heavily. As Timothy stood up from dropping the cigarette bucket at Wyatt's feet, the two of them locked eyes. They stared for a few seconds and Timothy felt uncomfortable, standing in front of Wyatt, startled at how much bigger he actually was. Wyatt's stare wasn't intrusive; it was almost curious.

Timothy swallowed and broke the silence. "So, what do you need my help with, Wyatt?"

"I thought it was obvious," Wyatt said with a smile. "I want you to find him."

"What?" Timothy stuttered. "I'm not Batman, Wyatt. If you found this, we can show Dad and—"

"No!" Wyatt's voice was sharp, and even though he didn't advance toward Timothy, he still took a step back, away from the bigger man. "Sorry," Wyatt said, apologizing quickly. "No. We can't tell your dad." Wyatt stepped over to the table, cigarette balanced in one hand, and stuffed the pages into his backpack.

"Wyatt." Timothy smiled carefully, and without realizing it, he reached out to gently touch Wyatt's arm before he stopped himself. "Dad will have a ton of resources I don't have. I'm a student, not a cop." Timothy smirked and spoke under his breath. "As my dad keeps reminding me."

"What?"

"Nothing." Timothy shrugged, paused for a second, and then narrowed his eyes. "Is there a reason you don't want me to tell my dad? You said you did something wrong?"

"What? No. No way would I hurt Bobby. He was... he was a friend, and I wouldn't hurt him. I swear it. I meant... I don't know what I meant." Wyatt dropped the cigarette in the bucket but didn't grind it out, and the two of them watched the last of the smoke curl in the air. "Do you think he's okay?"

Timothy looked away for a minute before he found himself able to look at Wyatt. "It's hard to say. To be honest, despite what TV shows say, if this was a kidnapping, those are pretty rare, and pretty likely to be solved. If he ran away, well, I know lots of times where runaways get in contact with friends, even if it's only to say they're okay. You haven't gotten any hang-ups or anything on your cell phone, right? No weird texts?"

Wyatt shook his head. "Nope. Nothing like that." Wyatt sat down at the picnic table, facing Timothy, who was still standing by the bucket. "You sound like one."

"One what?" Timothy picked up the bucket and looked at Wyatt. "Do you want another one?"

Wyatt shook his head. Timothy noticed a bead of sweat falling down Wyatt's neck. "You sound like a cop. Is it what you want? To be a cop?"

"Not according to my dad." Timothy rolled his eyes and put the bucket back down. "I'm not"—he raised his fingers in air quotes—"right for the job. I guess it doesn't matter what I want."

"So help me anyway. Prove to your dad that he's wrong."

Timothy's mouth curved up in a smile. "You're smarter than you let on."

Wyatt smiled back, and Timothy saw a row of bright white. The cigarettes hadn't begun to yellow his teeth yet.

Timothy shook his head, thinking Wyatt had won the genetic jackpot. "I'll think about it. Let you know in a couple of days, okay? It's the best I can offer right now."

Wyatt nodded. "Want me to leave everything with you?"

Timothy nodded back.

Wyatt passed him the papers and headed toward the gate. He stopped right next to Timothy, placing his hand on Timothy's arm.

Wyatt's hand was rough and callused, bigger than Timothy would have imagined. "Thanks, Timothy."

Timothy waved in response as Wyatt walked into the driveway and out to his truck.

CHAPTER TWO

TIMOTHY HAD finished almost all of his homework and was stirring a bunch of vegetables into a bowl of eggs, when the phone rang.

He picked it up and could hear a car horn on the other end of the receiver. "Get out of the way, jerkwad!"

"Belle?" Timothy set the eggs aside, pulled open the refrigerator, and grabbed the butter.

"Hey, squirt! What's up?"

"I don't know," he replied. "You called me. And is Mom seriously okay with you using the phone while you drive?"

"Mom is sitting here, holding the phone, and I'm driving in LA, so I'm supposed to be on the phone."

"Hi, Mom." He leaned against the counter. "How's California?"

"Hi, honey." Timothy could hear the edge in his mother's voice, which meant his sister had been driving like a maniac. "How are you?"

"I'm fine, Mom. Hey, when you come home, can you bring me some cookies from the place on Glendale?"

"I have a box for you already."

"You're the best mom ever. How's school, Belle?"

"It's fine, squirt. Mom and I had quite a weekend, but my classes start back up tomorrow. We're headed for a big dinner tonight before I put her on the plane."

"You can tell me the truth. You miss me, don't you?"

Belle laughed. "Yeah, sure. You're a treat." The two of them got along pretty well, actually, though they'd had some tension years ago because she'd been the one to introduce him to Ethan. "How's hot and swampy South Carolina?"

"It's made a little duller by your absence," he replied, his voice dry. A car door slammed in the driveway. "I think Dad's home." Timothy pulled a large pan out of the oven and started the burner. He dropped a small pat of butter in the middle, then stuck his head out of the kitchen and looked toward the front door. His father walked in and took his hat off, then tossed it on the couch and looked up at his son. "Mom and Belle."

Timothy spoke into the receiver. "Love you, Belle. Love you, Mom. See you tomorrow. Study hard, Belle. Try not to disgrace the family."

His father held out his hand for the phone. "Hi, Isabelle. Hi, Lovely Wife. How's Los Angeles?"

Timothy went back into the kitchen and dropped the eggs into the pan. He wasn't much of a cook beyond breakfast foods, and, even that he could claim only because of spending the last two summers doing morning shifts at Daisy's Diner. Most of the time he was waiting tables, but she'd put him in the kitchen now and then. As he was getting ready to flip the omelet, his father came into the kitchen and dropped the phone on the counter.

"I'll make the toast in a minute." His dad grabbed himself a beer and popped the cap off the bottle. He allowed himself one beer a night. Sometimes two, if he was technically on vacation.

"Why do you smell like cigarettes?"

"Hmmm?" Timothy sniffed his sleeve. "Oh, Wyatt Courtland was over today. He had one in the backyard."

"You didn't partake?"

"C'mon, Dad." Timothy reached behind his dad and put the bread in the toaster himself.

"Just checking. Why was Wyatt here?" His father leaned against the counter. He'd already taken off his gun belt and locked the weapon away while he was talking to Timothy's mother and sister.

"He needed some help with a school project."

His father snorted. "Surprised he's still in school."

"He's not dumb, Dad."

"No. He's not, but since it's only him and his mother, he tries to help her out with the bills. He skips half the school days so he can take extra jobs around the county."

The toast popped, and Timothy split the omelet in half and handed one plate to his father. The two ate in an easy silence. His dad wasn't a generally talkative person, and Timothy took after his father. As they were finishing up, Timothy took a deep breath.

"Hey, Dad, I wanted to run something by you."

His father answered with a cautious smile. "Sure thing, kiddo."

"I was thinking of pitching a column to the school newspaper on crime. Things that would affect the students. Like how drug use affects the community. You know, those kinds of things."

"Sounds interesting enough." His dad picked up the plates and brought them to the counter. He scraped the remnants into the trash before placing them into the sink. If it was the whole family, he would have put the plates into the dishwasher, but when it was only the two of them, they did the dishes by hand.

"Maybe," Timothy said hesitantly, putting the butter back into the refrigerator, "maybe even do something on some of the kids in the school who've been affected. Like, say someone's gone missing—"

His father turned around sharply and dropped their silverware into the sink. "Is this some complex way for you to try and get your hands on my old case files?"

"It would be for the paper, Dad."

"You're not getting near any police files." His father wasn't much taller than Timothy, but he was broader, and he was used to intimidating people. He crossed his arms across his chest. "You're not going into law enforcement in any way, shape, or form, Timothy."

"You do realize I'm almost eighteen, right, and I don't need your permission—"

"If you want your mother and me to pay for your education—"

"I don't—"

"Unless...." His father's face was turning red. "Unless the next words out of your mouth are 'you're right, Dad. I don't listen to anything you say,' then I don't want to hear it."

"That's not fair." Timothy crossed his arms over his chest, the same way his father did.

"Life isn't fair. And before you pull the I'm-almost-eighteen card, you should know you won't get a cent from me for your school if you think of studying criminal justice or the like."

"You're being ridiculous. I'm not stupid—"

"No, you're not." His dad scowled and pointed as his son. "You're too smart for your own good. You're smart, but you're impulsive, you don't listen, and you think you're the smartest person in the damn room, when you're not!"

"I don't even know why I try talking to you," Timothy shot back, his voice rising.

"Do not raise your voice to me."

"You're the one who's yelling, Dad."

"Go to your room!" His father pointed at the stairs.

Timothy looked as if he'd been slapped. "You're kidding, right?"

"Upstairs and finish your homework. Now." His father turned his back on Timothy and ran water into the sink.

It took all of Timothy's inner strength not to prove his father right by stomping up the stairs and slamming the door. He closed his door carefully and quietly, lay down on the bed, and burned. He didn't know why his dad was so damn set against his own damn son following in his footsteps. Most dads would have loved their sons to want to be them, but not Benjamin Mitchell. Timothy was not going to cry. He would show his dad. He'd figure out what happened to Bobby LaFleur and show his father exactly what he was capable of doing.

CHAPTER THREE

LACEY WAITED for him in her usual spot on top of the short ledge in front of the school. She wore a short jean skirt with red stockings covered in black diamonds. Her shirt was white and puffy, and her hair was in a long ponytail.

"You going for a Harley Quinn vibe?"

"Eh, I thought I'd try out some sort of mainstream nod," Lacey replied, before applying bright red lipstick and smiling.

"I admire your compromise." He smiled at her and helped her down off the short ledge.

"Hey, Tim," Bo called out from behind the two. "Sorry, Timothy," he said after seeing the look Timothy gave him. "Here's your money."

Timothy took the money from him and smiled casually. "Thanks, Bo. I appreciate it. Here's the file you're looking for."

Bo took it and stuffed it in his backpack without looking. "Hey," Bo said, looking down at the ground. "You're not going to tell anyone—"

"Client confidentiality, Bo. I didn't tell you about the stuff I've done for other people, did I? Promise."

Bo still wouldn't look at him. "Yeah, man, thanks."

"Congratulations," Lacey said as Bo walked away. "You managed to actually make him sort of polite."

"Yeah," Timothy replied as he put the cash away and hefted his bag onto his back. "I feel like a jerk how it happened, though. Can you remind me not to be an asshole next time?"

She laughed. "I'll do my best."

The bell rang, and they separated in the hall, him going to English, her to Spanish. Clomping footsteps came up behind him, and he turned to make sure it wasn't Bo or a friend, but it was only Wyatt.

"Hey, man, did you decide?" Wyatt was wearing his usual jeans and boots. The shirt today was still sleeveless, but it was a gray tank top, and Timothy kept his eyes forward, heading toward his classroom.

"Yeah, I'll help, but we have some things to work out." He was at the doorway of his class and turned to Wyatt. "Meet me at the track after school. I've got to get a run in today." Wyatt was about to say something, but Timothy cut him off. "Go. You'll be late, and I don't want tardiness on my conscience."

Wyatt shot Timothy a smile and then ran toward his own classroom.

AT 4:00 p.m. Wyatt sat on the bleachers as Timothy pounded out a steady rhythm on the track. Wyatt never liked running. Seemed like too much effort for too little. He liked working out in the school's weight room. It helped him in the construction jobs he was able to get, but what happened when you ran? Nothing. Wyatt liked the feel of the barbell in his hands. The challenge of weight plates against his muscles. The push and pull of powering against gravity. He liked the strength it gave him. He wasn't really much for attention, but he was already tall and he gained muscle easily, so he kept working out. He was one of the biggest guys in school and that meant people left him alone. They'd look and stare, but they'd stay away. It wasn't like they were afraid of him. He wasn't a bully, and everyone reacted to him as if he'd told them to leave him be. And they did. There was a kind of respect Wyatt got from his height and weight and muscle.

"Hey, Wyatt." Timothy was breathing heavily, his chest heaving as he gulped in air. "Thanks for meeting me. Let me grab my bag out of the locker room and we'll talk."

Wyatt followed Timothy and watched his back for a minute. He knew Timothy would keep his secrets. Timothy would never say anything, but he couldn't take the chance that Timothy might tell his dad. Wyatt had dealt with Sheriff Mitchell a few times and, while he seemed like a good guy, he wasn't going to risk it. After all, he was still a cop, no matter what. Besides, what would it get him? Why would Timothy want to be around him in any way? Wyatt was so rough and ugly and stupid compared to Timothy. Compared to—

"Wyatt? You ready?" Timothy had his messenger bag and was standing at the edge of the school parking lot. "Sorry you have to give me a ride again. If you don't mind taking me over to Burt's garage, I can pick up my car. We'll talk on the way."

"Sure." Wyatt never bothered to lock his pickup when he was at school. They had cameras, but he also knew his truck was a piece of shit and no one would bother. Plus, everyone knew it was Wyatt's truck, and no one wanted to piss off Wyatt.

"So, tell me what you know about Bobby," Timothy said, pulling the door closed and rolling down the window.

"He was a nice guy. Real nice. Quiet."

Timothy looked over at him from the passenger seat. "How did you meet Bobby?"

Wyatt paused. "Just at school."

"And you two were friends?"

"Sure." Wyatt stopped at a light in the center of town and looked over at Timothy. "Why?"

"I'm wondering how that happened. That's all."

"What do you mean? How what happened?"

"C'mon, Wyatt," Timothy said, sounding a little annoyed. "You're a C student. Vocational track, no college prep classes. You've played football every year, except this one. You're a jock. Or you were, anyway. Bobby was college prep all the way, A student, liked poetry, talked about moving to either San Francisco or New York as soon as he graduated. Quiet, sweet kid. Picked on a bit. Sounds like he was a gay kid planning his escape as fast as possible."

"How do you know all that?"

"You asked me to look into something. You think I don't do my own research?"

"I guess. Bobby was a good kid. I don't know anything except what I told you yesterday."

"Sure. Okay." Timothy pulled his sunglasses out of his bag and sat back as Wyatt turned into Burt's. "Come on. I have to get my keys, and then I'll follow you out to the house where you found the stuff."

"Okay." Wyatt sat back and followed Timothy across the lot.

"Hey, Burt!" Timothy called out, waving.

"Well, look who finally came by to pay me a large sum of money."

"C'mon, Burt," Timothy said, laughing. "It was only the alternator."

"Damn, how does a homosexual know about cars?"

"We're a well-rounded group of people, Burt." Timothy pulled out his credit card. "Keep in mind, my dad looks at all my charges, so if he wants, he'll ask for an itemized bill."

Burt ran the card while Timothy asked about his wife and kids and Burt asked about Timothy's mom. "Keys are in the car kiddo.

Hey, with your sister gone, are you interested in picking up some babysitting jobs?"

Timothy shook his head. "I like kids, Burt, but I'm not as patient as my sister."

Burt laughed again. "I figured." He wiped his bald head with a red bandanna and left a grease stain across the top of his forehead. "Let me know if it's not running the way you want."

"Thanks, Burt," Timothy said.

"Nice car," Wyatt said with a little smile.

"Yeah. It's a treat. A hand-me-down from my mom that spends more time in the shop than on the road."

"I bet it's faster than my truck," Wyatt said as he jingled his keys.

"I bet I'll seem shorter in the car than I seem standing next to you."

"What?"

"Just pointing out I'm short, Wyatt." Timothy opened his car door. "I'll follow you."

TIMOTHY WAITED for Wyatt to pull out, and he followed the pickup. Wyatt led him out of the main part of town, onto a long road bordered by overgrown grass on both sides. The short driveway was gravel and rocks, and Timothy parked right behind Wyatt's truck. Timothy stepped out of his car as Wyatt climbed from his truck with a half-finished cigarette dangling his mouth.

"You really should quit, Wyatt. It's a bad habit."

"I promise it's my only one." Wyatt turned red and looked away.

Timothy's eyes narrowed.

"C'mon, we can get in through the back."

They walked through the overgrown lawn, and Wyatt led Timothy up the two-step porch. Wyatt pushed the back door open, and the air was stale, smelling of dust and plaster.

"Very nice. I suppose early nineties crack den is a solid design choice."

"Is that supposed to be funny?" Wyatt smiled at Timothy. He wasn't sure if it was a joke or not, but he found he liked the fact he couldn't tell the difference.

"Not really. Show me where you found the box."

The kitchen they passed through was still relatively intact, but the living room was almost totally demolished. Only the support beams in the wall stood. There were small piles of drywall on the floor, but the walls were nonexistent.

Wyatt pointed to a corner of the room. "They took most of the drywall and plaster away in a truck the other day, but there wasn't anything else in the wall. I found the box over there."

Timothy headed over to where Wyatt was pointing and bent down to look at the beams in the area. "Who owns the place?"

Wyatt shrugged. "Tommy O'Leary. Big Tommy." Big Tommy was one of the rich guys in town. O'Leary assumed they called him Big Tommy because he was a big deal, but it was actually because his big belly hung over his belt.

"Did he ever live here?" Timothy pulled a flashlight out of his messenger bag and shone it around the dark corners.

"I doubt it. Seems too far out of town for him. He owns the bar and likes to drink. This'd be a little far for him to drive, right?"

"Yeah, I guess so." Timothy sighed and stood up. "What's the upstairs look like?"

Wyatt led him up the stairs, where it looked even more demolished than the first floor. There were no walls and only a few wires hung from the ceiling.

"No one found anything up here. Least, they didn't tell me."

"Would they have?" Timothy poked around, but there were no real places to hide anything, just a wide-open space, punctuated by support beams.

"Maybe not. It was two guys I've worked with before. Will and Brian. If they'd found something stupid, like old girlie magazines or something, they would have, but if it was worth something or locked in a box, like Bobby's stuff, they might not've told me."

"Okay, fair. Ask your boss if Big Tommy ever lived here and let me know what he says?"

"Sure. Big Tommy wants to build a bigger place here. Before we took out the walls, there were only two bedrooms here. He wants to use the original frame and make it a four- or five-bedroomer. Word is he's thinking of trying to make it a hotel for tourists."

"What tourists?"

Wyatt rolled his eyes and pulled out another cigarette. "He seems to think he can make this a real hot spot, I guess."

"Hotlanta part two, I guess."

Wyatt waited quietly as Timothy looked around. When he stared out the window, Wyatt cleared his throat. "Find anything? Clues?"

"No." Timothy shook his head. "But I didn't expect to." He led the way down the stairs and pulled out his cell phone, taking a few pictures along the way.

They went outside, and Wyatt took a deep breath.

"Do you know Bobby's mom?" Timothy looked up. Wyatt took a step back when he realized how close he was standing to Timothy.

"A little bit."

"Good. You want to come with me when I talk to her?" Timothy opened his car door and dumped his messenger bag on the passenger seat.

"Why do you need to talk to her?" Wyatt dropped his cigarette and ground it out under his boot.

"Because I want to find out what she knows. When a child disappears, it's likely a parent or relative who did it."

"Not Bobby's mom. She's really nice. Always has been. Even after he… disappeared, she would stop and say hello to me at the grocery store."

Timothy leaned up against his car and crossed his arms across his chest. "Wyatt, is there something you want to tell me? Because you're kind of tying my hands every time I try to do something here. You won't let me tell my dad. You won't take it seriously when I tell you sometimes parents have something to do with their kids disappearing. Do you know for sure Bobby didn't run away? Maybe his mom found out something, and he ran. Maybe he really was gay—"

"Fine, don't fucking help!" Wyatt lost his temper and barked at Timothy. Timothy flinched but didn't move, except to uncross his arms. Wyatt took a breath and stepped back. "Sorry."

"It's fine."

Wyatt felt guilty and hoped Timothy would tell him to forget it, but he kept talking.

"I've got some homework, and my mom should be back home soon. Let's talk tomorrow." Timothy got into his car and buckled his belt.

Wyatt rested a hand on the roof of Timothy's car as he started the engine. "Seriously, I'm sorry. I didn't mean to yell."

"It's fine, Wyatt. Don't worry." Timothy put his car in reverse and pulled out onto the street.

Wyatt stared at the back of Timothy's car and pulled out another cigarette.

Chapter Four

By the time he got home, Timothy's mother was putting the last of the plates onto the dinner table.

"Are you actually cooking?" Timothy stuck his head into the kitchen. "Hi, Mom. Welcome back."

"Honey!" Crossing the kitchen to hug and kiss her son, Janelle Mitchell shook her head. "Of course I'm not cooking. Your father's bringing home something from Daisy's Diner. He said he'd surprise us, so I'm guessing burgers and fries." She turned back to the sink. "I am, however, washing some carrots, so we'll at least have a vegetable."

"We're not back in California, Mom. They fry vegetables here."

"Well, you've only got one year left and then you can go back to California, like your sister, if you want." His mother sighed. "I'm not sorry we moved here. Grandma needed us, but I know you kids weren't thrilled."

"Mom." Timothy sighed back. "It's fine. It's not like it's a big deal." He sat down at the table and ate carrots from a bowl his mother put in front of him. "It's good we got to spend some time with Grandma before she passed. And Dad had his job. Sheriff is pretty cool."

She leaned forward and pinched his cheek. "Such a good boy."

"Ouch. Please don't ever do that again."

"Honey," his father called from the front door, "I'm home!"

Timothy's mother was laughing and waited in the kitchen doorway for her husband. Timothy waited until they were hugging before he took the bags of food out of his father's hand and unpacked them while his parents were saying hello.

"Seriously," he said while he was putting the Styrofoam packages on the table. "You guys can have your welcome home tonight once I put on my noise-canceling headphones, okay?"

"I can only hope that you're still in love with your partner after this many years, the way your mother and I are." The sheriff took off his gun belt, opened the refrigerator, grabbed his beer, then popped the top. He took a sip and then went to lock his weapon away.

"Come on. Let's eat, okay?" His mother took a roll of paper towels from the counter and placed it in the center of the table as his father came back in.

"Anything happen at school today, kiddo?" his father asked, putting a french fry into his mouth. "Who gave you a ride out to Burt's place?"

"Wyatt." Timothy was mixing both mustard and ketchup on top of his burger.

His dad raised an eyebrow. "Second day in a row. Something going on between you two?"

"What?" Timothy looked up from his food. "Dad!"

His mother turned to look at Timothy as well. "Wyatt Courtland? Are you and he a couple?"

Timothy sighed, and his parents smirked at each other, used to hearing dramatic sighs since his sister had turned thirteen. "No. Nothing is going on. Wyatt is straight, and I'm helping him out with something at school. Now, if we can eat in peace without my wonderful parents asking me about my nonexistent love life, that'd be awesome."

"What?" His mother looked shocked. "And ruin the time-honored tradition of parents making their children uncomfortable and awkward? Never!"

"Seriously. The two of you are terrible parents." Timothy smiled at them. "I'm going to be in therapy forever."

All three of them laughed and enjoyed dinner, simply being together.

IT WAS almost 8:00 p.m. the next night when Timothy stuck his head into the living room, where his parents were watching a news channel. "Hey, I'm heading out. I will drive safely, all my homework is done, and I will be back before eleven, so I can get a full night's sleep before I tackle Saturday."

His dad was up off the couch and into the small foyer before Timothy could even get his coat on fully. "Whoa. Hold it, sport. Where are you going?"

"I'm meeting with Wyatt for a school thing. It won't take too long."

"What school thing?" He shifted from concerned dad to interrogating cop, and Timothy recognized the subtle difference.

"I'm helping to tutor him in English." Deciding it was better to play offense than defense, he shifted slightly over the line. "If you want, I'll bring you his paper when he's done with it."

"No need to get snarky, kiddo." The sheriff softened a little bit and lowered his voice, leaning in slightly so Timothy's mom wouldn't hear. "This is only a homework thing, correct? Is there something going on between the two of you?"

"Dad," Timothy said, lowering his voice as well. If he had to have this conversation with someone, he'd rather it be with his dad and not his mom. "I already told you, he's straight. There's nothing going on between us."

"And there's no, how shall I put this? There's no apps on your phone and you're meeting some stranger?" His father blushed but kept eye contact when Timothy blushed even brighter.

"Are you seriously asking if I'm going to hook up with some stranger on a back road for a little suck and—"

"Do not finish that sentence, young man."

"No, Dad, I'm not meeting some random dude I know nothing about. I'm going to help a friend with something. Can I go now?"

"Call me when you're on your way home. And I want you in the door by eleven, not on the way home, understood?"

"Yes, sir. Understood." Timothy opened the door and called out, "See you later, Mom."

"Bye, honey. Are you going to hook up with one of the guys from the app on your phone?"

The sheriff looked at his son as Timothy froze with his hand on the doorknob. "I'm going to pretend I never heard that."

MADDY LAFLEUR'S living room was small and worn, just like her. She was smaller and thinner than Timothy imagined. Her hair was wild and dry and too long in some places as if whoever had cut it was half-asleep. She was nice, exactly the way Wyatt said she would be, but her eyes, blue as the sky, were haunted and hollow. Wyatt sat in the chair across from the couch.

Timothy noticed the couch was worn thin in some places, and he knew if he pulled the crocheted blanket from across the back, he'd see the cushions even more ripped than Maddy knew. He'd grown up in police stations and seen more than one parent who'd lost a child, and he knew the look in Maddy's eyes came from someone sleepwalking through life.

Maddy LaFleur had invited them in, seemingly happy to see Wyatt, but wary of his visit. Timothy kept his voice even and calm.

"Thank you so much for taking the time to speak with us, Ms. LaFleur. I can't tell you how much I appreciate it. I wanted, if you're okay with it, to speak with you about Bobby."

"Bobby?"

"See, Miss Maddy," Wyatt said, "the other day, I found—"

"We found the school paper was looking for some new stories," Timothy interrupted and ignored the look Wyatt shot him. "I was thinking I would do a series about crimes that have affected the schools in the community, and since I wasn't here when Bobby was, with your permission, I'd like to write a piece about Bobby."

"Bobby," she repeated.

Wyatt leaned forward, and Timothy could see his knuckles whiten as he clenched his fists. "Please, Miss Maddy. It'd really help." Wyatt looked over at Timothy. "Help for the paper, I mean."

She sighed. "What do you want to know?"

"Can you tell me a little bit about Bobby?" Timothy was curious about what she'd say. All he knew about Bobby was what Wyatt told him and what he'd found out when he'd asked around the school.

She smiled. The only genuine smile he saw from her the entire night. "He was sweet. That's Bobby in one word. He would pick flowers for me every day. He'd bring them in and make sure they were on my nightstand every night when I came back from work." She looked up at Timothy, who smiled gently. "He was good at school. I always insisted he get good grades, and he never let me down." Maddy leaned forward and picked up a red mug. It had a chip on the handle and the string with a tea bag label clung to the side. Her hand looked too thin for her small frame, her knuckles pushed against her skin, and even from the other end of the couch, Timothy could smell the whiskey in the mug.

"He liked poetry and music. I have no idea where he got that from. I know jack about poetry, and his father sure didn't. But even when he was little, he would drag me into the library and he'd sit there for an hour or two, picking out three or four books. Always had to find something he thought would be perfect. Marie, that's Marie Whitley, the librarian, she used to watch him, and I would head over and get my hair done, or do some shopping, and by the time I came back, she would have checked out a few books for him, and he'd be standing right in front of the desk, quiet as can be, waiting for his mama. Wanted to be a writer. So sure he'd become famous." She sighed quietly. "When he was about eight or nine, I suppose, he found a book on gardening. He was after me for almost two months before I would let him plant some flowers out back. You should've seen how he took to that little space."

Timothy looked over at Wyatt and saw Wyatt smiling. "I bet it was beautiful."

"It was. I try to keep it up, but with work and everything…." She drank again, and Timothy waited for her to speak. After a minute she inhaled deeply. "I don't even know what happened to him. How could a mother not know what happened to her own child?"

"Whatever happened to Bobby, it wasn't your fault." Timothy wanted to reach out and put his hand on hers, but he held back.

"I was always so grateful, the way you looked out for him, Wyatt. You made sure he wasn't picked on too much." She looked back and forth between Timothy and Wyatt, her head going between the two of them like a curious bird. "I never told no one this, but I sometimes thought that Bobby might be a homo. He was a bit of a sissy boy." She looked at Timothy quickly, worried. "No offense. I just mean he was sensitive."

Timothy smiled to let her know he didn't take it badly.

"I wouldn't have cared. He was my baby. I loved him. 'Course nothing would've changed that. But it made it so important to me that Wyatt here looked out for him. Made him feel safer."

Wyatt blushed redder than Timothy had ever seen him. "It was nothing, Miss Maddy. He was my friend."

"Do you remember the day Bobby disappeared?" Timothy's voice stayed calm and soothing, even though he wanted to ask Wyatt a few questions.

"Sure. It was a regular day. I got up and woke Bobby up for school. I made Bobby his lunch and got ready for work. I yelled through the bathroom door while he was in the shower. He told me he loved me. I told him same. That was always how we said goodbye. Always, even when he was mad at me, he said he loved me. The last thing I remember about my baby is he was half-asleep in the shower." She got up and looked at them both. "Do you want some water? Coffee? I think I might have some soft drinks left."

"No, thank you, Miss Maddy." Wyatt smiled up at her. "I'm fine." Timothy noticed Wyatt's accent was a little bit stronger than when they talked between themselves.

"Water would be great, actually, Miss Maddy. Thank you." Timothy stood up and followed her into the kitchen, gesturing for Wyatt to follow him. The kitchen was smaller than the living room with a table, barely big enough for two, in the center. There were cow salt and pepper shakers on the table, and Timothy remembered the same ones on his grandmother's kitchen table. "Miss Maddy, do you remember anything strange happening the week before Timothy disappeared? Strange phone calls or hang-ups? Something in the mail."

She shook her head as she dropped some ice into a tall glass. "No. Nothing like that. Bobby… well, I guess I should have believed him."

"I'm sorry," Timothy said as she turned on the faucet. "Believed what?"

"Bobby said he kept seeing the same car around town wherever he went. He said he didn't know anyone with that type of car." She passed the water to Timothy. "I didn't see anything. Nothing parked outside the house, nobody creeping around."

"And did you tell the police about the car?"

She snorted a laugh. "The police. Those idiots." She looked up at Timothy, a slight blush on her neck. "Sorry. Your dad. This was before he got here. They came out and sat in the kitchen here and told me he'd run away. Bobby would never have run away. I knew he wanted out of this town. I'da been a fool if I didn't know that, but he had a plan. Study hard, get a scholarship, and go to either California or New York. He wanted to find an apartment big enough for me to come live with him, and I'd find some cashier or waitress job, and he'd work some job during the day and write his poetry at night. He had it all planned out."

She sniffed, but even though her eyes were wet, she didn't cry. "Sorry. The police. Sheriff Bates at the time, he came out here with some deputy, asked me two or three questions, said he'd look into it, but he was sure Bobby would come back the next day. I didn't sleep one wink that night, called everyone I could, even you, Wyatt. You remember?" Wyatt nodded at her and Maddy continued. "Never really slept well since then. I went to the police station almost every day for three months. Nothing."

"Miss Maddy, this is, well, kind of uncomfortable, but is there any way, I mean, could the person in the car have been Bobby's dad?"

"That bastard, pardon my French. No. He was gone long before Bobby was born. Probably in prison by now."

"Bobby sounds like a great guy." Timothy gave her a little smile.

"He was." She frowned slightly. "He was moody. Right before he disappeared. A typical teenager, I guess."

"Yeah. I guess." He paused for a moment. "Do you have any of Bobby's things that I could take a look at? I mean, it'd be nice to add a little personal color to the article."

"I left his room the way it was when he... you know." She gestured down the hall. "Go ahead and look. Second door."

"Really?" He didn't give her a chance to change her mind. "Wyatt, why don't you visit for a few minutes, and I'll be right back." Timothy walked down the hall and quietly opened the door.

Timothy felt around on the wall until he found a light switch and flipped it on. He could see a layer of dust on the dresser next to the door. He shut the door behind him and looked around the room. A couple of posters on the wall, New York City's skyline. A map of the United States with a few cities circled. New York. Los Angeles. San Francisco. Orlando. Portland. Everything was neat and put away, and Timothy wondered how often Miss Maddy came in to sit down on the edge of the bed, crying, waiting for Bobby to come home. There wasn't a closet and Timothy pulled open a couple of drawers of the bureau. They stuck a little bit. Socks and underwear, T-shirts, jeans and pants, plain and threadbare and patched with bad stitching. Timothy ran his hands under the drawers, checking to see if something was taped underneath. Nothing there. He pulled his flashlight out of his bag and got down on the floor to check under the bed. Dust bunnies and a lost sock.

He flashed the light on the bed frame, hoping for a diary or something where Bobby had written down his escape plans from home. Anything to point the way. No journal, but an old workout magazine. Timothy smiled. A fourteen-year-old's jerk-off material. He carefully lifted the mattress slightly and ran his hand underneath. Nothing there either. He didn't want to take too much time, so he tried one quick thing and checked to see if there was a cut in the mattress. Was he so cynical that he assumed he wasn't the only one hiding things from his parents? He didn't find anything, so he carefully pulled the workout magazine

down, slipped it into his bag, and took one last look around. Maybe
Bobby had written something in the margins. There didn't seem to be
too many other obvious places to hide things, and he wasn't about to
start checking for loose floorboards or wall panels. He frowned when he
looked at the bed and went back to smooth it better. Timothy sighed and
sent a silent thought to Bobby LaFleur.

I'll find out what happened to you, Bobby. Promise.

WYATT AND Timothy were quiet during the first part of the ride back to
Timothy's car at the Save-Mart parking lot, where they'd met up. It was
halfway between their houses, and Timothy had wanted to meet Maddy
LaFleur with Wyatt.

"What'd you think?" Wyatt said finally, exhaling a plume of
cigarette smoke out the window.

"Of Miss Maddy? She was nice," Timothy said, shifting so his
back wouldn't stick to the seat of Wyatt's truck.

"I meant about Bobby being followed."

"Did he mention something to you?" Timothy looked at Wyatt's
profile as he drove carefully.

"Nope. Not to me." Wyatt shrugged and looked over at Timothy.
"But I can't imagine he would've."

"Why not?" Timothy asked.

"He always felt like it was too much trouble, me watching over
him and all."

"Really?" Timothy kept looking at Wyatt. He had to admit his
parents were partially right. It would be easy for him to crush on Wyatt.
Sure, he was big and strong, but he was also really kind. Timothy knew
Wyatt was hiding something, but the way he truly cared about Bobby
meant something. He might play the dumb jock, but Timothy could see
how he was during their conversation with Miss Maddy. Wyatt was laser
focused, following Timothy's questions and Miss Maddy's answers
with single-mindedness. And, no, it didn't hurt that his eyes were a soft
chocolate brown, his jaw was square, and his hair soft and almost blond.
Timothy could tell from his eyebrows that when Wyatt got older his hair
would shift from dirty blond to a mousy brown.

Wyatt's deep voice finally broke the silence. "So, now what?"

"Now, you drop me off at my car and I go home."

"I meant about Bobby." Wyatt's voice held a little humor. "Should we figure it out tomorrow?"

"I have plans tomorrow. Saturday, no school, so Lacey and I are going to Greenville."

"Okay. Hey, maybe I could come by tomorrow night and check in?" Timothy and Wyatt looked at each other as they pulled up next to Timothy's car. "If it's okay."

Timothy shrugged. "Sure. We'll be home by eight." He hopped out of the car. "Thanks for the ride." He half shut the door and then turned around. "Hey, Wyatt. I'll do my best. For Bobby."

Wyatt didn't answer, but he nodded. "I'll follow you till you get toward home. Make sure your car's fixed right."

Timothy smiled.

CHAPTER FIVE

AT NINE the next morning Timothy and Lacey were heading out toward Greenville, drinking soda and eating chocolate. Lacey was wearing a neon green half shirt that hung off one shoulder and jean shorts with high black boots, while Timothy wore jeans and a white polo shirt.

"Damn," she said, her Southern accent coming through strong. "I shouldn't be eating this stuff." She waved a half-eaten brownie in the air. "It's going to go right to my ass. If only it'd go to my tits."

"Don't tell me you're subscribing to the societal pressures of being told what your body should look like in order to be considered attractive." He looked over and smiled at her as they pulled onto the highway.

"Says the gay dude who works out and runs so he can post shirtless selfies on Instagram."

"Mom would never let me have an Instagram account." He slipped carefully into the fast lane and sped up, passing a few cars.

"Too worried about stalkers?"

"Too worried I'll post a bad pic of her."

"Movie tonight after we hang out with my aunts?"

"I've got a little bit of work to do on a project at the library, so I'm going to drop you off and catch up with you after noon. I have to see how much work I get done."

"If you don't spend time with them, they'll be pissed." Lacey's father had a lesbian sister, who, last year, had married and bought a house with her wife. Lacey had introduced them to Timothy quickly after they'd become friends. Her aunts were funny and smart and about the only people who'd ever made Timothy think he might actually settle in a small town. "They haven't seen you in about a month."

"I promise I'll get lunch with you guys. I just have something to do."

"Does this project have anything to do with why you've been spending so much time with Wyatt?" Lacey shot him a look, which he saw out of the corner of his eye as he pulled back into the center lane, allowing a motorcycle to pass him.

"I'm helping him out with some research, and I need to stop by the library. It'll probably be an hour at most."

"You have a crush."

"On Wyatt? Please. Sure, he's hot, but he's straight."

"And he's not too smart."

"I'm not sure about that," Timothy replied, speeding up a bit. "I think he's actually smarter than he pretends."

"He's not smart enough to pretend to be dumb." She laughed, and Timothy smiled but didn't agree. He pushed a CD into the stereo, and they sang a mixture of '80s music and show tunes for the rest of the forty-five-minute drive.

TIMOTHY STEPPED inside the library and let the AC cool the sweat dripping down his back. He shivered a little bit and walked up to the counter. He waved at Shirley Carver, the main librarian, as she was using the computer in the back. There was a library near the sheriff's station his father worked at, but he liked this one better. Not only was it bigger, because Greenville was bigger, but Shirley didn't treat his requests for LGBT books as if it was odd. If she was able to get ahold of any book he wanted, she'd get it and shoot him an email. Shirley had bleached blonde hair and dressed as if she was about twenty years younger and thirty pounds lighter than she was, but that was another reason he liked her.

She casually ambled out of the back and smiled big. Her voice was quiet in reverence for the library and the books Shirley felt like she brought to the community. "How are you, Timothy?"

"I'm good, thanks, Miss Shirley. How are you? You look great. I like the color on you."

"Well, aren't you a sweetheart?" She leaned on the counter and picked up a pen, knowing his requests were always weird enough that she'd need to write it down. "What can I help you with today, hon?"

"Strange one today, Miss Shirley." Timothy reached into his bag and pulled out an envelope.

She sniffed in a breath of air. "Aren't all of yours?"

He passed her the article about Bobby LaFleur. "This article got cut out without any of the banners or anything from the specific paper. Any idea where it's from? The article's from four years ago."

She slipped on her glasses and glanced at the article. "I remember this kid. So sad. Hmmm, I'm guessing it's from the *Courier*. They use this heavy black border. See here on the side?"

"Do you have papers from back then?"

"Back then," Shirley said, peering over her glasses. "As if it were seventy-five years ago." She gestured for him to follow her to a computer in the back. "Let's see, he disappeared in, was it June?"

"May."

"May." She nodded. "That's right." Shirley sat at the computer and typed a few keys while he peered over her shoulder. "Mind if I ask why you want this stuff?"

He kept looking over her shoulder as she pulled up the archives from the newspaper. "Um, school stuff. Newspaper article."

"Mmm-hmm. Here." Shirley pushed herself out of the chair and let him sit. "All set up for you with the correct year and month. Knock yourself out, hon. And, if you need to print anything, it's set up for the printer on the desk."

"Thanks, Miss Shirley. As always, I owe you." He paused for one quick second. "Listen, if anyone asks—"

"It's our secret. You know, there's a code among librarians that we take very seriously. Never gossip about any requests."

"You're the best."

She walked back toward the front counter, leaving him in peace. He pulled up the article he had a copy of and flipped back a couple of days, looking for any mention of Bobby going missing. Timothy found a brief mention and went to the main search bar, looking for anything about Bobby LaFleur.

While he waited for the search to run, Timothy pulled out his phone and opened up Grindr. It was something he only did when he was in Greenville, not wanting to find anyone too close to home. He set his profile to private so no one could see him unless he messaged them, but he could see them. There were two guys within a mile of him. One guy was over sixty years old, and the other seemed like he might be a student at the community college. Maybe he'd drop the college guy a hello. It had been a long time since he'd been on a date. He could sure use one. He left the app running in the background while he texted Lacey to let her know he might be done sooner than he thought, when the computer popped up with one article he hadn't counted on finding. It was an article from the month after Bobby disappeared.

Still No Information On Missing Boys

When Bobby LaFleur, 14, disappeared just over a month ago, the police assumed it was another case of our young people running away from home. With Andrew Madden missing over a year, some in our community are wondering if there is something else happening. Since the two young teens lived in different jurisdictions, the police didn't make any connection and have still denied that they are looking at the disappearances as related.

Julia Madden, 43, Andrew's mother, told the police "Andrew would never have run away. He was looking forward to a summer art program he'd be teaching at. He was so excited."

Andrew seemed to vanish into thin air one afternoon, which is a story repeated by Madeline LaFleur, 32, Bobby's mother. She also told police in no way did Bobby give any indication he would have ever run away.

TIMOTHY FROWNED as he kept reading. What was it his dad would say? When it comes to crimes, there are very rarely coincidences. There was no byline, so he pulled up the masthead of the *Courier*. Just a list of writers and an editor. He texted Lacey again, saying he had another errand to run, printed up the article, and wrote down the address of the newspaper.

He shut down the computer and deleted the browsing history, stopping long enough to say goodbye to Miss Shirley and ask for directions to the newspaper.

By the time he pulled his car into the parking lot, it was almost noon. There were only a few people in the office, so Timothy smiled at the first person who looked his way. "I'm looking for the editor?"

She didn't seem interested in who he was or why he was there, but she jerked her thumb at a man in his midfifties, so Timothy didn't offer any information.

"Excuse me," Timothy said politely, dropping his voice as deep as he could and smiling. "You're the editor?"

The man nodded, a bit of his gray hair flopping back and forth. It took him a minute to look up at Timothy, but when he did, the man smiled back. "Frank Carroll. How can I help you?"

"My name is Timothy Mitchell. My dad's the sheriff of the next county over. I'm working on something for the school paper, and I'm hoping you can help me find the writer of a particular article, Mr. Carroll." Timothy pulled the envelope where he'd stuffed everything out of his bag.

The older man frowned for a minute. "Did we print something wrong? Retraction requests need to be sent certified mail."

"No, sir. Nothing wrong at all. I happened to come across this article. It's about four years old, and I was hoping you could help point me to the person who wrote it." Timothy handed him a photocopy of the original article Wyatt had found. "Any ideas?"

"Oh, jeez. I remember this." Frank looked at Timothy. "Do you have any information?"

"No, I'm afraid not. Like I said, I came across the article and wanted to write something about Bobby for the school paper."

"Really? You know, if you're interested, we have an internship coming up for the summer."

Timothy raised an eyebrow. "I'd love some information about that."

Mike gestured for Timothy to follow him and handed the article back to him. "Well, I'm afraid the writer doesn't work for us anymore. He's, I think, he's teaching now. Left kind of abruptly too."

"Did he say why?"

Carroll stopped at his desk and opened a drawer. He didn't look up as he started riffling through it. "Not sure. He said he needed to leave. Here's the info and application for the internship. You can also fill it out on our website."

"Thanks. Can you give me the writer's name?"

"Sure thing. Matt. Matt Thompson."

"Any idea where I can reach him?" Timothy put the application in the envelope with the articles he'd gotten from Miss Shirley's computer.

"Not really. He used to live over on Cranberry but moved a while back. He said he was going to be teaching at the high school in Union, but that would've been three years ago. Lots of teacher burnout and moving around school districts in these parts."

"Great." Timothy couldn't hide his disappointment. He'd been on a roll this morning and was hoping to get more information, but his dad always said the only thing you needed when doing an investigation was patience, so he was willing to learn that virtue.

"Good luck trying to find him. God only knows where he is now. He was kind of a flake."

Timothy furrowed his eyebrows. "What do you mean?"

"He was a good writer, could make almost anything readable. Then, he calls me, no notice, just says he has to get away from the newspaper, as if we were the *New York Times* or something." Carroll sat down on the edge of his desk. "Rarely went out with us, even though we always invited him." He shrugged again. "Sometimes he'd say he'd meet us and then never show up. He was kind of weird. Bit of a loner, I suppose."

"Thanks so much for this, Mr. Carroll. I really appreciate it."

As Timothy turned to leave, Frank called out. "Hey, kid. If you get any more information…."

"I'll let you know. Promise." Timothy didn't wait for a response but headed out the door as fast as he could. It was after noon, and he drove over to Lacey's aunt's place, hoping they hadn't gone to lunch without him.

IT WAS almost eight by the time he dropped Lacey off at her house, and he looked at his phone while he was parked in front of her house.

If ur back b4 9, Im at the park near statue

Wyatt had the back of his pickup down and was leaning on the edge, smoking a cigarette in the dark when Timothy pulled up. Wyatt flicked his cigarette onto the concrete when Timothy got out of the car, and then he grabbed a paper bag to pull a long drink from whatever he had inside. There was a dog by his side, big and furry and his head resting on Wyatt's foot. When Timothy closed his car door, the dog sprang to his feet, cautiously looking at Timothy.

"You shouldn't be drinking and driving," Timothy said. There was a small edge to his voice, and he saw Wyatt squint at his own face, half in shadow.

"It's only pop, Timothy." Wyatt held up the bag and shimmed it down the can inside. "See?"

"Aren't you afraid the cops are going to come by?"

"Nope," Wyatt replied. "People stopped coming here when the cops busted a big party about a year ago. Everybody goes out onto the fields near Access Road 3 now, and the deputies head out there." Wyatt took another swig from his can. "I'm surprised you didn't know."

"I'm not really popular, Wyatt. The girls tolerate me, but their boyfriends aren't happy, so I don't get to go to parties. Most of the guys don't want to hang out with a homo."

"You can come with me, if you want. No one'll say nothing if I'm there."

"I'm good, Wyatt. Thanks."

"Sure." He paused a minute. "This is Colonel." Wyatt ran his hand along the dog's head and Colonel nuzzled it. "Colonel, this is my friend, Timothy."

Timothy bent down and held his hand out toward the mutt, who looked up at Wyatt.

"It's okay, buddy. He's a good guy."

Colonel went carefully over to Timothy and sniffed his hand. He looked up at Timothy and then back at his hand. The dog licked him, and Timothy giggled when the tongue tickled his wrist. Colonel backed up a few steps and then sat down and offered Timothy a paw.

"Well, aren't you polite," Timothy said, shaking Colonel's paw. "It's very nice to meet you, Colonel."

The dog barked and then went back to Wyatt, who picked up the big dog and placed him into the truck bed. "He likes you," Wyatt said with a smile. "You like him, don't you, buddy?" Wyatt laughed when Colonel barked a few times before lying down.

"He's sweet," Timothy said, smiling at Wyatt.

"Yeah. My best friend."

"Is that true, Colonel? Does he tell you everything?" Timothy said, standing up. "What kind of dog is he?"

"I'm not sure," Wyatt responded, shrugging. "I know he's part German shepherd. I can tell from his coloring, but I'm not sure what else is in there. Did you have a dog back in California?" Wyatt sat back in the bed of the truck.

"No." Timothy shook his head slowly. "Mom's allergic. I had a fish once, but it died after about two weeks."

Wyatt stared at the parking lot for a minute. "Find anything out today?"

"I'm not sure. Maybe. Do you know a kid named Andrew Madden?"

"Nope. Why?"

"How about a guy named Matt Thompson?"

Wyatt shook his head. "Sorry. Should I? Know these guys?"

Timothy's phone beeped, and he ignored it. "Not necessarily. Just curious."

Wyatt and Timothy looked at each other for a minute. Wyatt's mouth opened as if to say something, then closed again. He pulled a cigarette out of the pack sitting next to him on the back of his pickup. "I, uh, I, you know, thanks."

"For what?" Timothy hoisted himself up onto the truck bed, leaning his back against the side and bringing his legs up, crossed in front of him. "I haven't really done too much." Colonel stood up, walked to Timothy, and lay back down, resting his head on Timothy's feet, the way he'd been with Wyatt when Timothy pulled up. Timothy ran his hand over the dog's head.

"More than the cops ever did for him." Wyatt took a deep drag off his smoke, a gulp from his drink, and then tossed the empty toward the cab of the truck. He shifted his body until his back was on the opposite side of the truck and he was facing Timothy. Wyatt stretched out his long legs, his boots banging against the flatbed when he brought them down. "So, thanks."

"Mind if I ask you a question?" Timothy's phone beeped again, but he was too busy trying to catch Wyatt's expressions in the dim light.

Wyatt shrugged, then answered anyway. "Sure."

"Why? I mean, how did you and Bobby meet? Why are you so concerned?"

Wyatt snorted a laugh without humor. "That's more'n one question. Fair enough, though, I guess." Wyatt pulled his baseball cap off, scratched his head, and then put his cap back on. "Bobby was in my gym class, back when we were freshman. He was so small, and we were supposed to play some football. You know Bo, right?" When Timothy nodded, Wyatt raised an eyebrow. "Asshole, right? So, Bobby and me, we ended up on the same team, and Bo's on the other side with some of his buddies. He tosses Bobby the ball and his buddies all pile on top of Bobby. Kid looked really hurt. Like not just a little in pain, but really hurt. Next time Bo tried it, I grabbed the ball from Bobby and took Bo down myself." Wyatt shook his head. "Asshole," he repeated. "Bobby was a kid. Kind of helpless. He needed someone to look out for him. He was... sad."

"Sad? Troubles at home?"

"No, nothing that bad." Wyatt nudged Timothy's foot with his own. "Not everybody's you, Timothy."

"What is that supposed to mean?"

"C'mon, Timothy. You're not from here. You don't know what it's like. You're from California. People accept, you know, gay people. You guys aren't rich, but you're out of here as soon as you can be. We both know that. Go to some fancy college. Most of us can't do that. We're gonna be here forever. Bobby wasn't like you at all. He was gonna be here for life. People were always gonna make fun of him. His house, even his mom's car, people'd spray-paint shitty words where he'd see them. You got some muscles. You're a karate guy. Your dad's the sheriff. Bobby didn't have any of that. No matter how much he planned or what he said, Bobby was stuck here, and he knew it." Colonel looked up as Wyatt kept talking and left Timothy's side to go over to Wyatt. He nuzzled the side of Wyatt's face as if he wanted to comfort his owner.

Timothy didn't say anything. He stared at Wyatt. His voice had gotten more intense and Timothy wondered what was going on behind his tone. He knew Wyatt was right, at least about him.

"You never know, Wyatt. He might've gotten out."

"No." Wyatt's voice was as intense as Timothy's, but quieter, filled with something that tugged at Timothy's gut. "People like me? We never get out. Trust me." Timothy kept quiet, listening to Wyatt breathe in and out. "I wish I was more like you."

Timothy snorted. "Why the hell would you want that?"

"This is my life, Timothy. Saturday nights are gonna be sitting here in this parking lot. Maybe hanging out at Big Tommy's bar, getting drunk, waiting for Monday to start the damn week all over again."

"You're way too young to think like that. And you sure as hell don't want to be me." Timothy pulled his knees closer to his chest, trying not to disturb Colonel, who had his eyes closed. "I'm not an idiot. I know if I wasn't the sheriff's son, I'd have the shit kicked out of me every day."

Wyatt's voice was low and deep. "I wouldn't let it happen."

"Thanks, Wyatt." Whatever was going on between the two of them was making Timothy confused and unsettled. "I've got to head home. Some research. I found an article in the Greenville paper about another missing kid. Same age as Bobby when he went missing. He disappeared a year before Bobby." Timothy frowned. "We also need to see if Big Tommy can tell us who was renting his place four years ago." Timothy flung his legs off the side of the truck and hopped down. "I've got to get home," he repeated, but he yawned this time. "Get some sleep."

"See you tomorrow?" There was something more in Wyatt's voice than just curiosity, but Timothy couldn't place it, and he was too tired to figure it out.

"I've got to do some extra reading for homework, and all the stuff I have to find out for Bobby's case, I'll have to do at my computer. Unless you want to spend a couple of hours online looking for one guy who used to live in Union?"

Wyatt laughed. "You're funny, Timothy." He helped Colonel out of the truck bed and slammed the back of his pickup back in place. The dog barked a goodbye to Timothy before scrambling into the front seat of the truck. Wyatt lit another cigarette. "See you in school."

"Yeah. See you then."

Timothy's parents were asleep by the time he got home. He set the alarm and got ready for bed before he pulled out the papers from the lock box. They were mostly poems, a few short stories, all in Bobby's careful, measured handwriting. Timothy had to admit they were pretty good, especially for a fourteen-year-old. A little sentimental, but they were meant to be, he assumed. None of them were dated, but Timothy felt pretty sure he could tell what order they were written in by their style. The first few were about isolation. They were melancholy, angsty, and Timothy could almost feel sadness radiating off the page. The last few were hopeful, sweet, and painfully romantic. Timothy wasn't sure if it was his California cynicism or the difference of the years between Bobby's fourteen and his seventeen, but they were almost too sweet. When Bobby wrote these ones, he was obviously in love with someone. Timothy smiled and hoped it meant Bobby didn't have an unrequited crush. Maybe he'd met someone, somehow.

He packed the pages back in the envelope, put it in his messenger bag, and turned out the lights. Timothy tried to focus on figuring out what might have happened to Bobby, but his thoughts kept floating to Wyatt.

Wyatt's watery brown eyes came to Timothy's mind. He was handsome, his jaw square, his arms big and strong. Timothy could feel himself getting hard, thinking about feeling Wyatt's weight on top of him. He grabbed himself and inhaled sharply. He shoved the covers off and imagined his lips on Wyatt's neck, inhaling Wyatt's smell, earth and tobacco and salty sweat. He could feel Wyatt lift him off the ground, holding him in the air, their tongues wrestling in their mouths, their breath coming hitched and fast. Wyatt lacing his big callused fingers in Timothy's smaller, softer hands.

"Fuck!" Timothy hissed out the word carefully as he felt the warm, wet splatter on his stomach. "Fuck," he repeated quietly, his voice just above a whisper. He reached over and grabbed tissues from the package on his bedside table and wiped himself off. He rolled over and was drifting off to sleep when his phone beeped again. He grabbed it from his bag and opened it up, wondering what was going on. Timothy realized he'd left Grindr open from today in Greenville and the notifications kept beeping. Usually he was only notified if someone was within 200 feet of him. He smirked to himself and realized he was probably sitting next to Lacey and her aunts, while accidentally ignoring a hot guy. The app opened up as he pressed it, and he saw a profile labeled "Country Boy" with a headless, shirtless torso pic. Whoever it was, was big and muscled and Timothy couldn't help but open the profile and look at more pictures. No face, but a couple of shirtless shots. There was something strangely familiar about the slope of those shoulders. Timothy sat up in bed and enlarged a small section of the picture.

Timothy's voice was harsh as he blurted out, "Son of a bitch." There on the headless torso's arm was a yin and yang tattoo.

CHAPTER SIX

TIMOTHY WAS quiet through breakfast with his parents, wondering what to do about Wyatt. As soon as he finished eating and doing his chores, Timothy texted Wyatt.

Need to talk. Someplace private. Meet me in 30 minutes?

It took Wyatt under three minutes to respond.

U ok? House where I found the stuff?

I'm fine. Just some stuff came up. See you then.

Timothy told his parents he had to go out and run a few errands and he'd be back before three. His father asked him to bring home some snacks for the second half of some football game. Timothy had tuned him out and didn't pay attention to which team was playing which team.

As he drove out to meet Wyatt, Timothy felt himself torn between anger and curiosity. He wasn't sure how he was supposed to feel, and that made him feel worse. Why had Wyatt lied? What had happened between Wyatt and Bobby? Had Wyatt done something to Bobby? He hated it, even as it came to mind. He turned the radio up to drown out the thoughts running through his head.

Wyatt was sitting on the hood of his truck when Timothy pulled into the driveway. He pulled up behind Wyatt and took a deep breath before he got out of the car. He kept the door unlocked and the keys inside, just in case. Wyatt had a temper, and since Timothy didn't know which direction this conversation was going to take, he decided to play it safe.

Wyatt hopped off the hood of the car. "Everything okay? Did you find something out about Bobby?"

"No, Wyatt." Timothy pulled his phone out and flipped the case open. "I need to talk to you about something, and I need you to not lie to me."

"What's that mean?" Wyatt shoved his baseball cap up, taking the shadow off his face. "I didn't lie to you."

"Tell me about this." Timothy held his phone up for Wyatt to see. Wyatt's face went white, then red, then white again.

"I... I don't know what that is."

"It's a picture of you, on a gay app, saying you want to meet someone 'real.' And I need you to tell—"

"It's not me," Wyatt interrupted loudly. "Lots of people have a tattoo like that." He was breathing heavily. "It's not me," he repeated.

Timothy sighed, trying to keep his own voice steady. "Wyatt, I don't care if you're gay or bisexual or pansexual. It doesn't matter to me, unless we're dating. I don't care if you're straight and making some extra cash hooking up with gay guys, as long as you're not rolling anyone, but I told you not to hide anything from me." Timothy shut the app down and put the phone back in his pocket. "So, tell me what's going on."

Wyatt took a step forward and put his finger in Timothy's face. "You better not start spreading rumors about me!" He raised his voice, and Timothy took a quick step back. "I swear to God, I'll kick your ass if you start saying shit about me!"

Timothy took another step back and kept his voice soft and easy. He put his hands up in a conciliatory way. "Wyatt, take it easy. I'm not interested in spreading rumors about anyone. I swear. It's not important to me."

Wyatt was towering over Timothy and he took a step back, as if he was starting to scare himself. His own voice dropped, and Timothy could see a look of sheer terror in Wyatt's eyes.

"Please don't tell my mom. Please. Please promise me you won't tell my mom."

Timothy reached out and carefully put a hand on Wyatt's arm. "Wyatt, I swear. I won't tell anyone."

Wyatt looked at him with wet eyes.

"Please don't worry. I won't tell anyone. Just relax." He reached into his car without turning his back on Wyatt. "Here. Have some water." Timothy handed him a bottle.

Wyatt took a couple of tentative sips from the water bottle. "Thank you. For not telling anyone." He took a huge gulp of water, then pulled a cigarette out of the pack in his pocket. "Shit. I'm sorry. I'm sorry I yelled. I can't let anyone find out."

Timothy nodded and let Wyatt smoke down almost half of the cigarette before he said anything. "Were you and Bobby a couple?"

Wyatt didn't do anything except bring the cigarette back to his lips, and his shrug was so subtle, Timothy almost missed it. "It's not like that. Not exactly. We were kids. Only thirteen or fourteen. I don't remember exactly. Fourteen, I guess." He paused. "It wasn't like we, you know, hooked up or anything."

Timothy nodded in understanding. He kept right out of Wyatt's reach.

"He was so nice. We used to sit up in my attic and look out the window, watch the moon. He always wanted to sit right next to me, close as he could. Said I made him feel safe." He snorted angrily and lit another cigarette. "Like I kept him safe when he needed it." Wyatt looked at Timothy. "I wasn't there when he needed me."

"That's not true, Wyatt. You know that." Timothy felt comfortable relaxing a little, and he hoisted himself up onto the hood of his car to sit. "That's not true." He repeated it, not because he thought Wyatt hadn't heard him say it, but because he felt Wyatt needed to hear it again. "I promise."

"It doesn't matter. He's gone. He never got out of this shithole town." Wyatt ground his cigarette into the ground. "He's dead, isn't he?"

Timothy looked Wyatt in the eyes and paused. "Most likely, yes."

Wyatt nodded.

"I'm sorry. It would be extremely unlikely—"

"Don't." Wyatt held up his hand. "It won't help." Wyatt turned and walked around his truck. Timothy watched him make two full revolutions before he stopped on the side of the truck bed. Wyatt was breathing heavily as his fist shot out and he punched the side of his truck. He slammed his hand as hard as he could, and the sound of skin on metal came once, twice, three times. Wyatt winced and grabbed his hand, hissing in pain. He leaned against his truck and Timothy could see his shoulders shaking.

Timothy waited until Wyatt seemed to calm down. Wyatt didn't move, so Timothy slid off the hood of his car and grabbed another bottle of water. He walked up to Wyatt and gently took Wyatt's larger hand in his own. Wyatt turned and watched without saying anything as Timothy poured the water over the cuts and bruises on Wyatt's hand and then took the hem of his own shirt and carefully blotted the small wounds.

Timothy held Wyatt's hand flat. "Can you move your fingers?" When Wyatt did, Timothy let Wyatt's hand fall. "They're not broken."

"Don't matter." Wyatt seemed defeated about something, about everything. He sank down to the ground, his back propped up against the side of the truck.

Timothy sat down next to him, his back resting against the tire. "Did you and Bobby date?"

Wyatt picked up a few small rocks from the gravel driveway and tossed them onto the grass. "Everybody wants something. Parents want you to be whatever they expect. Grow up. Get a job. Get married. Have babies. Teachers want you to get good grades. Friends want you to be fun all the time." More pebbles went flying into the grass and one went over Timothy's car. "Not Bobby. He just let me be whatever I wanted to be. You'd never know it, but he was funny. Really funny. You could fail a test, and he'd still have you laughing like crazy." Wyatt wiped at his eyes. "He wasn't like you. He was really shy. Like, really. Sometimes he'd be, I don't know, maybe afraid. Hard to describe. He didn't hide, but he didn't, wouldn't… he didn't stand up for himself. Not like you. He wouldn't ever have told people he was gay." Wyatt took the water bottle from Timothy and drank. "Him and me were in the same English class. We had to write a poem and his was really good. Really good. I told him I liked it, and we hung out for lunch."

"He sounds sweet." Timothy didn't look at Wyatt. He stared out at the trees across the way.

"He made me feel special. Like I was worth something."

Timothy turned his head and bumped his shoulder gently against Wyatt. "You are worth something."

"I've done stuff. With guys, I mean. I've met some guys through Grindr. It's not like Bobby." Wyatt pulled off his hat and scratched his head, dropping the hat into his lap. He paused, looking at Timothy, who took his hand off Wyatt's arm. "They want me to yell at them. Call them names, do things to make them feel bad. It was good with Bobby." Wyatt's forehead was furrowed, like he was trying to figure out the best way to say something. "Bobby wasn't like that. We never really did anything 'cept kiss. That was it. But he liked being next to me. He'd always want me to put my arm around him, hold him. He wanted to feel safe." Wyatt turned to Timothy, staring him in the eyes. Wyatt's eyes softened as he talked more about Bobby. "The first time we kissed, he asked me. He really asked me. We were sitting up in his attic, looking up at the moon. His mom was at work, and mine, this was right after Dad died. She was drinking a lot. It was hot, and we both had our shirts off and he put his hand on my arm and left it there, pointing out some stars. He looked at me, and he asked me if he could kiss me. I might've nodded. I don't know. But he kissed me. Best thing that ever happened to me. Seriously. It was like everything good all rolled up into one thing."

"Must've been some kiss." Timothy grinned at him, and Wyatt knocked against Timothy's shoulder, mimicking his earlier move.

"It was." He grinned back. "Yeah, it surprised me. Maybe it was 'cause I wanted it so bad, but it was sweet. Started out soft, and then it was like he needed me so much, he couldn't get close enough to me. It was like he wanted to curl up with me forever. Ever seen a hungry dog get a whole bunch of food in front of him? He looks around to make sure you ain't gonna take it away, and then he attacks it. That was kind of how Bobby kissed me." Wyatt traced a pattern on the leg of his jeans. "Didn't think about it much till after he went away, but I hope he wasn't afraid of me. You know what I mean?"

"Yeah, I do." Timothy paused. "Look, Wyatt, is there anything else I need to know?"

"No." Wyatt shook his head. "Nothing else."

"You sure?"

"Why the hell does it matter what went on between me and Bobby?"

Timothy sighed heavily and rolled his eyes. He stood up and wiped dirt from the back of his jeans. "Because, Wyatt, it makes you a suspect." Timothy watched the way Wyatt's face changed. It wasn't fear or anger. Just massive confusion.

"What do you mean?" Wyatt stared at Timothy.

"When someone goes missing, the first thing the police do is look at the people who are closest to the missing person. Family, friends, romantic partners. I'm guessing the cops already looked at his mom, but since they didn't know about you and Bobby…. Did anyone know about you and Bobby?"

"No. No one." Wyatt pushed himself up to his feet, and Timothy noticed a dirt stain on the side of his jeans. "It was just for us. Just about him and me." He narrowed his eyes, thinking about something for the first time. "You don't think I did something to Bobby?"

"No." Timothy didn't hesitate for a second before he responded. "No, not at all." Timothy narrowed his eyes at Wyatt. "But someone, most likely someone who knew Bobby, did hurt him. You don't remember anyone else he was close to? This is important, Wyatt. Think."

Wyatt shook his head slowly. "He didn't have many friends, a couple of guys he used to watch science fiction movies with. He liked his English teacher from the year after him and me had the same class."

"Miss Ricker?"

"No. It was someone different. Some guy. I was in a different class year."

"And these guys Bobby hung out with?"

"Mark, Adrian, and I think Andrew. That's about it."

"Okay." Timothy's phone beeped, and he pulled it out to see a text from his mom, asking him to pick up a few other things, since he was stopping off for chips anyway. He sighed. "I've got to go. I have to pick up a few things for my parents." He walked around to the side of his car and opened the door. "Wyatt? I want to figure this out. For Bobby." Timothy paused but started speaking again before Wyatt could respond. "For you too. Text me if you think of anything else." He got into the car and turned it on while he yanked his seat belt over his shoulder. Timothy was distracted and almost missed the turn into the parking lot of the grocery store when he went to grab the list for his parents.

"Timothy!" His mother stood behind him, hands on her hips. "I've been calling you for the last five minutes."

"Sorry, Mom." He stood up and stuffed his phone in the pocket of his jeans from where he'd been staring at the picture of Wyatt. He felt pretty sure he'd wasted an hour memorizing the placement of each hair on Wyatt's chest, and he blushed red at the thought. "What's up?"

"I need something out of the closet."

"I came out of the closet years ago." They both laughed as he went into the hallway closet.

"The box on top, please," she said, pointing to what she needed. "It's so nice to have such a tall, strong son."

"You don't need to compliment me, Mom. I'm always happy to help out my beautiful, loving mother."

"Such a sweet and obnoxious child." She opened the box he held for her and pulled out a few smaller boxes of photographs. "Okay, this is all I need. You can put the rest back."

He shoved the larger box back in the closet and joined her as she sat down at the dining room table. "Mom, can I ask you a question. A hypothetical one."

"Yes, honey," she replied. "Once I make an album for Isabelle to remember her childhood, I'll make one for you too."

"According to Dad, I'm still a child."

She paused and put the pile of pictures in her hand down on the dining room table. "Harsh."

"I guess it's not a question so much as... well, I sort of found out this guy at school is gay."

She raised an eyebrow. "You're right. It's not a question?"

"Ha. Ha." Timothy rested his chin in his hands. "He's a little, what's the best word? Paranoid that I might say something and out him."

She looked at him carefully, figuring out her next words. "You wouldn't, would you?"

"Mom. No. I'm not that much of a jerk." He frowned. "Am I? He could come out on his own. It's not that big a deal."

She brushed a little bit of hair off his forehead. "Honey, you're my son and I love you." His mother paused. "But sometimes I think you haven't figured out how lucky you are."

"Mom," Timothy said, breaking in fast as he could. "I know that."

"I know you do a bit, Timothy, but keep in mind not everyone is your father or me." Placing her hand on top of his she squeezed it gently. "When you came out, your father and I, and Isabelle, all—"

"I know, Mom."

"All I'm saying is you might want to learn a little patience, honey. Not everyone is as lucky as you are. You might want to remember it might not have been a big deal in our house, but it is a very big deal to some. You do understand that, right?"

He paused, looked down at the table, and kept silent. "Sure, Mom. Do you need anything else from the closet?"

"First of all," she said, looking at her son, "don't think I didn't notice the evasion, and secondly, is this something I need to know about? We're not dealing with another Ethan situation, are we?"

"I'm not seeing anyone, Mom. And Ethan wasn't perfect, but he wasn't all bad. We were barely old enough to date, so I'm not surprised it didn't end well."

She sighed, stood up, and walked into the kitchen. "I only want to make sure you're okay." Raising her voice slightly louder so it would carry, his mother continued. "As far as the question, it would depend, I guess." She came back with two glasses of lemonade. "I would say to ask yourself if you could help them somehow."

He exhaled quietly. "Okay, Mom."

She leaned forward and brushed hair off his forehead again. "If you want to be an adult, then you have to accept the fact that life decisions aren't easy. Sorry, kiddo."

He smiled. "Thanks, Mom."

"Now," she said, dropping her smile, "let's talk about the crack you made toward your father."

"I'm a minor, but I'm not a child, Mom."

"I know, but—" She shook her head. "You're his child, and he wants you to be safe, honey." She kissed the top of his head, picked up her stack of photographs, and sorted them into two piles. "Your father is a lot of things, but unreasonable isn't one of them. He knows you're growing up, and it's a bit scary for him. You're his baby."

"I thought fathers were only supposed to feel that way about their daughters."

She laughed. "You do know he cried when you were born and he finally had a son, who he could play football with and teach to fish."

"If only I cared about either of those things." He smiled at his mother. "Maybe for Father's Day I could ask him to play baseball while we're on a riverboat?"

"He adores you just the way you are." She picked up an album and smiled at Timothy. "It would be funny, though." She stared at him, and he looked back, confused.

"What?"

"I can't get over how much you look like your father. Same eyes, same chin." Her smile was soft and careful. "You're so handsome."

He blushed. "Thanks, Mom." He raised his voice to be heard over the game his dad was watching. "I'm going to try to become more sports-minded for my father!"

His father shouted back from the living room. "I love you exactly as you are, kid."

The three of them were laughing as Timothy went upstairs.

THE NEXT morning, Timothy sat in his car for an extra five minutes as he called the high school over in Union.

"Hi," he said when the secretary answered. "This is Julian Carter, from the *Greenville Courier* and I'm looking for Matt Thompson. I believe he's teaching English there."

"No," the secretary replied, her voice thick with a Southern accent and cigarette smoke. "I'm sorry we don't have a Matt Thompson here. Have you tried the middle school?"

"Not yet, thanks so much. Have a good day."

He hung up and ran to spend a few minutes with Lacey before the school bell rang. As he went through the parking lot, he looked for Wyatt's truck but didn't see it, and he frowned, wondering why he wasn't there yet.

The morning went by quickly, and when Timothy got to his locker right before lunch, Wyatt was waiting for him.

"Hey." Wyatt tilted his chin in a greeting.

"Good. You're here. Come on," Timothy said, grabbing his lunch and his afternoon books. "We have to go to the library."

"Why?"

"Research, Wyatt." Timothy led the way down the halls and noticed Wyatt eyeing the people around them. "Tell them I'm tutoring you. Or tell them I ran a background check on someone for you. Relax."

Wyatt looked at him, slack-jawed and awkward. They reached the library, and Timothy paused, his hand on the doorknob.

"Here's a little free advice: if you want to keep your secret, become a better liar." He opened the door and went to the desk, waiting for the librarian. He didn't like Mrs. Willett as much as he liked Miss Shirley. Mrs. Willett disapproved of him, but she disapproved of everyone, so he didn't take it personally.

"Yes, Timothy," she said, her voice much too high for someone her age. "What can I do for you today?"

"Hi, Mrs. Willett. Could I see the yearbooks from four years ago and five years ago, please?"

"Why would you want to see those?" She sniffed, and Timothy thought it might be because she was trying to be snobby, but it came across as if she had a cold.

"Just helping Wyatt do some research. Nothing special."

Mrs. Willett rolled her eyes, went into the office, and pulled open a closet door. She pulled out two books and closed the door behind her.

She passed Timothy the two books and opened her mouth to say something, but he cut her off. "Thanks, Mrs. Willett. You're the best." He turned and went to the table farthest from the desk. Wyatt followed silently and watched as Timothy placed one book in front of himself and the other in front of a chair across from him.

Wyatt sat down when Timothy pointed at the book. "What am I doing with this?"

"Find the teacher Bobby liked so much." Timothy pulled out a sandwich his mom had made and passed half to Wyatt. "Here. You didn't bring lunch."

"Thanks, Timothy." Wyatt took a bite and then put the sandwich down on the napkin Timothy passed. "And thanks for earlier."

"Sure." Timothy was flipping through the pages, looking for the section highlighting the teachers. "Okay, is this him?" He held up the page for Wyatt to see.

Wyatt squinted. "Mr. Matthews. Yeah, looks like him." Matthews was thin and tall and had a receding hairline on top of a boyish face. His smile was awkward and goofy.

Timothy stood up. "Okay, see if he was teaching the year before." He took a picture of Mr. Tom Matthews with his phone and passed the yearbook back to Mrs. Willett. "I have another question. Mr. Matthews here. How can I find out where he's teaching now?" She raised an eyebrow at him. "It's for an article."

She nodded, not believing him for a second. "You could try the state board of ed, but keep in mind, if he's teaching at a private school, he may not be registered." She tapped a few keys on her computer. "Here's the number you want. Ask for Clara, and she'll help you out. And you didn't get her name from me."

He nodded. "Thanks, Mrs. Willett. I appreciate it. Really."

She smiled strangely. "You got Wyatt Courtland to come into the library, Mr. Mitchell. I'll do what I can to help out. If you can get Bo Watterley in here, I may marry you."

"I'll keep it firmly in mind." He turned around, and Wyatt waved him over. When he got back to the table, Timothy leaned over at Wyatt's side. "What'd you find?"

"He's not here. I mean in the yearbook."

"Weird." Timothy was about to say something else when the bell rang. "I have a test tomorrow, so I've got to get to study hall. I'll catch up with you after school tomorrow."

"Hey." Wyatt grabbed Timothy's arm as he turned. "Thanks. Seriously. For everything."

Timothy was silent for a minute. Why was he noticing the way Wyatt's eyes seemed focused on him, how beautiful they were? He nodded, afraid he might say something wrong, so he didn't say anything. He nodded again and left Wyatt standing there in the library.

TIMOTHY WAS trying to go over his calculus notes before tomorrow's test. He'd called the middle school in Union after classes and, with the same name and story he'd given the high school, asked for Matt Thompson and received the same answer as before. He sat at the kitchen table, listening to jazz music in the background. The mathematics of jazz usually inspired him to concentrate on his math work, which was probably the subject he had the most trouble with, though he was still getting an A. He wasn't really worried about the test. He wasn't the type to have to cram the night before a big exam because he studied every subject every day. Even Lacey thought it was a bit extreme, but he was competitive by nature, which was why when he joined track, he focused on the events that were individual, not team. He sighed and pushed the thoughts of Wyatt running through his head to the side. No way did he want to be thinking of Wyatt and the way his palm was callused and dry and strong when they shook hands. He certainly didn't want to be thinking about Wyatt's arms and wondering how strong they might be. And no way in hell he was going to think about the shirtless photo on Grindr and the pattern of hair on Wyatt's chest.

"Test?" His father's voice startled him, and he jumped a little. "Sorry, son. Didn't mean to scare you."

"It's okay, Dad. I'm a little distracted. And yeah, calculus."

"You've always been good at math," his father said as he reached into the refrigerator for his nightly beer. "Something else on your mind, kiddo?"

"No," Timothy said quickly. Too quickly, and his father knew it.

Father and son stared at each other, and Timothy noted how similar they were: the same dark hair and eyes, the same slight spray of freckles across the back of the neck. His mother always teased the two of them as to how alike they were. They both denied it, but Timothy knew his stubborn streak firmly marked him as his father's son.

"Mm-hmm." His father's raised eyebrows made Timothy flush red. The sheriff sat down at the table. "Would this distraction happen to be named Wyatt?"

"Dad. Please." Timothy went back to his notebook, looking at anything but his father.

"I can't help but notice you didn't deny it."

"Dad, I'm not—Wyatt is only a friend. Someone I'm helping out. There's nothing romantic going on. First of all, you'd kill me. And second, I'm not exactly redneck fantasy material. And… he's not…." Timothy hated hiding something from his dad. Especially considering everything else he was already hiding, but he'd promised Wyatt he wouldn't say anything. "He's not gay, Dad."

His father reached across the table to pull the pen out of Timothy's hand. He placed it on the table and then put a finger under Timothy's chin and tilted it so they would be looking at each other. "First of all, redneck is a derogatory word, and I expect better from you, especially given the things you've had to hear in your life. Secondly, I would never kill you about the guys you date. As much as I had problems with Ethan, I trust your judgment, and if you tell me you like someone, I'm going to trust they're a good person. Wyatt's not a bad kid. He's been respectful of me, the law, and you. He has been respectful of you, correct?"

Timothy nodded, answering the way he did when his dad stopped being his fun dad and turned into sheriff dad. "Yes, sir."

"Good. Now, I'd like to know what you mean by 'fantasy material.' Have you and Wyatt slept together?"

"Dad." Timothy sputtered, but the sheriff cut him off. "He's not—"

"I'm asking a question of someone, who, while age of consent in this state, is still under the age of eighteen, as well as my son, and I think I do need to know if you're sleeping with someone."

"No, sir. No sex. With anyone. I'm still pure as New York snow."

"I'll ignore the bad joke." His father sighed. "I would hope you feel comfortable enough to tell me and talk to me before you decide to have sex. Of any kind." He picked up Timothy's pen and handed it back to him. Standing up, his father put his hand on Timothy's shoulder. "And if that 'fantasy material' crack was about you thinking that you're not a good-looking kid or you're not worthy of someone like Wyatt, we have a lot more to discuss."

"Can we talk later, Dad? I really do have to study."

His father nodded and started out of the room.

"Hey, Dad? You won't say anything, right?"

That got him an eyebrow raise. Timothy knew his dad wouldn't, but he had to make sure.

"Thanks."

His dad nodded again and left Timothy to study calculus.

CHAPTER SEVEN

TIMOTHY WASN'T too worried about his test. He finished it early and went back over his answers, only finding a couple of mistakes. He and Lacey were having lunch, laughing over her new boots, which were covered in flowers, when Timothy's phone buzzed.

Meet me after school??

4 at my house. Rents will be at work.

C u.

Lacey raised an eyebrow. "Is there a reason you're hanging out so much with Wyatt?"

"Just doing some work for him on a couple of background checks. No big."

"Seriously," Lacey said, "if I find out you're crushing on him and not telling me, I'll be pissed."

"I tell you everything." Timothy shrugged. He felt bad lying to Lacey. But he wasn't lying, really. Wyatt seemed more confused than gay, and Timothy was pretty sure he was not anywhere near Wyatt's radar.

He was still thinking that when he dropped Lacey off at her place. He had time for a quick run before Wyatt was coming over, so he threw on shorts and sneakers and headed out for a fast, mind-numbing, body-crushing run. Something to kill the thoughts in his head and give him some inspiration as to where he was going next with Bobby's case. He wasn't sure of the best way to go, so he wanted to burn out his brain until he was forced to figure out something new. The run was exactly what he needed, and by the time he was back at cooling-off speed and coming back up to his house, Wyatt was outside. Wyatt dropped his cigarette onto the street and ground it out underneath his boot, and Timothy walked the last block to his house, sweat dripping down his bare chest. Wyatt was staring at him, and Timothy suddenly felt self-conscious, thinking how scrawny his lean body must look to Wyatt.

"Hey." Wyatt stood on the sidewalk, and Timothy thought he was staring at his chest, when Wyatt looked away, clearly embarrassed about something. "Sorry."

"About?" Timothy raised an eyebrow. Since the day he came out, he'd learned not to back down from feeling afraid or anxious. He pretended he didn't care and made damn sure the person who was making him anxious knew he didn't care. So far, his parents were the only ones he couldn't fool.

"Um, making you come back from your run?"

"Is that a question?" Timothy walked toward the backyard, and Wyatt followed.

"No. It's not really a question."

"Relax, Wyatt," Timothy said, holding open the gate. "I was making a joke. Be right back." He ran in the back door and grabbed two bottles of water from the counter. Stepping back outside, he tossed one to Wyatt, who caught it one-handed. Timothy pulled a tank top over his head and sank down at the table. "So, what's up?" He opened up the water bottle and started drinking.

"When we talked about Bobby the other day, I didn't tell you everything."

Timothy clenched his fists. "Why do you keep hiding things from me?" He shook his head. "I will never figure out what happened to Bobby if you keep hiding things—"

"It's not a big deal—"

"Wyatt, do you actually—"

"It's not a big deal!" Wyatt raised his voice slightly, and both he and Timothy sighed at the same time.

"Fine." Timothy pouted. "Go ahead."

"Mostly Bobby just wanted to kiss. The first few months that was it. Just kiss. Sometimes he'd want me to hold him." Wyatt scratched the side of his head. "The last couple months, though, he started getting real aggressive."

"What do you mean?" Timothy's eyebrows furrowed.

"We'd be kissing, and then he'd start to reach for my pants. So he could undo them. He'd want to...." He trailed off, his face red. "He'd try to do stuff a fourteen-year-old shouldn't do."

"Wyatt, we both know what two guys do together. Spare me the modesty and spill it."

"Bobby would grab my dick and try to blow me."

Timothy narrowed his eyes. "Okay."

"That's not Bobby. It's not something he would've done." Wyatt ran a finger along the picnic table. "He wasn't like that. I wanted to sleep with him, but Jesus. We were only fourteen." Wyatt scratched at the stubble on his cheek. "It wouldn't have been right. It would've been getting off. It wasn't how either of us wanted to have sex. We'd talked about it, and then a few months later… it was the only thing we ever fought about."

Timothy grunted a small noise. "Okay. Let me think on it." He rubbed his eyes. "Please stop hiding things from me. It wastes my time."

Wyatt mumbled, "I'm sorry."

"Why do I always feel bad when I yell at you?" Timothy meant it as a joke, but even he shook his head when he heard it out loud.

"You don't need to do that." Wyatt was looking down at the ground, and his hands were fidgeting back and forth.

"Do what?"

"Did you mean it the other day?" Wyatt reached into his pocket and pulled out his cigarettes, and then stuffed them back in his pocket. "Did you mean it?"

"Hold on, Wyatt." Timothy shook his head and held his hand up. "What are you talking about? You're not making any sense."

"Can I smoke? I need to smoke." He pulled out his cigarettes again and waited until Timothy nodded.

"You really should quit," Timothy said while Wyatt was lighting up. "Those things are no good for you."

"Yeah, I know." Wyatt sat down at the picnic table across from Timothy, then stood back up again. When he finally looked up at Timothy, his eyes were worried, Timothy thought. Almost haunted. "Did you mean it?"

"Okay, you've got to tell me what you're asking because you're freaking me out here."

"Did you mean it when you said it didn't matter unless we were dating?"

Timothy looked at Wyatt, who wiped his hand across his forehead. "You don't remember?"

"Yeah, I remember, but I don't know what we're talking about. You're not making any sense."

Wyatt reached out and pushed the sweaty hair plastered on Timothy's forehead back. He took a step toward Timothy, who was forced to look up to keep eye contact. They stared at each other for almost a minute, and Wyatt licked his bottom lip, right before he reached out and grabbed Timothy's arms. Timothy tried to back up, but Wyatt pulled him close and kissed him.

It wasn't soft or gentle. It was full of need and passion, and it took Timothy's breath away. Wyatt's hands wrapped around his arms, pulling him closer, their bodies pressed together. Timothy's arms were bent at the elbows, his forearms tight against Wyatt's torso. Timothy could feel the heat from Wyatt's body, and when he stepped back, the slight breeze felt cold. Wyatt broke the kiss and reached up with one hand, running the back of it across Timothy's cheek.

Wyatt pulled his hand away and looked at it for a moment. His mouth dropped open and he stammered, "I'm sorry." He backed away two steps and then ran for the gate that led to the front yard, his booted feet landing heavily on the ground and then the concrete of the path.

"Wyatt, wait." Timothy took a step forward, but Wyatt barely turned his head as he barreled down the driveway.

"Sorry!" Wyatt shouted as he yanked open the truck door. He hadn't even closed his door before gunning down the street.

WHAT THE hell was that? Timothy stopped at the gate as Wyatt drove down the street. He went back into the yard and sat down at the table, leaning back and staring into the sky. Why had Wyatt kissed him? More important than that, why did he run away? Timothy was pretty sure it had nothing to do his kissing abilities, but he wasn't positive. Maybe it did. Ethan always said he was a good kisser. Timothy'd never kissed anyone else, and Ethan sure as hell wasn't known for his honesty. Timothy stood up and paced around the yard, ignoring the shivers he got as the sweat from his run dried on his skin in the cool air. He bent down and grabbed Wyatt's cigarette butt and dropped it in the can. His head was spinning with questions, and he went inside and upstairs to his room. He dropped on his bed, holding himself back from texting Wyatt. It wasn't until his mom came home and opened the front door that Timothy realized he hadn't kissed back.

WYATT SAT on the hood of his truck, with an unopened beer in his hand and a headache. He looked at his hand, the cuts open again, because once he'd driven away from Timothy's house and gotten back to his own, he'd punched his truck over and over. He went into his house, ignoring his mother passed out on the couch, and grabbed one of her beers. He held it over his cuts and bruises, the condensation gathering even though the night was chilly. He didn't bother finishing any of his homework, just went back outside and sat on the hood of his truck, his face and neck hot every time he thought about what he'd done. How the hell could he be so damn stupid? He closed his eyes and pushed the thought of the shocked look on Timothy's face into the back of his mind, away from everything. Wyatt thought about what would have happened if he'd stayed. If Timothy had grabbed Wyatt and squeezed his arms tight around Wyatt's waist, pushing against him. He felt himself, even embarrassed as he was, getting hard in his jeans. He put the unopened beer down and pressed his hands against his eyes as if he was trying to push Timothy out of his brain. What was he thinking? It wasn't until he'd dropped a blanket over his mother, put the beer back in the refrigerator, and gotten into bed that he realized he hadn't even given Timothy a chance to kiss him back.

TIMOTHY WAITED outside the school until the last bell was ringing for Wyatt to show up. Timothy was tempted to call him, but he needed to get inside before he was marked as late, so he ran in and barely made it before Mr. Ridley walked through the door. Lacey shook her head at him and smirked. He turned red and kept his head down. One thing Timothy had learned from his father was how to focus. He pushed Wyatt and the kiss into the back of his mind and concentrated on school. When lunchtime rolled around, Timothy went out to the parking lot and called Clara at the board of education.

"Hi. My name is Timothy Mitchell, and I'm calling from Burton High. I'm looking to contact a teacher. Thomas Matthews. He taught here four years ago."

Clara Drake's voice was soft and thick with a Southern accent. "Why are you looking for him?"

"Just wanted to do an article for the school paper and catch up with a couple of former teachers, and he's the only one I can't locate."

"Hmmm," she replied. He could hear her typing in the background. "I can't seem to find any current employment or address. The last address he had is in Monroeville, but that was four years ago when he was teaching at Burton. Sorry," she said, and Timothy had to strain to hear her voice. "I can't find anything more recent."

"Thanks for checking. I'll see where else I might be able to dig it up. Hey, could you tell me if there's a teacher with the name Thompson at Union Elementary? Thompson is the last name."

She typed a few more moments on her computer. "Nope. Sorry, hon. I don't see anyone with that last name ever at any of the Union schools."

"Hmm, weird." Timothy looked at his watch. "Thanks so much. I really appreciate it. Have a great day." He hung up and ran to the cafeteria to grab something to eat and spend some time with Lacey before afternoon classes started.

BY FRIDAY, he'd seen Wyatt a couple of times in the hallways of school but only from a distance, and he was getting angry.

"Earth to Timothy." Lacey was sitting on her bed, painting each fingernail a different color. "You haven't been paying attention for the last five minutes."

"Sorry, Little Edie. I've got a headache." He smiled and could feel the tension. Even he wasn't fooled by his own smile.

"Don't Little Edie me. Ohh, do you want to watch *Grey Gardens* tonight? We haven't seen it in about eight months."

He shrugged. "We could do that. Do we have enough snacks to get through the main movie and the extra footage?"

"I doubt it." She set one bottle of nail polish down on her bedside table and picked up another. "Dad hasn't been shopping this week, and they don't trust me enough to shop for the whole family on my own." She stopped painting a nail and looked at him expectantly.

Timothy sighted and stood up. "Fine. I'll go get snacks. It's not like I've got anything better to do on a Friday night."

"It's not night. It's still late afternoon," she replied. "And you love it."

"This means I get whatever I want, and I don't want to hear about you not liking stuff."

Lacey rolled her eyes. "Whatever."

Timothy was out the door before she could tell him anything specific about what to buy. He was almost at the grocery store when he saw Wyatt's truck at Big Tommy's bar. He frowned and cut the wheel sharply, pulling into the lot. Timothy parked in front, hoping his parents wouldn't be driving by in the next ten minutes, while he was yelling at Wyatt. He pushed open the front door and felt the eyes of the after-work crowd staring at him. Timothy could see a couple of guys shift in their seats, and he knew they were wondering what the hell the sheriff's gay son was doing in a bar. His eyes adjusted to the dim light, and he saw Wyatt sitting at the bar talking to Big Tommy, with an open half-empty beer bottle next to him. He walked toward Wyatt and realized he was behaving like a stupid jealous boyfriend, which was the last thing he wanted. He was upset Wyatt had run after the kiss, but he and Wyatt weren't a couple. They weren't even friends, not really, and he couldn't get mad at someone who kissed and ran. He inhaled deeply and walked over to Wyatt, standing a respectable distance. He lifted his chin in greeting when Wyatt looked up, face flushed bright red, even in the low lighting.

"Hey, Big Tommy. How are you?"

"Well, well. Is the sheriff sending you in to bust me?" Big Tommy folded his arms over his chest, resting them on his big belly.

Timothy laughed. "Not at all, sir. I was wondering if you were able to give Wyatt the information we needed."

Big Tommy leaned forward against the bar. "Information?"

Wyatt looked like he was about to bolt out the door, and Timothy couldn't help but feel the tiniest bit of satisfaction, so he drew out the moment a little longer than he needed to. "Yeah. He didn't say anything? We're working on a project. You mind if I ask you a few questions?" Timothy waited for Big Tommy to shake his head before he sat down. "Wyatt found an old diary in the wall of the house you're having renovated. The last entry was about four years ago, but there's no last names, and he asked me to help track down the owner."

Big Tommy looked mildly suspicious as he reached over, grabbed a glass, and poured some club soda.

"I went back through the old yearbooks, but the names I can find don't match up with any of the people. Either too young or they don't know the other names in the diary. I was really hoping you'd help, if you can. It'd be a great story for the school paper."

Big Tommy relaxed a little bit, and Timothy could see he was trying to figure out if this had anything to do with the fact he'd served Wyatt a beer. He downed his club soda and poured himself another one.

"I was hoping you'd remember who was there about four years ago?"

He shook his head. "I suppose I could look through some records for you fellas."

"Thanks, Big Tommy. I'd really appreciate it."

"And you won't—"

"Won't say a word, sir. See no evil and all that." He turned to Wyatt. "Don't drive drunk, buddy."

Timothy shook Big Tommy's hand and headed out, ignoring Wyatt. It bothered him how easy it had become to lie to people. It was one thing not to tell his parents about a dating app or two, but he'd—

"Hey!" Wyatt's voice interrupted the thought. "What the hell?"

"What are you talking about?" Timothy pulled open his car door as Wyatt came around to the driver's side.

"Was that you trying to fuck with me? You told me you wouldn't tell anyone—"

"I haven't said anything to anyone, Wyatt." Timothy leaned against the doorframe and shook his head. "I didn't say—"

"Are you trying to mess me up?"

"I'm pretty sure you're doing a great job of being messed up all on your own."

"You know what I mean," Wyatt said, clutching the door.

"No, Wyatt. I really don't. Right now the only thing I know is that you're the king of mixed messages. Now let go of my door. I have somewhere to be."

FOUR HOURS later Lacey turned to Timothy as she rolled up the last bag of chips. "Want to tell me what's going on?"

Timothy looked up at her, startled. He frowned. "What do you mean?"

"First of all, you didn't laugh once. Not once. And secondly you barely ate anything. And you haven't mentioned my nails at all."

"Maybe I was just trying to be polite."

She smiled. "You?"

"Yeah, that's fair."

"You okay?" She was still smiling, but he knew she was worried. "You're not usually so scowly and broody. Even when you're being a bitch."

He looked at Lacey, horrified. "I'm never a bitch." His whole face softened. "Well, maybe sometimes. And nothing's wrong. I'm tired. That's all. It's been a long week."

She looked at him like she didn't believe him at all, but she didn't say anything, just handed him a bag of chocolates. Sometimes Lacey knew he was so stubborn, she needed to let him tell her things in his own time.

WYATT HAD finished six beers after Timothy left him standing in the parking lot. It shouldn't have been a big deal for someone his size, but he downed them quickly. He also wasn't really a drinker, even with his mother being a drunk. The last time he'd been drunk was the night his dad died. His mother had passed out after she'd finished off one of the two bottles of Jack Daniels she'd bought at the store. He'd gotten wasted in the backyard, crying most of the time as the alcohol burned his throat. He'd thrown up several times, and even though he hated the feeling, it pushed all the sadness out of his mind for a short time.

He was sober enough to know he wasn't sober enough to drive, so he was walking home, not quite stumbling, but his head was spinning, and he knew his feet would hurt like hell by the time he got home. He was about halfway there when a car came up behind him. He moved to the side of the road to let it pass, but it stopped beside him and the window rolled down.

"Wyatt." Sheriff Mitchell nodded at him.

"Sir." Wyatt smiled back, not trusting himself to nod without pitching forward.

"Everything all right? Your car break down?"

Wyatt opened his mouth to say something when the sheriff held up his hands.

"I can smell the beer on you from here so be very careful with what you say."

Wyatt stared at him, and his eyes were so much like Timothy's in the dim light of the setting sun, Wyatt's breath caught in his throat. "I left my car in… a parking lot, sir. So I wouldn't… you know."

The sheriff sighed heavily and leaned over to open up the passenger side door. "Get in."

Wyatt felt tears behind his eyes, and he was tired and worn down. "Please don't arrest me, Sheriff."

"Get in, Wyatt. I want to get you home safe. I'm not interested in busting you."

Wyatt didn't say anything as he climbed in and shut the door behind him. He carefully pulled the seat belt around him, clipped it in place, and then leaned his head against the window, feeling the cool glass against his head.

"I'm guessing I don't have to give you a lecture about underage drinking and how damn lucky you are I'm not pushing that fact? And I'm also guessing you're going to feel like shit tomorrow, so let's consider that your punishment, hmm?"

"Thanks, Sheriff." Wyatt breathed deeply, trying hard not to let his head fall forward. He was silent the rest of the way to his house, and when Sheriff Mitchell pulled into the short, overgrown driveway at Wyatt's house, Wyatt unbuckled his seat belt and sat in the police cruiser, not moving.

"Do you need me to come in and speak with your mom, Wyatt?"

Wyatt looked up at the sheriff and again saw Timothy's eyes staring back at him. But it was so much more. There, reflected in the man in front of him, was Timothy's jawline, his ears, his nose. It was harder, more angular, more masculine than Timothy, but he was there nonetheless, and Wyatt's eyes were tearing up again.

He shook his head and then spoke before he could stop himself. "No thanks, sir. But would you do me a favor? Would you tell Timothy I'm sorry, Sheriff? Tell him I'm really, really sorry."

The sheriff's eyebrows furrowed in concern. "For what? Did you—you didn't hurt Timmy, did you?"

Wyatt shook his head sharply, instantly regretting it. "I wouldn't hurt him. Ever." He started laughing his breath hitching in his chest. "He lets you call him Timmy?"

Sheriff Mitchell snorted his own laugh out. "No. He'd never let me call him that. Sometimes it slips out, reminds me of when he was a little boy."

"I wouldn't ever hurt him. Never." Wyatt's head stopped spinning, but he laid it back against the seat. "Timmy. Timothy. Timmy Tim Tim." He rolled the words around his mouth, letting it rest on his tongue, feeling every syllable in his body. "Timothy."

Sheriff Mitchell sat silent for a moment and shifted the car into Park. "Wyatt. I'm not sure what or if there's anything going on between you and Timothy, but he's my son. I don't want him involved in underage drinking. Do we understand each other?"

"Yes, sir." Wyatt nodded an affirmation. He opened the car door and carefully stepped out, making sure he didn't land flat on his ass. He leaned on the car door as he turned around to face the sheriff. "And there's nothing going on between me and Timothy. He deserves way better than me."

Wyatt shut the door and stumbled up his front steps before Sheriff Mitchell could call out to him.

He walked through the door to find his mother sitting up on the couch, a glass in one hand, the dim light of the television reflecting off the half an ice cube left.

He took a deep breath and carefully walked over to the chair. As he sank deep into the cushion, Colonel came out from his bedroom. Wyatt scratched Colonel behind the ears. The dog rolled over for a belly rub, but Wyatt couldn't bend down without falling over, so he sat back in the chair, listening to Colonel whine for a minute before the dog went back into the bedroom.

Wyatt watched the television; the sound was almost completely down, and he had no idea what show was playing.

His mother held out her glass. "Wyatt, get me another." He didn't say anything but stood up and grabbed the empty. He was still a little unsteady on his feet, and he walked carefully into the kitchen, as she called out. "Three ice cubes, Wyatt. You know how I like it."

He sighed. *Yeah, I know how you like it*, he wanted to say. *I've always known since I was first getting you your damn drinks when I was eight. And after having to drag your sorry ass to bed since Daddy died, and cleaning up the puke all over the bedroom, and making excuses with my teachers when you didn't come to conferences, or answer phone calls, or emails, and picking you up after Big Tommy's closes....* And the first thing Wyatt did when he was afraid was go and get drunk. He cursed silently and rubbed his eyes.

Wyatt poured her drink and went back into the living room. He held out the glass. "Here you go, Momma."

"Thanks, sweetie. How was your day? Where did you go after school?"

He sighed as he lit up a cigarette and sat back in the chair. He sure as hell wasn't going to tell her he'd been drinking. And she knew he wouldn't hang out by himself without Colonel. He told her what he wished he'd been doing.

"I was hanging out with Timothy."

"Timothy?"

"The sheriff's son," he said, his voice flat.

His momma paused for a moment and then finished her drink in one gulp. "He's the homosexual."

Wyatt stared at her, the light from the television too dim for her to see him flush red. He shrugged.

"I don't want you to be friends with someone like that." Her voice had no tone. The only thing that colored it was the whiskey.

"Why not?"

"Because he's a sinner." She leaned forward and held out her hand for him to pass her a cigarette. "I taught you that."

He pulled his pack out and handed her one and his lighter. "He's a friend of mine."

"People like that, homosexuals, they only want to corrupt you." She inhaled deeply on the cigarette and handed him back his lighter. "Don't let him drag you down, Wyatt."

Wyatt grabbed it from her and ashed into an empty can they were using as an ashtray. "No one's corrupting anyone. He's a nice guy and he's my friend. I'm going to bed." He dropped his butt into the can and went into his bedroom. He lay down on the bed with his shoes still on and fell asleep with Colonel right next to him.

Chapter Eight

His mom had already had breakfast and headed out for her weekly errands before Timothy even got out of bed. It was the latest he'd slept in a long time, and the truth was, he wasn't even sleeping. He'd mostly tossed and turned for reasons he couldn't even truly understand. It was partially the fight with Wyatt, but it was also about the fact he'd hit a dead end on figuring out what happened to Bobby.

It was most likely Bobby was dead. He knew that. He hated to admit it, but he knew it. Timothy thought he had two good possible leads. The first was the teacher, Tom Matthews. The other was finding the writer at the newspaper, Matt Thompson. One knew Bobby, and the other had information about other missing kids. He frowned at the fact he couldn't find either of them. It was as if they wanted to disappear. He decided to try to find the mom of the other kid from the article, Julia Madden. Her son Andrew disappeared from the Greenville area. He frowned again as he booted up his computer. It wasn't unheard of for children to go missing in clusters over periods of time. It happened, and Timothy wanted to know if there were more children who went missing around the same time.

After logging on to a couple of missing persons databases, he set search parameters and let the computer run its search. Timothy scratched his head, not sure where he was going wrong. His dad said sometimes you had to look at a puzzle when you were in the middle of it in order to make some sense of it. He pulled some index cards from his desk drawer and laid them out in front of him, grabbing a pen.

He sighed heavily. Okay, what did he know?

Bobby LaFleur disappeared almost four years ago.

Andrew Madden disappeared about a year before.

According to Maddie LaFleur, Bobby wouldn't have run away and he wouldn't have killed himself.

Bobby was dating Wyatt Courtland.

Wyatt had a bit of a temper, but Timothy couldn't imagine him hurting Bobby, never mind killing him. The way he'd talked about

Bobby was so sweet, so sincere. He couldn't imagine Wyatt even yelling at Bobby, let alone laying a hand on him.

Matt Thompson wrote an article implying more children had gone missing.

Tom Matthews took an interest in Bobby's poetry.

Timothy turned back to his computer and clicked on the first window. There were thirty-four girls and forty-seven boys between the ages of twelve and sixteen who'd gone missing around the same time Bobby and Andrew went missing. First, he eliminated the girls. Bobby was white, so was Andrew, so he eliminated everyone who wasn't. Bobby and Andrew were both fourteen so he took out the older boys and was left with sixteen possibilities. Too many to track down and not use his father's name. The school newspaper article thing would only get him so far and there would be no reason for a school paper to be interviewing parents from fifty miles away four years later. Timothy noted each child's name on top of separate index cards and looked up whatever newspaper stories he could find on any of these new names. He wondered why Bobby's behavior changed so much, according to Wyatt. He'd dismissed Miss Maddy's talk about Bobby being moody to teenage angst, but Wyatt had a different perspective and it made him curious.

About Charles Williams: *Possibly ran away.*

About Ryan Bolger: *His parents are asking the public for any help.*

About Rob Lewis: *He didn't run away.*

About Joe Freeman: *He was feeling depressed because of people picking on him at school, but he would never hurt himself.*

About Joey Travis: *He was bullied, but I didn't think it was so bad he'd run away. Please come home.*

Timothy read the articles and knew his eyes were tearing up a bit. What he was reading was hitting close to home. Even growing up in California, having parents who'd accepted him when he came out, some of the attitudes he'd had to face at school were things he'd rather forget.

He ran the back of his hand across his eyes. This was more than hitting a dead end on an investigation he wasn't even supposed to be doing. He opened up another window and let it search for any Julia Madden in the area and turned off the monitor. He grabbed his running shoes and iPod and jumped down the stairs. He stuck his head in the living room long enough to tell his mother he was going for a run and then headed off down the street. When Timothy ran, everything seemed to fall into place. The world made sense. The rhythm of his music matched the rhythm of his feet as they hit the ground. The feeling of his muscles and his lungs as he pushed them, shoving every thought out of his head. He didn't think of anything but going faster, taking longer strides, and burning everything out of his brain.

He hit his stride, letting the sweat run down his neck and back. He wasn't sure how much time had passed before he got back home, but he went right to the kitchen and grabbed a water, then headed into the backyard. He opened up the bottle and gulped half of it, then upended it over his head, letting the cold water shock him as it ran over his head, down his shoulders and arms. He shivered and drank the rest of the water. He stood in the backyard, staring at the fence, the branches of the trees in the neighbor's yard reaching toward the sun, bending over the fence, twisting around each other, watching the leaves flutter slightly in the breeze.

His mother popped her head out of the back door. "You getting hungry, sweetie? We were going to wait a bit, unless you're feeling like you need to eat now."

"No," he replied quietly. "I'm good, thanks."

She frowned at him, her mom instincts kicking into high gear. She stepped out into the backyard and went over to him. "Are you all right?"

"I had a weird day, Mom. That's all." He sat down at the table. "Mom, I have a strange question I need your expertise on."

She raised an eyebrow and sat down opposite him. "I'll try."

"Why would a teenager go from being shy with someone they had a crush on to being pushy?"

"Pushy?"

"Like really aggressive. Like trying to take someone's pants off aggressive?"

His mother was a laid-back woman, but when she needed to, she became more of an interrogator than his dad. "Is something going on—"

"No, Mom. It's no one I know. It was a psych paper I was reading online, and I can't figure out how the subject changed so quickly from one type of person to another." That was the worst excuse he'd ever come up with, and he almost flinched when he said it.

She nodded, as if she didn't believe him. "If there's something going on at your school—"

"No, Mom. I swear. It's no one at school."

She inhaled deeply. "Well, I was an education major, not a psychology major, but we had enough psych classes that it sounds to me as if there was some sexual abuse going on with this person. Children who are abused often act out sexually, especially with other children."

"I… hadn't thought about that." He frowned and looked at the table. Was someone abusing Bobby? It wouldn't have been Miss Maddy. His mother's voice pulled him out of his thoughts.

"If there's something happening that you can stop, I trust you to stop it and tell an adult." She stood up and kissed his forehead. "I do trust you, honey."

"Thanks, Mom." He watched her go back inside and sat at the picnic table for a little while.

When he finally felt ready, he took a long hot shower and went back into his bedroom to stare at the faces of missing children, feeling as if they were begging him to help. He found himself angry at Wyatt for pulling him into this and then, just as fast, he felt really sad. Wyatt was hurting every day, stuck not being able to talk about who he really is. Not able even to really grieve for Bobby.

Timothy knew the tears were close to falling again. Maybe his dad was right. Maybe he wasn't cut out for this. Maybe he wasn't strong enough for police work. He clicked over to the window where he'd been searching for Julia Madden and copied the two addresses most likely to be Andrew's mother, then grabbed his phone. He texted Wyatt.

Be at my place tomorrow at 10. We have to head over toward Spartanburg to find someone.

Let Wyatt figure out what to do with that. Timothy opened up an Excel file and entered data. Names, dates of disappearance, age, location, whatever information he thought might help. He sorted it as many different ways as he could think, cutting and pasting and adding tabs, so he could click back and forth easily.

There were too many coincidences for all of this to be unrelated. Somehow this had to be connected, right? Or was he trying too hard? Maybe he was seeing patterns where they didn't really exist. Maybe Bobby wandered off and got hurt. There were plenty of woods around the town. Easy to get lost in and easy to get hurt. He saved his files and page links and then closed his computer. Timothy went downstairs to start the homework he hadn't finished, so he wouldn't be rushing back from Spartanburg tomorrow to finish. He made a pot of coffee and sat down at the table, pulling books out of his backpack.

His dad walked into the room to grab his Saturday beer. "Any plans tonight?"

Timothy shook his head. "No. Just hanging out with my amazing parents. Unless you guys are going out, in which case, I'll be hanging out on my own."

"No, we're in tonight. What do you want for dinner?" His dad was randomly opening and closing the cabinet doors, as if in search of something specific.

"Pizza? I went for a run earlier, so I'm not too worried about calories."

"I think we can do pizza. A-ha." He pulled a package out of the cabinet and smiled at Timothy. "Your mother's been hiding cookies from me. She says I'm getting a little soft."

"You can always come running with me, if you want. I'll take it easy on you."

"You're so nice." His dad ate a couple of cookies. "I ran into Wyatt last night. He said to tell you he was sorry."

"Really?"

"Any ideas what he's sorry about?"

Timothy shook his head slowly. "Nope. Sorry."

"You know," his dad said, sitting down at the table, "there seems to be quite a lot going on between you and Wyatt these days. You're spending all sorts of time with him; he's walking home drunk and apologizing to you through me."

"Drunk? Did you run him in?"

"No." The sheriff yanked the top off his beer bottle.

Timothy hesitated for a minute. "Glad to hear it."

"I figured you would be." His dad stood up and rested a hand on Timothy's shoulder. He paused before he spoke. "Study hard."

Timothy had a hard time focusing on his homework for the rest of the night.

CHAPTER NINE

TIMOTHY STEPPED outside Sunday morning after a restless night's sleep. Wyatt stood on the sidewalk in front of Timothy's house, leaning against his truck. Timothy opened up the passenger's side door on his car and then walked around to the driver's side. He put his coffee in the cupholder, buckled his seat belt, and started the car. He adjusted the seat on the passenger side to push it back as far as possible, then waited for Wyatt.

Wyatt sat down in the car, pulled his seat belt on, and shut the door. Timothy backed out of the driveway and turned on the radio to some country music station.

Neither of them said anything until Timothy was on the highway, headed toward Spartanburg in search of Andrew Madden's mother, Julia. Almost twenty minutes of silence passed before Timothy glanced over at Wyatt.

"Pass me my sunglasses please. They're in the glove compartment."

Wyatt handed the glasses over and Timothy took them.

"Thanks. Dad said you asked him to apologize to me."

Wyatt waited for a few moments before he finally responded. "Yeah?" His voice was flat.

"Yeah."

"Don't remember. I was pretty drunk." Wyatt didn't look at Timothy. He kept staring out the window. Timothy signaled to pull off the two-lane highway and slowed the car. The crunch of gravel on the side of the road made Wyatt sit up in his seat.

"What the fuck is wrong with you," Timothy snapped as he put the car in Park and flipped on the hazard lights.

"What're you doing?" Wyatt turned around and stared at the scattered cars speeding past them. "You're not far enough off the road. You're gonna get us killed."

"What's going on, Wyatt?"

"With what?"

"Stop acting like an idiot! You flirt with me, you tell me you're gay and had something going on with Bobby, and now you hook up with guys on Grindr. Then you show up at my house, kiss me, and run away. What the hell is that about? And then you're drinking and apologizing to my dad. Just tell me, Wyatt. Please tell me what's going on. Just tell me."

"I don't know, okay? I'm sorry. Jesus, I'm sorry. I don't know what's wrong with me." Wyatt covered his face with his hands and leaned forward, as if he was going to throw up. "I don't know what's wrong. I want to be around you, Timothy. I want to be your boyfriend and kiss you and fuck you, and I know I'm some piece-of-shit redneck who you wouldn't even look at twice. And I kissed you because I couldn't not kiss you. I mean I didn't… I don't know what I mean." Wyatt kept his face in his hands, breathing heavily.

Timothy stared at him for a moment, then another. He put the car in drive and signaled to pull back onto the highway.

He waited until Wyatt's breathing evened out before he spoke quietly. "Sounds like we've got a lot to talk about on the way to Spartanburg."

Wyatt still wouldn't talk for a few minutes, and Timothy waited quietly, patiently, needing to hear Wyatt before he said anything. "My mom. She told me that gay people go to hell."

"And what do you think?" Timothy surprised himself by sounding more gentle than he felt inside. "Seriously, what do you think?"

"Why am I gay? Why are you gay?"

Timothy paused. "I don't know. It's how it is, I guess. To be honest, I've never really thought about it."

"Really?"

"Nope. I don't know if that makes me stupid, but I've never wondered why I am the way I am. I don't wonder about what things might be like if something were different. That doesn't do anyone any good. This is the world I live in, Wyatt, and the only thing I can do is live in it. If I want to change something and I can, I will, but otherwise? Living a lie? Hiding my feelings? That's all bullshit. Not something I want to be part of."

Wyatt snorted a laugh. "It's that easy, huh?"

"Not all the time, no, but usually it's other people who make things complicated. We are who we are. If someone else doesn't like me, it's not my problem. It's theirs. And you never answered my question."

"What?"

"You said your mom said gay people go to hell. I asked what you thought. You never answered."

Wyatt smiled. "You hear something every day, it's hard to not believe it." Wyatt leaned up against the door and shifted his body as best he could in the small car. "Can I say something? I mean without you getting pissed at me?"

Timothy laughed. "Great way to start a conversation. Sure, I'll do my best."

"Not everyone is like you, Timothy." Wyatt took a deep breath. "I don't mean that bad, but face it: you're lucky. Your parents are cool with you being, you know, gay, and you have enough money to go wherever you want to go to college and you're strong. Stronger than me."

"That's not true."

"C'mon, Tim—"

"It's not true." Timothy interrupted him and kept talking rapidly. "Yeah, the me being lucky part is true. I hit the jackpot with my parents, but you're strong, Wyatt. First of all, you can bench-press me—"

"That's not what I mean," Wyatt shot back.

"I know. I was making a joke." He sighed heavily. "Look at what you've dealt with, Wyatt. If I heard the kinds of things your mom said, I don't know if I could have shown the slightest bit of kindness to someone like Bobby, and here you are, trying to find out what happened to him. I don't know if I could do something like that."

"You could've done it standing on your head." Wyatt leaned over. His voice got quieter, huskier. "You like the fact I can bench-press you?"

Timothy's grip on the steering wheel jerked slightly. "It's… intriguing."

Wyatt laughed, really laughed, deep and throaty, and sat back. He poked Timothy in the arm. "So, I'm your type? You know, I don't know anything about the guys you've dated."

"Not much to tell, I'm afraid." Timothy checked the mirror and pulled over into the middle lane to let a car pass. "I've only dated one guy. Ethan."

"What was he like?"

"Are you sure you want to hear this?"

"You've heard about Bobby. And I'm not a jealous guy."

Timothy nodded. "Well, Ethan was smart. Really smart. He was serious and sarcastic. Shorter than me."

"What happened? I mean between the two of you?"

"We moved. We tried to do a long-distance thing, but we were fifteen years old. I mean, there he was, all alone in California, and I was here." He checked his mirrors and moved back into the fast lane. "It didn't end well."

"He was an asshole."

Timothy laughed and glanced at Wyatt. "No need to be indignant on my behalf. We were fifteen. It's not like it was so long ago. You remember what it's like. You're convinced you're going to be together forever. I did love him, though. Really."

"I can tell."

Timothy frowned. "I wasn't saying anything about you and me."

"Yeah," Wyatt said. His voice sounded sad. "I know that. Whatever. I mean, whatever happened between me and Bobby, it's… I mean, what I thought about Bobby, what I think about you, it's not the same."

"Yeah. I understand."

"Really?"

"I think so. Maybe." Timothy turned to Wyatt for a second before looking back at the road. "So, where does that leave us? You and me?"

"You tell me."

Timothy spoke carefully, slowly, knowing each word was important. "I would never out you, Wyatt. Your secrets aren't mine to tell. But I won't hide for you. I won't go back into the closet. I mean, not that I could, but I won't lie about who I am."

"But you'd be okay with not saying much other than hello at school? Meeting me in a quiet part of the town? Never hanging out at my house?"

Timothy drew in breath, getting ready for a fight.

"Yeah, I'm asking for a lot. I'm sorry, but I can't tell my mom. I don't have anywhere else to go. I don't have anything. But if I had you, it'd be something." He paused. "Something."

"I'm… I'm not making any promises, Wyatt." Timothy pulled off the highway toward Spartanburg and slowed the car down as he waited at the top of the exit for a minivan to pass. "I like you. Yes, I'm attracted to you, and yes, I want to get to know you better, so we can take things one step at a time. See what happens. If you're good with that."

"For you? Yeah, I'm okay with that."

"One thing," Timothy said as he pulled out a piece of paper from the cupholder, underneath his coffee. "We have to tell my parents." He handed the paper to Wyatt. "That's where we're heading."

"No. No way." Wyatt shook his head. He pulled off his baseball cap and ran his hand through his hair. "We can't tell anyone."

"Wyatt, my parents know how to keep a secret. Besides, no dating anyone until my parents meet the potential boyfriend. He has to come over for dinner before anything. House rules." Timothy gulped down the last bit of coffee. "My dad's a cop. He knows how to keep his mouth shut." Wyatt didn't respond, so Timothy continued. "When you do have dinner with us, you might want to wear sleeves. You do own a shirt with sleeves, right?"

"You're not funny." Wyatt slumped down in the seat as best he could and crossed his thick bare arms over his chest.

"I'm hilarious," Timothy replied. "The funniest guy you know."

"I should meet more people."

THE FIRST Julia Madden they found lived in the city proper, and she was barely in her early twenties. She was thin and sweet, and her brown hair fell around her face. She thought it was funny they thought she might have a kid. It took them longer to find the other Julia Madden. Spartanburg would have been her post office, but she lived out on a dirt road, almost a half hour out of the city itself. They turned down three different rocky roads before they found the correct one.

Wyatt stretched when he stepped out of the car, shaking out his legs after the ride. Timothy grabbed his messenger bag, set his notebook and pen within easy access, and headed toward the door. They both glanced around. The grass was more brown than green, and there were patches of dirt in the small front yard. The house itself was run-down, and Timothy glanced over at Wyatt. Wyatt seemed unconcerned about the house and its state. Timothy realized he didn't have any idea about Wyatt's house and where he lived. Before they could get to the porch, the door opened and a woman stepped outside. Her hair was brown with thick streaks of gray, and she moved as if every part of her body hurt. She scratched the back of her head, careful not to light her hair on fire with the cigarette held daintily between two fingers.

"Help you?"

Timothy smiled carefully. "I'm Timothy Mitchell. I'm writing an article for my school paper, about crimes that affect local communities and especially high schoolers."

"Yeah? You a reporter?" Her accent was thick and she crossed her arms across her ample breasts and stayed where she was on the porch, blocking them from coming closer and staring down on them. Her eyes were glazed as if she was asleep, and Timothy wondered if they'd woken her up. He narrowed his eyes as he realized that the sleepiness came from inside her. It was something he'd first seen back in California. There was a woman who was at the sheriff's office. He'd been barely ten years old and was sitting out with the officer at the front desk, and a woman walked in. Her face was bloody and she had a split lip, but he'd noticed her eyes. Timothy didn't know what had happened, but when he looked into her eyes, it seemed as if she was dead already. The only thing about her that proved she was alive was the fact she was breathing. It was the same thing he saw in this woman's eyes. The same internal death.

"Well, it's a school paper, but it's something I'm hoping to major in at school. See where it leads me." He tried to sound businesslike and calm.

"Lucky. Lots of kids in these parts don't get to go to school."

"I am lucky," Timothy said as his eyes flicked over to Wyatt. "I was hoping to ask you a few questions about Andrew, your son. Would you mind?"

"He's with Jesus now."

Wyatt and Timothy glanced at each other. "He's passed away? Did you find him?"

She shook her head and pulled a pack of cigarettes out of her pocket, chaining the new one with the old and flicking the butt onto a patch of dirt in her yard. "Pastor Steve told me."

"I'm sorry. Pastor Steve? Who's that?"

"You're not from around here, are you?" She shook her head again. This time at him.

He stared at her. "About an hour away."

"Community must be something pretty big to you. Usually people only mean their own town when they say that. You said crimes that affect the community." She was almost smirking at him.

Timothy opened his mouth to say something, but Wyatt jumped in first. "Ma'am, whatever happened to Andrew might've happened to a friend of mine. My friend Bobby, he went missing about a year after Andrew. We were trying to find out if they might be, you know, connected somehow."

"Ah. That's what the other reporter said. He was a real reporter, though, not a kid."

"Matt Thompson?"

She nodded in reply. "I think that was his name. He was nice. First time I saw him, I wasn't even sure he was out of high school himself. He looked so young."

Wyatt stepped a little closer. "Bobby's mom, she's not doing so well. If you can think of anything that might help her, we'd like to know."

"What makes you think I might know something?" She kept smoking and staring at them, and Timothy couldn't tell if he was annoyed or unsettled with her attitude.

"Well, you said Andrew's with Jesus." Wyatt shrugged. "You know for sure?"

She exhaled a plume of smoke. "That's what he said. Said he was able to save Andy's soul in time."

"In time?" Wyatt pulled out his own cigarettes and lit one. "What do you mean in time? And who do you mean? You mean you know where he was?"

"Nope. Not at first." She sat down on the porch, rested her feet on the top step. She was responding better to Wyatt, so Timothy kept his mouth shut, figuring he'd jump in if he really had to. "Pastor Steve told me later on. He's helped lots of kids. Mostly boys. Kids like Andrew. You know, artsy and…." She snapped her fingers. "What's the word? Sensitive. Andrew was sensitive."

"He just took him?" Wyatt's face was getting red. "You let him?"

"No!" Julia snapped at him. Her eyes brightened for a minute. "I wouldn't have done that." Timothy watched her eyes die again. She shrugged and flicked the second cigarette onto the dirt. "He was my son. When the reporter came by, I still didn't know. Didn't find out till a month or so later." She sniffed, and her eyes were wet with tears. "I wish I had known, though. I would've visited. I loved him. He was my baby."

"You didn't find out he was dead or that Pastor Steve had taken him?" Wyatt flicked his own cigarette onto the dirt, half smoked.

"Either. Both." She was speaking faster now, and Timothy could tell from the way her body was shifting that she was jumping back and forth from past to present in her head.

"Can you tell me exactly what happened, ma'am? Bobby's mom's been out of her mind for four years. I sure would like to tell her something." He stepped closer to the bottom step and knelt down, so they were almost on eye level.

"Andrew up and disappeared one day. I knew he wouldn'ta run off or nothing like that. He wasn't strong enough to be on his own, but I couldn't find him. I was outta my mind for days. Cops came by. Useless. Nothing they could do, least that's what they said. I drove around the town for hours hoping I'd find him." She seemed like she might cry, and Timothy felt a stab of sympathy for her. "I about gave up any hope of finding him when Pastor Steve came by. Said he'd found the boy out near that pervert's house. He took my boy to beat the sin out of him. That's what he told me, but—"

She paused, and Wyatt's voice was so quiet and soft Timothy could barely hear him. "What pervert?"

"That sissy florist, Mike Chamberlain. I guess Andrew used to go by his house." She pulled another cigarette from the pack, stared at it, and put it back. "I don't think he touched Andrew none. Andrew, he woulda told me that. But Pastor Steve, he thought that Mike might've been leading him astray. That's what he said. Astray. Pastor Steve, he took Andrew back to his place to push the devil out of him. Andrew, well, according to Pastor Steve, he fought back, so when the punishment got more strict, Andrew, he couldn't take it. I wanted to tell someone. Tell the police, but Pastor Steve, he told me I didn't have no proof. He'd told me, but he said I couldn't prove it. He said the police wouldn't believe me. That I only had this story and he'd deny if anyone asked." She looked up, tears in her eyes. "I tried to tell that reporter, but he never called me back. Never. I called him at least ten times. Nothing. Do you think I did something wrong? Do you think it's my fault?"

Wyatt ignored the question. "Where can we find Pastor Steve?"

"I loved him, you know," she said as she stood up and wiped the dirt from the back of her shorts. "I loved him. I don't want you to think I didn't."

THE DIRT was still stirred up from his car when Timothy drove up the long dirt road. They'd gotten lost on the way here, and Timothy felt as if his heart was beating loud enough for Wyatt to hear.

"I'll make sure you're safe," Wyatt said, like he was reading Timothy's mind.

"I'm fine."

Wyatt nodded. "Uh-huh. Is that why you're white knuckling the steering wheel?"

"If my dad knew I was here—"

"He doesn't. That's why we ended up here instead of him, right?" Wyatt traced his finger along the rim of the window. "You wanted to prove your dad wrong, right?"

"I figured I'd find out what happened, not let my idiot ass be talked into going to find a possible murderer."

"I'll make sure you're safe," Wyatt repeated.

They pulled up, and Timothy turned the car off but left the keys in the ignition. He took a deep breath and then opened the door. Wyatt opened his own door, and Timothy gestured at him. "Don't lock your door. Just in case we have to get out of here in a hurry."

"You worry too much."

"You don't worry enough." Timothy shook his head. Wyatt clearly didn't have enough sense to be afraid, but Timothy had heard enough stories from his dad to know how things happened.

The sign in front of the small building was hand-painted, not too well, with the words LAMB OF GOD MINISTRY, and the first thing Timothy noticed were three smaller buildings in the back. There was a fence along the property line with what seemed like barbed wire along the top.

Timothy frowned and pointed it out to Wyatt. "Pretty extreme for a church, right?"

"And there's three cameras in the front of this building alone." Wyatt shrugged when Timothy gave him a glare. "I had some friends who wanted me to be a lookout a couple of times."

"Don't tell me, Wyatt," Timothy said. "There are some things I shouldn't know."

A screen door opened, and he turned to see a thin older man step out of the main church. "Can I help you boys with something?" His accent was thicker than anyone's Timothy had ever met.

"Is Pastor Steve around?" Timothy kept his sunglasses on and focused on the churning anger in his gut from when he'd first spotted the barbed wire. Anger. It helped keep the fear away.

"Naw," the old man said. "He's out right now, probably spreading the word. You fellas here about services?"

"You could say that. I'm looking for this kid." He reached into his bag and pulled out his cell phone. He had a picture of a photo Julia Madden had shown him. He walked closer to the old man, holding out the picture. "Seems like he was seen around here a few years back. His name was Andrew."

The old man squinted at the picture. Timothy saw the blood drain out of his face when he stared at the photo. The way his eyes opened a bit wider. The way his breathing slowed down a bit.

The man shook his head. "Nope. Sorry. Don't ring no bells with me, and I've been out here with the pastor since the beginning of the ministry."

"How about this kid?" Timothy scrolled to a picture of Bobby. "Seen him?"

The old man barely blinked at the picture this time, but he shook his head anyway. "Nope. Can't say he's familiar either." He licked his lips. "Want to tell me what this is about?"

"Missing kids who seem to keep ending up around here." Wyatt spoke up, his voice thick with anger.

"We're looking for these two kids," Timothy interrupted before Wyatt said anything else. "They both went missing years ago."

"Sorry to hear that." The old man took a few steps back. "I'll think on it."

"You do that. Maybe we'll get the sheriff to come out with us next time," Wyatt said.

The old man nodded. "I'll let the pastor know."

"Sure thing," Timothy said. He turned on his heel and walked toward the car. He stopped, and, turning back around, said, "Hey, is Pastor Steve out kidnapping more gay kids to beat to death?"

The man spit toward Timothy, who was too far away for the gesture to be effective. "Sodomites. Go burn in hell!" He opened the door and reached inside to grab at something. He pulled out a shotgun, and Timothy swallowed hard when the old man tightened his grip on it.

"Might not want to do that," Timothy replied as evenly as possible. He realized his voice wavered a little and hated himself for it. To him it sounded weak. And he hated feeling weak. "The sheriff he mentioned? My dad. If you want me to give him a call now." Timothy held up his cell phone. He didn't say anything else, but gestured to Wyatt, who seemed like he was about to rush the old guy, to get into the car.

They were driving down the dirt road back toward the main part of town before Wyatt said anything. "So, at least we found out what happened to Bobby and Andrew."

Timothy didn't respond.

Wyatt smirked. "And you said *I* was a shitty liar."

"You are a shitty liar. He was a shittier one."

A heavy silence filled the air between them. "Do you hear that every day?"

"What?" Timothy glanced at Wyatt quickly and saw he was staring out the window.

"Do you get called sinner and sodomite a lot?"

Timothy shook his head. "Not so much. Usually it's faggot. Queer. Pussy. Others are less charming."

"I'm sorry."

Timothy shook his head. "Nothing to be sorry about. It's not your fault and it's fine. I'm tough enough. And it's not like it's everyone I meet. There are only a few guys like that. And I have my parents."

"You're lucky, Timothy. To have them, I mean."

"I know. Even if I don't always act like it."

BY THE time they found a diner, ordered food, and started eating, Wyatt had asked, insisted, demanded, and pleaded they go back to Pastor Steve's at least two dozen times.

"No," Timothy said. "We're not going back there. We're going to tell my dad. If some guy is taking kids off the street and they're dying? That's not something you and I are taking on." He drained the last of his coffee as Wyatt dragged a french fry through a small pile of ketchup on his plate.

Wyatt looked more unsettled than he had on the day Timothy had confronted him about his Grindr pics. The day he'd told Timothy about what happened between him and Bobby. "You know, between the two of us, we could take this guy."

"This is not 1932, Wyatt. We're not going to storm some side-of-the-road church and drag Pastor Steve out to the lawn for a public whipping. Dad'll know what to do next. We did what we set out to do, which is figure out what happened to Bobby."

Wyatt snorted. "We should—"

"No, Wyatt. A thousand times, no."

Wyatt sat back in the diner booth and didn't say anything else for the rest of the meal. Timothy was fine with the silence and didn't do anything except stare out the window and play with his phone for a few minutes.

After Timothy paid for their lunch, Wyatt followed him outside, where Timothy suddenly stopped in front of a black SUV with a red crucifix bumper sticker. Wyatt had to stop short in order not to bump into Timothy's back.

"I'm sorry," Timothy said, his voice soft and sympathetic. "I know what you want and I'm sorry."

Wyatt looked up, locking eyes with the guy behind the wheel of the SUV before turning back to Timothy. "Yeah. I know you get it. I'm sorry too."

Timothy smiled and started moving again. He didn't accept Wyatt's apology, not out loud, but he was already over it. Timothy had the car doors unlocked and was headed out toward the highway before he said anything to Wyatt.

"How are you going to deal with having an out, stubborn boyfriend?" He smiled at the word.

Wyatt took a deep breath. "Boyfriend, huh?" He laughed out the breath he'd inhaled. "Sorta hate to admit I like the sound of that."

"Why hate?"

"Well, you're kind of a jerk sometimes. Obnoxious. Kinda snobby. If I say I'm looking forward to dating a guy like that—"

Timothy interrupted Wyatt with fake indignation. "Obnoxious, snobby, and a jerk? Wow. What you must think of me."

"Well, you know, your ass makes up for it." Wyatt waggled his eyebrows at Timothy, who felt heat rise on his neck.

"Wow. You are objectifying me, and we haven't even been on a real date yet." Timothy pulled back onto the highway.

"Um, you're not heading home." Wyatt glanced behind them as Timothy slowed down slightly to merge into the traffic.

"Nope. We got one more place to stop. It's only a few towns away."

"What do you want to do?"

"We have one more family to meet with. The Bolgers." Timothy sped up a little. "Remind me to get gas before we head home."

"I meant on our first date. What do you want to do?"

Timothy glanced over at Wyatt before turning his eyes back to the road. "I told you, it'll have to be dinner with my parents." His fingers carefully gripped the steering wheel. "Don't take this the wrong way—"

"Breaking up with me already?" Wyatt tried to make a joke, but even his smile was a little strained.

"Well, you being in the closet makes an actual date a little... difficult. I mean, it's one thing to tell my parents or your mom I'm tutoring you or helping you with a paper."

"So? We'll just tell people at school the same story."

Timothy shook his head. "Too easy for them to check, Wyatt. They all know we don't have any of the same classes together."

"Man, you really know how to lie."

"Not sure that's a compliment."

"I didn't—I meant that you know how to lie. I mean—"

"Relax," Timothy said gently. "I know what you mean." He slowed down, waiting for the car in front of him to speed up a little. "I've always wanted to be a cop, but it's not something my dad wants me to be. Even when we were back in Cali, I used to visit him at the office, and I'd pull out the files on his desk. I'd look through them." His voice got softer and Wyatt kept silent. "Sometimes, not too often, I'd sneak them into my bag so I could take them home to study them. I had to learn to lie to my dad about stuff like that. It's not my proudest skill."

Wyatt reached out gently and pulled Timothy's right hand carefully off the steering wheel. Timothy let his hand be pulled down onto the cupholder area between the two seats.

Wyatt traced his finger back and forth across Timothy's palm. "Didn't mean to bring up bad memories. Sorry." He paused for a second. "I keep saying that to you." He snorted a laugh. "Guess I'm kind of a failure as your boyfriend right out of the gate."

"Wyatt, shut the hell up and don't say stuff like that." Timothy sighed, realizing even though he was trying to be supportive, it didn't come out the way he wanted. "My turn to be sorry. I don't know why you're down on yourself. You're a great guy. Really. I don't want you to say shit like that. You really think I'd want to date a failure?"

Wyatt shook his head silently.

"Then shut the hell up." He signaled and they pulled off the highway, gliding to the end of the onramp. "You're great. Trust me."

It was almost two minutes before Wyatt responded. "I trust you." The blinker clicked for a turn as he spoke. "You're gonna go away to school."

"What?"

"You're gonna go away to school and do great. And I'll still be here."

"Let's… let's see what happens." He laughed to try to lighten the mood. "It's not like I'm a great catch. Give it a week. You might break up with me. I'm not special at all."

"See," Wyatt responded. "You *are* a good liar."

Timothy didn't respond.

RYAN BOLGER'S house reminded Timothy of his own. It was on an average street and seemed as if it held an average family in an average town. Wyatt took his hand away from Timothy's, and Timothy shivered from the air cooling off his skin, which had been warm from the constant contact. Timothy chugged the cold remains of his coffee and slipped out of the car. Wyatt was right behind him as they walked up the porch steps to the front door. Timothy rang the bell and they waited.

"Hey, does our school even have a paper?" Wyatt looked curious as a girl a few years older than them opened the door. Timothy smiled and ignored Wyatt's question. Her hair was red, and she was built like a weightlifter with broad shoulders and thick arms. She was muscular enough to have taken Timothy out with one punch.

"Hi. I'm Timothy Mitchell and this is Wyatt Courtland—"

"We're not looking to be saved. Thanks." She started to close the door in their faces with a smile.

Timothy braced his hand firmly on the door. "We're doing an article for our school paper about some area students who've disappeared. Kind of a way to help people our age learn safety. I was hoping to speak with the Bolgers about Ryan. He disappeared about two years ago, right?"

The girl's eyes narrowed, and someone called out from the house. "Who is it, honey?"

"Just some guys from school, Mom. We'll be out on the porch." She shooed Wyatt and Timothy from the door and they backed up, stepping down off the porch and onto the lawn.

"I don't want you talking to my parents."

"We don't want to—"

"It took my mom almost a year before she stopped crying herself to sleep. My dad spent most of that time blaming himself, and I don't want you dragging up all that shit again." She pointed to Timothy's car. "Get the fuck outta here."

Timothy held his hands up. "Sorry. I didn't mean any disrespect. I swear." He turned away, but Wyatt grabbed his arm.

"My friend Bobby went missing four years ago, and we found a whole list of other guys around his age who're missing too. We don't want to hurt anyone, but we think we might have figured out where Bobby went. We want to see if maybe the same thing happened to Ryan."

Her eyebrows knitted together. "What do you mean where he went?"

Wyatt peeked around, as if to make sure no one was watching them. "A guy named Pastor Steve kidnapped him and killed him because he was gay."

"Ryan wasn't gay."

Timothy kept his voice low and quiet. "Did he ever tell you—"

"I asked him. If he was gay." She crossed her arms, then dropped them to her sides. "He was my brother. I thought he might be, but he wasn't."

"Would he have told you?"

She spoke without hesitation. "Yes. Absolutely."

Timothy paused, and Wyatt waited for him to ask another question. "Did people think he was?"

"Gay?" She hesitated for a moment. "Sure. Lots of people did. I mean, we wouldn't have cared—"

"But it doesn't help in school, does it?" Timothy scratched at his chin.

"No." She nodded in agreement. "It sure as hell doesn't. Pastor Steve? Never heard of him." She gestured to herself. "I'm Margaret."

"Nice to meet you, Margaret." Timothy noticed Wyatt's arm flex and release as he pointed at them. "I'm Wyatt. This is Timothy."

"Yeah," Margaret said with a flat voice. "Nice to meet you too."

"Did Ryan's behavior change at all before he went missing?" Timothy pulled out his notebook.

"What are you doing?"

"Making notes. So I can read them later. See if there are any patterns."

"You think somebody took him?" She looked back at the house and she shrugged when she turned back to them. "I want to make sure my parents don't come out."

"According to one mom we talked to today, Pastor Steve took her son to make him, well, not gay. It seems like a similar situation."

"C'mon," Wyatt said as he pushed the brim of his baseball cap back. "It's the same as Andrew. Let's go back and get this guy."

"No. We talked about this." Timothy shook his head. "If his mom was telling us the truth, then Pastor Steve knew Andrew. Would he have come this far?"

"It's not too far," Wyatt said quickly. "It's only, what? Twenty minutes away? It's bigger here. More restaurants. More bars. Towns like this? People always travel to them."

"He was acting funny," Margaret interrupted, as if she hadn't been listening to either of them. "Before he disappeared. He was acting funny."

"Funny how?"

"He was always a really sweet guy. Funny. Patient. Then he started getting short-tempered. Crabby. Secretive." She shook her head. "I thought it was him being a teenager."

Timothy shot a glance at Wyatt, but Wyatt didn't seem to register anything. "Was there someone he was close to? Someone he talked about a lot?"

She thought for a minute, pursing her lips. "He liked his English teacher."

"Do you remember his name?" Timothy asked quickly.

"No." Margaret tapped one hand against the other. "I was already a senior by then, and he was in the junior high. Mr. Mathis, I think."

"Hmm." Timothy couldn't keep the disappointment off his face or out of his voice.

"What?" Margaret narrowed her eyes at him.

"Just, there's a teacher I'm looking for. Different person." He shook his head. "It's nothing."

"There's this comic book store he used to go to in Greenville. Borderlands. Ryan spent time there playing Dungeons and Dragons." She jerked her thumb back toward the house. "I've got to get back inside. My parents have some friends over. Give me your phone." Timothy handed his phone over, and she typed her number into the contact list. "Text me. I'll see if I can find the teacher's name."

"And a picture too, if you can."

"I'm not gonna talk to my parents about this. I don't want to—"

"Yeah." Wyatt nodded. "I get it." He turned around and then back to Margaret. "We'll do whatever we can. Promise."

Margaret nodded but didn't say anything before going back into the house. Timothy walked slowly to the car and sat in the front seat. The two didn't say anything for a few minutes before Timothy started the ignition.

"We've got to get gas. And stop at a comic book store."

They went from Spartanburg back to Greenville and pulled into a shopping center parking lot. "You ever been here before?" Timothy asked.

"A while back," Wyatt replied. "Dad used to bring me here to pick up some when I was a kid. We'd read Batman and Spider-Man." Wyatt held the door open for Timothy, who walked through. "Haven't been since he died."

Timothy walked toward the middle of the store and smiled at the woman behind the register. She was about the same age as Timothy's mom, with the same sweet, open smile. She tucked a strand of her blonde hair behind her ear and adjusted her glasses.

"Hi, I'm Michele, welcome to Borderlands. What are y'all looking for today?"

"Hi. I'm wondering," Timothy said as he looked through his messenger bag. "Could you tell me if you remember this kid coming into the store?" He held up a picture of Ryan Bolger.

She looked for a second. "He looks familiar. Mark," she called to someone in the back. "You remember this guy?"

A tall, good-looking guy came forward from what Timothy assumed was the gaming section of the store where the tables were. He had salt-and-pepper hair and beard and a goofy grin. "Who is it?"

"His name's Ryan," Timothy replied with a smile. "He used to play Dungeons and Dragons here?"

"Oh, yeah." Mark adjusted his glasses. "He used to come in, I guess it was every other Saturday. Haven't seen him for a while now."

"Oh, right. He was the one who always bought dice when he came in, right?" Michele pushed her glasses to the top of her head. "I remember he was always forgetting to bring his dice."

Mark nodded. "Yeah. Nice kid. Everything okay with him?"

Timothy looked up at Wyatt, who stood with his hands in his pockets. "He's missing, and I was wondering if you remember anything strange about him. Anything out of the ordinary."

"Not really," Mark said. He scratched his chin. "He was here one day, and then he just stopped coming in. I guess I should've noticed before now." He tilted his head. "I do remember a guy coming in to meet him once after a game. I thought it was his dad at first, but he called the guy by his first name."

"You remember what that was?" Timothy crossed his fingers as he asked.

Mark shook his head. "Nope. Sorry. I wish I did. I just remember thinking it was, you know, off."

Timothy shrugged. "No worries. Thanks for your time." Mark smiled and turned back to the gaming area.

Michele waved at them from behind the register and reached for a customer's purchases to ring through.

Wyatt pushed the door open again.

"Is it the way you remembered?" Timothy asked Wyatt.

"Wyatt stood at the passenger door while Timothy unlocked the car. "I miss my dad."

Timothy stopped before he turned away to walk around the front of the car. "I'm sorry."

"Your dad...."

"Yeah. I don't act like it, but I know."

Neither of them moved. Wyatt finally opened the car door. "Let's just find out what happened to these kids."

Timothy smiled. "Sure thing. But we really do have to get gas first."

TIMOTHY WAS pumping the gas while Wyatt went into the small store attached to the station to get them coffee. Wyatt was adding sugar to his coffee when he looked up to see someone watching him. He wasn't tall. Maybe an inch over Timothy, but he was stocky, barrel-chested with thick arms and a bushy beard. And he stared at Wyatt. His eyes narrowed and then he turned around and walked out. Wyatt watched him stomp across the lot and get into a black SUV and pick up his phone.

He finished fixing his coffee the way he wanted it and got another for Timothy. By the time he paid for everything, Timothy was waiting for him with the car ready to go.

"We're going to tell your dad?" Wyatt set the coffee in the cupholders between them and then placed his hand, palm up, on top of his own cup.

Timothy smiled and reached out to hold Wyatt's hand over the heat of the coffee. "Yep. I'm thinking we open with 'Hey, Dad, remember how you told me I couldn't be a cop? Well, we think we figured out what happened to a bunch of missing kids, but we need you to get a warrant for some guy.' And then after he's finished blowing up about that, we throw in 'by the way, Wyatt and I are going to start dating.' It'll go over great."

"I know you're joking and all, but you really think your dad won't approve? Of me. You and me?"

"I'm kidding, Wyatt." Timothy took his hand back from Wyatt and went to grab his coffee but left it in the cupholder. Instead he put both hands on the wheel. "I get you're worried, but don't be. It matters more what my mom thinks."

"But no pressure, right?" Wyatt tried to make it light, but he could hear the nerves in his own voice."

"What are you nervous about? I'm sure my parents are going to be fine. If anything, they'll probably be pissed at *me* for this whole thing and forget you're even there."

"You mean about Bobby? How could they be pissed? I mean, you did something the cops didn't do. You found out what happened to Bobby."

"No. We found something that *might* have happened to Bobby. We're not positive about any of it. We have a theory. That's all." Timothy chewed his bottom lip while he paused. "I wish we had proof."

"We could go find—"

"Nope. Can you pass me my coffee? It feels like the lid is coming off when I grab it." Wyatt pushed the lid tighter and passed it to Timothy. He took a few sips. "I know you want to go find Pastor Steve and beat the crap out of him, but there's a process here, Wyatt. It's—"

"Yeah, yeah, the law." Wyatt sighed. "I know."

"It's not always fair, you know. I get it, but it's what we've got." Timothy didn't wait for Wyatt to respond. "What I don't understand is, why didn't Andrew's mother say anything? I mean, if Pastor Steve went to her and told her—"

"You're not from around here, Timothy. You don't know what it's like." Wyatt snorted out half a laugh, half a sigh. "Cops in these parts, they don't care. No offense, your dad, I mean. But most cops around here just wanna get through until they retire. Bust a few drunk drivers, break up a few out-of-control parties, that's about it. If you don't have to do something because no one's making a big fuss, then it doesn't matter. You don't know what it's like."

"It's not like that, Wyatt. It doesn't have to be."

"Then why did you do more for Bobby than anyone else?"

Timothy shook his head. "Wyatt, we've gotten this far, right? Let's keep going and see where it leads."

"Do you think... do you think I'm smart?"

Timothy took his attention off the road and looked quickly at Wyatt, then back out the windshield. "Of course I do. Where did that come from?"

"You know." Wyatt was staring out the window, watching the miles on the highway fly around them.

"No. I don't know. If I did, I wouldn't have asked." Timothy threw a quick glance to the side to look at Wyatt and Wyatt looked at him with a small smile.

"You think your parents'll like me?"

"Why don't you worry more about whether I like you?"

Wyatt's big hand landed on Timothy's knee, and he could feel the heat from Timothy's skin through his jeans. "You know what I like? I like the way you look when you run." His hand slid slowly up Timothy's leg. "You're sexy when you're all sweaty."

"You're getting me hot and bothered when I'm driving."

"So, pull off the highway." Wyatt pointed to the next off-ramp. "We're not too far from home and we can take the back roads. Stop off somewhere quiet. Make out a little bit. See what happens."

"Seriously?"

"Why not?" Wyatt asked, leaning closer to Timothy and squeezing Timothy's thigh lightly. "Making out in a car isn't something we can do when we're thirty."

Timothy laughed and signaled to pull off the highway. "Only making out. I'm not the kind of guy who does it in a car."

Wyatt turned around and looked into the back seat. "Not enough room here for both of us anyway. I'm a little bigger than you."

"Yeah," Timothy said as he headed toward a dirt road a couple of miles off the highway. "I noticed."

Timothy drove carefully on the unpaved road, and Wyatt pointed to a small area half hidden by trees.

"That looks good." Wyatt's voice sounded lusty, filled with desire.

"I can't pull over here. There's someone behind us, and there's not enough room to let them go by."

Wyatt glanced behind them and squinted, blinking twice. "Timothy, drive. Fast."

"What?" Timothy carefully pressed down on the gas, trying to avoid the rocks sticking out of the ground. "What's wrong?"

"That truck. That truck was the one I saw in the parking lot back at the diner."

"That's impossible." Timothy steered the car cautiously. "Why would someone follow us?"

"He's moving faster, man." Wyatt turned around and pointed toward the road, where it forked. "Take the left here. It'll be faster to get back to the main roads."

"You're sure?" Timothy pressed the gas pedal down harder.

Wyatt cursed himself that they'd taken Timothy's car. It was too low to the road for them to go much faster without worrying about hitting a rock or a tree root or something that would damage his car. He knew Timothy was tough and he could take care of himself, but he didn't know if whoever was following them, if they *were* being followed, had a gun or not. He didn't like their chances if he was armed. Dammit. They should have taken Wyatt's truck.

"Yeah, the bumper sticker is the same one. He looks like the guy who was at the gas station too." Wyatt pointed at the road. "The path's kinda long, but it should lead us right out to Mason Road. That'll lead us through Union and then back to home."

"Wyatt," Timothy said as he pushed down slightly on the gas and leaned his hip toward Wyatt. "Take my phone out. It's in my front pocket."

"What? Why?"

"We're going to call my dad." Wyatt pulled the phone out. "Password is *G-R-E-Y*." Wyatt keyed in the password and pulled up the contacts. "Use his cell number and then put it on speaker." The phone rang, and Timothy's dad answered on the second ring.

"Hey, kiddo. Are you on your way home? Could you stop—"

"Dad," Timothy interrupted, "I have a 911."

Even Wyatt could hear the way Sheriff Mitchell changed his demeanor. His voice got harder, and he could imagine him standing up straighter and walking somewhere he could speak freely. "What's going on?"

"Wyatt and I are being followed. There's a truck behind us we saw about an hour ago at a diner. Wyatt thinks he saw the driver at a gas station. I don't want to slow down enough to get a closer look."

"Where are you?" If Sheriff Mitchell was angry or scared, Wyatt couldn't hear it in his voice. He sounded calm and cool and professional.

"We're on a dirt road headed toward Mason Road in Union."

"See if you can get a plate number and make."

Wyatt spoke up. "It's a Dodge. I can't tell if it's a Durango or a Journey. Black. The plate's on the back."

Timothy's father didn't answer, and Wyatt figured he was writing any information down. Timothy had to slow to take a corner, and he swallowed down a taste of panic.

"Okay, when you get out onto Mason, head as fast as you can back home. One of the deputies is heading toward you now. When he sees your car, he's going to pull you over. Who's driving?"

"Me," Timothy said as much as he could, apparently ignoring the fact that the truck seemed to be gaining on them.

"Wyatt," Sheriff Mitchell said as something clanked in the background, sounding as though the sheriff was getting dressed. "Keep the line open. How far until you get to Mason?"

"Should be ten minutes. Maybe?" Wyatt flew a few inches off the seat as the car bounced. He hit his head on the ceiling. "Ow. Shit!"

"Timothy? Wyatt?" They both heard the concern in his voice.

"We're fine, Sheriff. I hit my head on the ceiling. He's getting closer."

"He could move faster. Why isn't he?" Timothy raised his voice. "Is he only trying to scare us?"

"Timothy," the sheriff said, his voice clear and controlled. "It doesn't matter what he's trying to do. Don't try to find out and don't slow down. Get out of there. Deputy Mike will meet you on Union as soon as he can."

"I'm going silent, Dad. Got to concentrate on the road." Timothy smiled without humor. "Wyatt'll keep you company."

"I'm still here, Sheriff. I won't let anything happen to Timmy."

His father must have known things were scary when Timothy didn't correct him.

No one said anything. Timothy was trying to move as fast as he could, and Wyatt's mouth was getting drier with every second. Wyatt knew the SUV could ram them, run them off the road, and he wondered why the hell it wasn't. Was it Pastor Steve, and was he trying to scare them? He tried to concentrate as Timothy sped the car up slightly. Wyatt blinked back some tears at the thought he'd gotten Timothy into this mess. *Stupid, stupid, stupid.* If he'd kept his nose out of this and hadn't asked—this wasn't helping. Wyatt pushed the thoughts aside and tightened his grip on the door handle.

The road got narrower and the trees were overgrown, blocking off more light from the sun.

Wyatt turned around carefully. "I can see his beard. I know it's him." He flipped back around and shook his head. "I should have just thrown that fucking box away. This is all my fault."

"Wyatt," Timothy said, voice tight and tense. "Shut the fuck up."

Wyatt's heart beat faster when the paved road came into sight. He resisted the temptation to tell Timothy not to push on the gas. They both knew the roots could be even worse and if they busted the axel on the car or punctured a tire, it wouldn't end well. He felt as though he was counting down as they got closer and closer. When they got to the paved road, Timothy didn't stop to make sure the road was clear; he gunned it the second the tires hit asphalt and concentrated on the road ahead, waiting to see Deputy Mike's patrol car.

Wyatt was staring behind them at the SUV pulling onto the road and coming after them faster.

"He's still following us," Wyatt announced, an edge of fright coming into his voice.

"Stay calm, Wyatt," Sheriff Mitchell's voice came through the phone. "Mike is on his way to you fast as he can."

Both cars picked up speed, and Wyatt thanked God there was no other traffic. A police siren grew closer, and Timothy carefully slowed down as flashing lights appeared. He hoped it was Deputy Mike and not someone else. He pulled completely to the side and tires screeched as Deputy Mike slammed on his brakes and pulled over to the opposite side of the road. The black SUV slowed down for a moment before it sped by both other cars as Deputy Mike stepped out of his car, cell phone out to try to snap a picture of the license plate.

"You okay, Tim?" Deputy Mike Ferguson was tall and lanky and had a full head of red hair. He was as tall as Wyatt but forty pounds lighter. He leaned down to peer inside the car.

"Hi, Mike. I'm better now that I see you." He didn't bother correcting Mike. He was too grateful.

He nodded. "You get his license number? My picture's too blurry."

Timothy frowned and shook his head. "It was too fast."

"The first three were A-3-7," Wyatt said, bending forward to speak to the deputy. Without thinking, Wyatt put his hand on Timothy's shoulder. "You okay? Do you need me to drive?" When Timothy smiled at him, Wyatt squeezed his shoulder and let the sheriff know Timothy was safe.

"C'mon, fellas," Deputy Mike said, turning back toward his car. "I'll follow you home."

Timothy waited until Mike had turned the car around and then started home, happy and scared to have to face his dad.

CHAPTER TEN

WHEN THEY got back to the Mitchell house, the sheriff was standing outside, fully dressed in his uniform, keys in one hand, and the other on the car door. Timothy pulled into the driveway, while Mike parked at the curb.

By the time Mike had slammed his door and walked up the front lawn, his father had Timothy wrapped in a hug. He let go and smiled at Mike. "Thanks, Deputy. I owe you one."

Mike smiled back. "No way, Sheriff. I'm glad to help out. Got to keep my little brother safe." He grinned down at Timothy who reached out to hug Mike.

"You okay, kiddo?" Deputy Mike asked him.

Timothy nodded. "Yeah. Thanks, Mike. Seriously. Thank you."

The sheriff cut off Mike's reply. "Why was someone following you?"

Timothy chewed on his bottom lip and shifted his weight to one side. "I've got to tell you something, Dad, but I need you to promise not to yell or interrupt until I'm done. Promise?"

The sheriff took a deep breath. "Let's go inside."

THE FOUR of them were sitting around the kitchen table, the sheriff's face by turns red or white as Wyatt and Timothy started at the beginning and told the two officers everything. Wyatt finding the box in the wall. Bobby and Wyatt's relationship. Bobby's changes in behavior. Andrew, Ryan, and the other missing children.

When they finished speaking, Sheriff Mitchell stared at the wall for almost two minutes. "Mike, Wyatt, would you mind waiting outside for a minute, please?"

Wyatt placed his hands on the table. "Sheriff. I should share whatever punishment Timothy gets. It's my fault. I was the one who pushed him toward this."

The sheriff's expression was poker-faced. "Wait outside."

Mike pushed his chair back and grabbed Wyatt's shoulder. "C'mon, Wyatt. We'll split a cigarette in the backyard." He leaned over and whispered something when Wyatt didn't budge. After a quick glance at Timothy, who was tracing patterns on the table, Wyatt stood up and let Mike lead him outside. They stepped down off the porch, and Mike grabbed the cigarette bucket, then brought it over to the picnic table. He held his open pack in front of Wyatt. "You need one?"

"I got mine here."

Both of them lit their cigarettes, and Mike took a long drag on his. "Don't worry about Tim. The sheriff—"

"Timothy."

"Right. The sheriff might bark a bit, but Timothy means the world to him. He'd never do anything bad."

"Yeah, I know." Wyatt was looking at the back door of the house, trying to hear the conversation between father and son.

Mike smiled at Wyatt. "Does he know?"

"Does who know what?" Wyatt turned to Mike, confused.

"Does Timothy know you're into him?" Mike stared hard at Wyatt.

"What?" Wyatt stammered as he fumbled with his cigarette. "I don't know what you mean?"

"Man, I've got eyes. And I'm not a fool. You've got it bad for Tim, so don't even try to claim otherwise."

Wyatt didn't respond. He just turned toward the house and ran a hand over his face.

"TIMOTHY JASON Mitchell, do you have any idea how furious I am right now?" The sheriff stared at his son, who didn't dare look up from the table. His voice was full of quiet fury.

"I'm sorry, Dad."

"I can't believe you'd do something like this." He was pacing around the kitchen. "You yourself in harm's way. You put Wyatt in harm's way. I think the worst thing is that you lied to me."

Timothy was tempted to go on the offensive and point out he hadn't technically lied to his father but quashed that thought as quickly as it came. He decided to repeat himself. "I'm sorry, Dad."

His father sat down at the table and shook his head. "The worst part."

"I'm sorry. I screwed up. I get it."

"Yes, you did." Timothy's father threw his hands in the air. "You poked around in something you shouldn't have. And you did it because you don't think. It's like you don't give a damn about me."

Timothy's head snapped up, his temper rising as quickly as his dad's. "That's not fair and you know it's not true."

"No, I don't know it's not true. I tell you not to do something, and what's the first thing you do? You go out and do the one thing I told you not to. Maybe you have a little too much freedom."

"I get it. I fucked up. I'm an idiot and I'm a moron and I'm a shitty son. I'm also the only one who found out what the hell is going on—"

"Watch your language and don't try to play this off as if I said you were a bad son." His father's face was red, and Timothy knew his own was as well. He briefly wished he'd inherited his mother's laid-back attitude instead of his father's temper. Timothy was about to say something, without knowing exactly what, when Wyatt came back into the kitchen.

"Sorry, Sheriff," Deputy Mike said as he entered the room behind Wyatt. "Got past me."

"I'm sorry, Sheriff," Wyatt said, his voice pleading. "I know you're pissed off, but it's not like Timothy didn't do something good."

"Good?" The sheriff stood back up and started pacing again. "You two got followed by someone who has your license number, who knows what you look like—"

"We know who it is, Sheriff. It's Pastor Steve, right? It's got to be." Wyatt stood his ground, even when Mike tried to pull him back out the door. Wyatt's voice cracked with raw emotion, and his eyes were wet. "Timothy found out what happened to Bobby, something the cops didn't do."

Wyatt's voice, his tone, his tears left Timothy's father speechless, and he stopped pacing. He leaned against the counter. "Go ahead."

Timothy spoke carefully and quietly. "If what we think happened really did, then we found something big, Dad."

The sheriff spoke just as quietly as Timothy. "Get me your computer."

Timothy nodded and ran up and down the stairs. He sat back at the table and booted the computer up, all of them standing behind him in anticipation.

Timothy opened up the file, and the sheriff's eyes grew wider as he studied what Timothy had uncovered and the reality of what Timothy had been doing hit. "It's weird, right, Dad? Seeing it like this and not just hearing about it." Sheriff Mitchell pulled a chair up and shifted the computer so he was working it. Mike crossed the room until he was standing behind Timothy's father. "Those are the most likely seven—if I include Bobby LaFleur and Andrew Madden—I can find. I didn't look for girls or go back much before Bobby disappeared. I can expand the search, if you want."

"No," came the quick reply. "I want to keep this as narrow as possible. Have you connected any of these others to this Pastor Steve?"

Timothy shook his head. "The only one for sure is Andrew Madden, and that's on Julia Madden's say-so. We talked to Ryan Bolger's sister too. She never heard of Pastor Steve, and we haven't had a chance to talk to anyone else."

Timothy took out his cell and pulled up his saved Google search on Pastor Steve from his phone. He'd done some searching while Wyatt used the restroom at the diner.

Mike looked over their shoulders. "*Change your son to a real man.* What an asshole."

Timothy smiled carefully. Mike was a good cop. He wasn't imaginative, but he was dogged and determined and loyal as hell. Timothy was always grateful Mike was his father's backup.

The sheriff pulled up the same search from Timothy's phone on his computer and added a few other words to the search engine to try to narrow down some results. "Wyatt," Timothy's father said calmly, "why don't you head on home? I'd like you to add my number to your contacts, especially given what happened today. Make sure you call me when you get home." He gave Wyatt his cell number and checked to make sure it had been entered correctly.

Wyatt nodded and looked at Sheriff Mitchell. "Yes, sir. I will." He leaned over to kiss Timothy on the cheek. The sheriff father raised an eyebrow, and Mike stifled a laugh. Wyatt straightened up and cleared his throat. "I'd also like to date your son, sir. I understand I'll have to follow all your rules, and I promise I will. I also promise to do everything I can to make sure Timothy's happy." Wyatt swallowed hard. "Also, please don't tell anyone I'm gay, because my mom will kill me. Seriously."

The sheriff nodded thoughtfully. "I will keep your secret, and you will come over for dinner so Janelle and I can get to know you better. That will happen before you and Timothy go out on any dates. Understood?"

Wyatt nodded and headed out the front door. Timothy rubbed his temples but kept his eyes off both the men left in the kitchen.

"Timothy, why don't you go up to bed? Mike and I are going to look at this for a few minutes."

"Yes, sir." Timothy stood up and started toward the staircase. "I'm really sorry, Dad."

"I know." His father nodded at him. "Try and get some sleep. You're safe, okay?"

"Thanks."

THE SHERIFF and Mike listened to Timothy head up the stairs and into the bathroom before they looked at each other.

"Sheriff," Mike said, "you've got to admit, this is, well, this is good work."

Benjamin nodded. "Yeah, I know." He held up some of the photocopies Timothy had made and handed them to Mike. "Do you remember any of these kids?"

"Well, Bobby was before I was on the force, but about twenty or thirty of us combed the woods looking for him. It was all on our own. The sheriff, before you, well, it didn't seem like he did too much to find the kid. These others, they're out of our jurisdiction, so I doubt any of them would have been a blip on our radar, so to speak." Benjamin grunted a response. "My sister-in-law's got family near where the Freeman and Williams boys disappeared, so I can ask if they remember anything."

"They're all pretty similar, these kids. Both in age and look." Benjamin piled everything up and closed Timothy's computer. "Make some inquiries but make them damn discreet. If this Pastor Steve has any friends in high places, I have no desire to find out until after we've got some solid information."

"You can count on me, boss." Mike stood up, and Benjamin walked him to the door, stopping before he opened it.

"And, Mike, thanks a lot for getting Timothy home safe."

"And Wyatt."

Benjamin laughed. "Yeah. And Wyatt. It means a lot to me."

"I meant what I said earlier, Sheriff. Tim is like a little brother to me. He's a pain in the ass, but he's also pretty incredible."

"He's like that as a son too."

Mike waved and headed down the front lawn toward his car. Benjamin waved and closed and locked the door. He locked the back door and set the alarm. He didn't like the feeling of having someone possibly know where they lived, but it wasn't the first time something in his work unsettled him. He went into the living room to tell Janelle what had happened and wait for Wyatt's call saying he got home safely.

THE NEXT morning Timothy and his father set up security cameras at the front and back doors—just in case, the sheriff said.

Timothy was quiet, waiting for a massive lecture and punishment to drop at any time. Father and son had hidden the front door camera carefully by a hanging plant, and as they dragged the ladder around the corner of the house to the back, Timothy could tell his dad was looking up and down the street for anything out of place.

Timothy braced the ladder while the sheriff climbed a few steps to figure out the best placement for the camera. "I think this is good." He held his hand out to Timothy for the screwdriver. "I'm not mad, Timothy." His father held one screw between his lips while he held the camera up to the wall. "I'm mad, but I'm not mad at you. I'm not happy you lied to me." He pulled the screw out of his mouth and worked it into place. "Your mother and I don't want you to put yourself in danger. Hear me out, okay?" He held his hand out for another screw. "Gay police officers face an incredible number of challenges. You work twice as hard to be considered half as good. You get passed over for promotions that you deserve." He held his hand out for one more screw and this time looked at Timothy's eyes and kept his attention. "I knew a gay officer who called for backup during a domestic dispute. His backup didn't show, and he didn't make it." He turned away from his son. "I can't have that happen to you. I just can't."

"It's not." Timothy swallowed. "It's not a teenage rebellion, Dad, and I swear, I'm not doing it to make you angry. I think... I think I can do something good."

"Just, look promise me you'll think of other things. Promise me."

"I promise, Dad."

"Good." Timothy's father finished with the last piece of setting the camera up, and they went inside to make sure the cameras were connected and recording before they took the ladder down. After they folded the ladder to take it down to the basement, Timothy grabbed his dad's arm. "I want my life to mean something, Dad. I don't want to be nothing."

The sheriff wrapped his arm around Timothy's shoulder and pulled him into a one-armed hug. "You'll never be nothing, kiddo."

They held the hug for a moment before breaking apart and carrying the ladder back inside. Halfway through the kitchen, there was a knock on the door. His father put his side of the ladder down on the floor and gestured to Timothy he'd be back. Timothy could hear Wyatt's voice from the front door.

"Hi, Sheriff. Since you said we'd have to share dinner before Timothy and I could go out, I thought I'd bring some food over." Wyatt smiled nervously and shifted his weight back and forth from foot to foot. "If it works for you, sir."

Waving Wyatt inside the sheriff took the bag from his hands. "Help Timothy get the ladder downstairs. I'll set the table. Janelle's at the store, but we can wait until she gets home."

"Yes, sir." Wyatt and Timothy maneuvered the ladder down into the basement.

The sheriff shouted down from the kitchen. "Not dating until we've shared a meal also means not making out in a dirty cellar!"

Timothy laughed and the two ran up the steps.

"We'll be outside until Mom comes back, okay?" Timothy grabbed Wyatt's hand and pulled him outside as his dad shook his head in resignation.

THE SUN was still high in the sky and the afternoon was hot. Sweat beaded on Wyatt's forehead. His usual baseball cap was on the picnic table and Wyatt swept his hand through his damp hair.

"Your T-shirt has actual sleeves."

"And you're still alive, so that's a good thing," he said as he tapped a cigarette out of the pack.

"Yeah." Timothy laughed softly. "I think Dad was more scared for me than anything else. Scared for us. You know what I mean."

Wyatt exhaled a plume of smoke. "I'm not going to let anything happen to you."

"I doubt it's something we need to worry about." Timothy gestured at the house. "I was freaked out last night, but Pastor Steve would be stupid to try anything."

"I'm just saying you're safe with me."

Timothy nodded slowly.

"He was scared, huh?"

"Don't get me wrong, he was pissed too." Timothy shifted in his seat. "He still doesn't want me to be a cop."

"Did he say what he wanted you to do?" Wyatt inhaled and exhaled on his cigarette.

Timothy laughed. "Anything else."

Wyatt's smoke disappeared into the air. "Can I ask a question?" He waited for Timothy to nod. "Why do you want to be a cop?"

Timothy rested his elbows on the table and played with one of his index fingers. "I had a hard time telling my parents. About me being gay, I mean. It wasn't that I was afraid of them, or even thought they'd reject me. It was more like I was afraid of what it meant for me." He looked away from Wyatt. "I think I felt it meant I wouldn't be strong enough. I didn't, well, I *don't* want anyone to think of me as weak." He snorted a laugh. "I guess you heard about what happened when I moved here, huh?"

"You mean about you beating the shit out of a couple of douchebags?" Wyatt ground out his cigarette and dropped it in the pail he and Mike had used last night. "Yeah."

"I'm not really a nice guy, Wyatt. Sometimes I'm an asshole, because I feel like if I'm nice, people will think I'm weak. If I'm an asshole so I can make someone else feel like they don't have to be afraid, then I think it means I did something right." Timothy sighed and shook his head. "That doesn't make much sense."

"Sure it does." Wyatt leaned forward so he could catch Timothy's eyes. "If you're strong, then the people you look out for don't have to be. I get it."

"Yeah. Maybe that's it." Timothy smiled. "I guess that's how it is with your mom. I felt as if I can't be nice and strong at the same time. Your mom thinks you can't be a good person and a gay person at the same time."

"Yeah. That's how it feels."

"Sorry."

Wyatt nodded.

"Boys!" Timothy's mom called from inside the kitchen. "Lunch!"

They stood up and walked toward the kitchen, and Wyatt stopped Timothy at the door. "You're not an asshole. And there's nothing weak about you." He didn't wait for Timothy to say anything. He just opened the door and waved his hand, then followed Timothy into the kitchen.

"WYATT," TIMOTHY'S mother said as she passed around the sandwiches he'd brought. "Tell me a little about yourself. You used to play football, correct?"

"Yes, ma'am," he responded as he took a sandwich and passed the plate to the sheriff. "I was a linebacker for a couple of years, but I wasn't very good."

"I'm sure you were fine."

"No. I was pretty bad. I could knock people down, but I wasn't too good at catching the damn—I mean darn ball."

"Does a lineman really need that?" she asked as she passed Timothy a bag of potato chips.

"On a team as small as ours was, yes."

"And you do some construction?" She took a sip of her water and nodded at Wyatt.

"I do. I'm hoping once high school's over I can work with a couple of the local guys. Get myself some full-time work. The pay's pretty good."

Timothy's mother sneezed and all three of the men looked up and spoke in unison. "Bless you."

"Sorry," she replied, nodding. "Wyatt, you have a dog, right?"

He nodded. "Yes, ma'am. Colonel."

She rubbed her nose daintily with her napkin. "I'm pretty allergic, and I think you have some dander on your clothes."

Wyatt stood up at the table. "I'm sorry."

Timothy and his father started laughing, and his mom silenced them with a glare as Wyatt turned beet red. "There's no need to be sorry and no need to back away from the table. We won't be able to have Colonel over with you, unfortunately." She shot both her husband and son a rather intense look. "And don't let these two bother you," she continued as Wyatt sat back down. "I haven't been able to teach either of them manners."

The sheriff took her hand and kissed it. "Sorry, my dear."

"Have you thought about going to college?" Timothy's mother smiled sweetly at her husband and then Wyatt while Timothy suddenly found a particular cabinet fascinating.

"I don't think… I mean, even if my grades were good enough, I don't think I could afford it, ma'am." He swallowed hard.

She opened the second half of her sandwich and started to spread mustard on the bread. "Please, Wyatt. Call me Janelle. And not 'Miss Janelle.' Just Janelle is fine."

His eyes widened. "Are you sure?"

"I am, yes."

He smiled at her. "Thank you." He put the sandwich down and leaned forward, his elbows rested on the tabletop. "I know—I mean, I know I'm not exactly what you probably pictured Timothy with. I know I'm not good enough—"

"Wyatt," Timothy's mother cut in, "that's ridiculous."

"Mom!"

"Finally, my son looks at me." She turned to her husband and sneezed again. "Excuse me. Wyatt knows I don't mean *he's* ridiculous. It means that he seems like a nice young man, who I'm very interested in getting to know better. Isn't that right, Ben?"

Sheriff Mitchell stood up. "Wyatt, I'd like to speak with you outside, please." He walked out the back door to the small yard.

"Dad!" Timothy pleaded with his mom who simply leaned back in her seat and smiled at him calmly. "Mom, please stop him."

"Relax, honey," she responded, petting his hand.

Wyatt stood up and followed Timothy's father outside. They got to the picnic table, and Wyatt nervously pulled out a cigarette and lit it.

Sheriff Mitchell clasped his hands behind his back, standing at attention. "I'm not going to lie to you, Wyatt. I've got some extremely serious reservations about whatever's going on between you and Timothy." He gestured with his chin to Wyatt's cigarette. "Not the least of which is that. I fully expect my son won't be pressured into picking up that habit from you. I also expect he won't be asked to engage in anything that he might not be ready for yet. Yes, I'm talking about sex, but I'm also talking about drinking and partying." He sighed and gently rolled his shoulders. "I do think you're a good kid, Wyatt. And your secrets are safe with Janelle and me, but I won't have Timothy have his heart broken because you can't have anyone find out about who you are.

If you find yourself unable to be seen with him in public or deal with the questions you will start to get when people notice you and Timothy hanging out, then you need to deal with that now. And they will notice, Wyatt. Don't fool yourself about that. I'm not trying to scare you, but I do want you to think about this before you go too far with either your feelings or Timothy's. Understand?"

"Yes, sir."

"I'm not trying to be an asshole here. I'm not, but I have a son to protect."

Wyatt laughed and the sheriff looked at him sharply.

"Is there a problem?"

"No, sir," Wyatt said quickly. "It's just that Timothy called himself an asshole earlier and I didn't realize how much you're alike till right now." His laughter died off, and he dropped his eyes for a moment before raising them back up to Timothy's dad. "I won't ever hurt him."

"I know you won't mean to, but it's not the same thing." The sheriff seemed almost as uncomfortable as Wyatt felt.

Wyatt took a big drag off his cigarette. He turned away from the other man and exhaled the smoke into the air. "I don't want to watch my mom drink herself to death and hate me because I'm still around and Dad's not. I want to have a place of my own and go to work and come home and get another dog, you know, to keep Colonel company when I'm at work." He shrugged. "And find someone to be there at night." His voice got quiet. "I know Timothy's going to go off and do great things. I want to be with him for a little bit before he realizes he can do better than me. Until he figures that out, I'll always be there for him."

When Wyatt finally looked back at him, the sheriff's eyes were concerned. He hadn't seen a parent's concern in a long time. "You're too young to be so disappointed in life, Wyatt." He pointed to the door. "Janelle will probably be getting some dessert together. Would you please ask Timothy to come out here? Put your cigarette out first."

"Yes, sir." He put his cigarette out and walked toward the door but stopped before he opened it. "I'll try to quit, sir."

HIS FATHER had just sat down at the table when Timothy stepped out the door. Timothy moved in front of him, at attention, and his father frowned.

"Sit down, kid."

Timothy dropped into the seat, shifting a little bit so he was in the shade.

"Do you like him, Timothy?"

"What?"

"Wyatt might seem like a big, strong guy, but he's lonely and hurting, and if you're thinking this is going to be some casual thing for you, then you should cut it off now." He stared at Timothy intently. "Do you like him?"

Timothy locked eyes with his father and nodded. "Yes, sir. I think I do."

"Good. I think I do too." He stood up, and they walked into the house together to find Janelle showing Wyatt some pictures of Timothy from California.

SHERIFF AND Mrs. Mitchell had gone out to give them some privacy, and Wyatt and Timothy sat in the living room with strict instructions that they were not to go upstairs under any circumstances. Wyatt was leaning against Timothy's chest, the two of them making out.

"Wyatt," Timothy said, pulling away slightly. "Wait. Hold on."

"What?" Wyatt sat up, worried. "Are you okay?"

"Yeah," Timothy said, pulling his legs up on the couch. "Fine. I mean, I'm good." He picked at an imaginary thread on the sofa cushion. "I wanted to ask you about something. Something my dad said."

Wyatt shook his head slowly as he spoke. "He doesn't want us to date, does he?"

"What? No. Wyatt, you worry way too much about my parents. He actually really likes you." Timothy paused, breathing deep, then letting it out, counting to ten. "He kind of got the impression you were, um, I think he said lonely."

"He said that?"

"Among other things." Timothy kept playing with the cushion and stayed quiet.

"Can we talk about something else?"

"You don't want to talk to me?" Timothy stopped picking at the cushion and pulled a pillow into his lap.

"I do. Just not about that stuff." Arms crossed over his chest, he looked intimidating. "Why do we have to talk about stuff like that?"

"Because when people date, they actually talk. You know they don't only make out, right?"

Wyatt sighed and fell back against the couch. "Fine." He sounded less annoyed than resigned. They studied each other from the opposite sides of the couch. "So, talk."

"Your mom—"

"No." Wyatt stood up. "I don't want to talk about her. I don't even want to think about her. And you're sure as hell not meeting her."

"Why do you think your mom would hate you?"

Wyatt snapped back at him. "Didn't you hear me when I told you she thinks gay people go to hell?"

"Yeah," Timothy replied, his voice calm.

"That's why. That's why she'd hate me."

"Things change when it's about your own kid." Wyatt snorted a laugh in response and tried hard not to show that he found that sentence strangely funny. "You think you know people, but sometimes they surprise you."

"Not her. I've spent every fucking day with her." Wyatt stood up, looking over Timothy, out the window.

"Okay."

"That's it?"

"That's it, Wyatt." Timothy smiled slightly. "I don't want to fight. I want to know you better, but I don't want to force you into anything. That's not what I'm after."

Wyatt sat back down at the edge of the sofa. "I like vanilla ice cream with chocolate sprinkles. I like driving when I don't have anywhere to go and Colonel's in the seat next to me. I like listening to music, but I hate when people sing along to my favorite songs. I liked hanging out with your mom, but your dad scares me."

Timothy looked at him for a second and then his smile broadened. "Vanilla, huh? Figures."

"With sprinkles. Don't forget the sprinkles."

"I meant what I said," Timothy said with a little bit of sadness in his voice. "I don't want to fight, but I do want to know you. Bad stuff and all. And I can't help being a little nosy." He shrugged. "It's kind of my thing."

"I noticed." Wyatt relaxed into the sofa and his voice softened. "I like you being nosy. And it's not like I'm trying to hide anything. I swear it. I just… sometimes my stuff is bad, and I don't want you to be caught up in it."

"I'm not afraid of the dark stuff, big man." He reached out and gently punched Wyatt's arm, leaving his fist touching Wyatt's arm. "And, of course, you'd do something stupid, like try to protect me from the dark stuff."

"Big man? Well, compared to you, slim, but yeah. I'd protect you." He reached up and took hold of Timothy's hand. "And that wouldn't be stupid. Besides, I promised your dad."

"I'm not looking for someone to protect me."

"That doesn't mean I won't do it if I need to." He pulled Timothy into his body. Wyatt cupped Timothy's face with his hands and kissed him. It was long and slow, and he took his time before sliding his tongue into Timothy's mouth. Timothy's tongue pushed back against his, and Wyatt moaned into Timothy's mouth. Wyatt pressed his lips tighter against Timothy's, and Timothy moaned back, and his tongue ran across the back of Timothy's teeth. Wyatt lifted his hand from where it was pressed into the couch cushion and ran it down Timothy's side. He pushed it under Timothy and grabbed at his ass. Timothy moaned louder, and Wyatt squeezed tighter. He worked his way to Timothy's neck, kissing and sucking the skin there.

"Wait." Wyatt pulled his face a little away from Timothy and said, "Hold on."

"Are you okay?" Timothy pulled away completely and smiled at him.

"Yeah, I'm more than good, actually." He kept running his hands up and down Timothy's side. "I don't want to leave a hickey." He laughed when Timothy did and then gently collapsed on top of Timothy. Timothy was breathing into the side of Wyatt's neck. "Plus, I'm not sure, you know."

"No, I don't know." He inhaled deeply, smelling Wyatt, who rolled off him, without separating their bodies completely. Timothy wanted to feel Wyatt's body, and he kept a hand on his arm. "Want to tell me?"

"I can feel how hard you are. And I'm pretty sure you can feel how hard I am." Wyatt turned away, then back to him. "I know myself, and I might not be able to stop if we keep going. Let's take a few minutes and chill. If you're okay with that?"

"I'm okay with whatever."

Wyatt smiled carefully. "I do have a favor, though."

"A favor?" Timothy pretended to think hard. "I suppose I could at least listen to your request. Boyfriends do stuff like that, so I'm told."

"When it's you and me, I want to call you Timmy."

"Yeah, not going to happen." Timothy stood up and threw Wyatt a smile over his shoulder as he headed toward the kitchen. "You thirsty?"

"Yeah." Wyatt stood up and followed Timothy, wiggling his eyebrows. "Your ass is kind of a thirst trap."

"I'll post it on Instagram." He gestured at the refrigerator. "Help yourself. I'll get glasses."

"So, I seriously can't call you Timmy?" Wyatt pulled a carton of orange juice out and put it on the counter, holding out his hand for the glasses. Timothy passed them to him. "Isn't everyone supposed to give their boyfriend a nickname?"

"You know," Timothy said as he leaned on the counter, facing Wyatt. "If you really want to find me a special name, you could wait until we get to know each other better and then pick one based on one of my charming habits."

"Or I could use a special name I know you hate, but you'll learn to love because you know it's our secret and you'll blush. Then whenever you hear me say Timmy, you'll get all red, and then think about kissing me."

"That's a very specific fantasy." Timothy smiled at him.

"Yeah, well," Wyatt said, handing Timothy a glass of juice. "What can I say? I've been crushing on you for a while now."

"Really?" Timothy raised an eyebrow and stepped closer to Wyatt. "Tell me."

"Well…." Wyatt was really blushing now. "I might tell you, for a price."

Timothy sighed dramatically. "Fine, but if you slip and call me Timmy when anyone else is present, the deal is off."

Wyatt held out his hand. "Deal." They shook on it, and Wyatt pulled out a chair. He sat down and stretched out his legs. Timothy looked at him, sprawled out in the kitchen, and smiled. Wyatt wore the same thing he always had: jeans, work boots, a T-shirt, and baseball cap. Timothy liked the consistency of Wyatt and drank in the man sitting before him. He pulled another chair a bit closer. Not too close, because he wanted to be able to see all of Wyatt, head to toe.

"So? Tell me. About the crushing."

"You know what a big deal it was when you moved into town?"

"Was it?" Timothy was perplexed.

"Shit, your dad was the new sheriff. You came in and told people you were gay, and you didn't take any crap from anyone." He laced his hands on top of his head, and Timothy's focus shifted to Wyatt's biceps. Wyatt noticed and popped them a few times, smirking in a sweet way. "When Billy and Jon came up to you after school, when they told you they didn't like fags... I heard you looked like your head was gonna explode." He shook his head, shifting his arms and upper body back and forth, keeping his legs spread out in front of him. "Tell me, I've gotta know, who challenged who?"

Timothy exhaled loudly. "They told me they didn't want a faggot hanging out with their girlfriends. I think Hannah only wanted to hang out with me because she once saw gay guys on TV and thought we'd go out shopping and talk boys."

"She should've met you first." Wyatt snorted. "You don't seem like a shopping and gossiping kind of guy."

"She did meet me," he replied flatly. "She's kind of a hurricane, though. They sweep through and don't consider anything else." He waved his hand as if he was brushing something away. "Anyway, I told them if they had a problem with me, we could handle it like real men."

"Bet that went over well."

"Oh yeah. I met them after school and—"

"I was there that day," Wyatt interrupted.

"You were?" Timothy was surprised. He knew half the football team was there and some of their friends, but he didn't remember Wyatt. Even though he knew Wyatt was a football player. Even though he knew Wyatt was friends with Billy.

"I was way in the background. Almost in the trees. I remember following a couple of cars headed over toward the park." The only place two or more hotheads could fight without a teacher or a cop breaking it up or busting everyone. "I figured I could step in if Billy got too rough. He's got a temper and a pair of fists."

"Yeah, he was pretty tough."

"But, damn, the way you moved, Timmy." Wyatt sighed and smiled and reached out to put his hand flat on the table near Timothy's hand. "It was like watching Jackie Chan or something. It was one beautiful ass kicking. I couldn't believe that Jon didn't jump in, but I think he was scared. After you knocked out Billy and told Jon to take a swing, I really thought he might shit himself. I didn't think he was gonna do it."

"But he did."

"Yeah, and I remember that too. You laughed, you know."

Timothy's leg touched Wyatt's and neither of them moved away. Wyatt pressed his leg slightly harder against Timothy's.

"You laughed when Jon started throwing punches."

"Did I?" Timothy frowned. "I didn't mean to. What a dick move."

"Yeah but you were having a good time, and he was getting madder and madder. I thought you were going to end the whole thing with some fancy move, but you gave him this roundhouse and caught him right on the side of the jaw." Wyatt laughed the way a kid does at something stupid.

"I'm so lucky Dad never caught me doing that. He would have grounded me for life."

"You were kind of a jerk back then."

Timothy nodded. "Yeah, I was." His voice became distant, detached and flat. "I really was."

"But even with you being so cocky, even though you were a jerk, you were also—"

"The only gay guy you knew?"

"Well, yeah," Wyatt said. "That, too, but you were also really nice. You never went after anyone because you could. You never beat anyone up. You weren't ever a bully. You were this guy who stood up for himself. And you always had, I don't know, something in your eyes. You were just special." Wyatt's voice got quiet, and Timothy leaned forward to hear him. "Special. I used to watch you. I don't mean I stalked you or anything," Wyatt said quickly, glancing up at Timothy. "It was watching you walk down the hall. The way you walked, there was something in the way you moved, like you were daring someone to say something. I don't know how to describe it." Wyatt sat up in his chair, pulled himself closer to the table, and held his hand out to Timothy, who grabbed it. "I used to think I'd figure out some way to get you to notice me, like scoring a ton of touchdowns or having something I made in woodshop win a trophy at the 4H fair. Yeah, I know it's stupid, but I wanted you to notice me. I think I wanted you to rescue me or something."

There was a heavy silence between the two of them as they sat at the table, not touching, except for their palms.

"Wyatt," Timothy said carefully, "I'm not looking to rescue anyone."

"No, I know." Wyatt nodded carefully. "But it kept me from thinking I was alone." He lifted Timothy's hand and kissed it, holding his lips against the bottom of the palm for a long time. "I didn't know you at the time, but I owe you for that. That hope." He leaned his head on their intertwined hands. "You're all red."

"You're embarrassing me."

"There's something else I'd rather be doing to you, but—"

"But?" Timothy's voice was teasing and sexy.

"But your dad would kill me. Seriously, he carries a gun. I think he'd actually kill me."

"Naw," Timothy said, still teasing. "I'd stop him. I kind of like you."

"Yeah? Enough to stay here when you go to college?"

"Hah. You're funny." Timothy untangled his hand from Wyatt's and took the juice glasses to the sink.

"I'm not trying to be funny." Wyatt's voice had a slight edge to it. "Don't leave. Stay here, at least for a little longer. A year or two. You could transfer after that."

"I'm not even looking at schools in the state right now."

"Soon as you graduate, you're out of here?"

"I told you before, Wyatt. We should just take things as they come."

Wyatt hesitated for a quick second. "Yeah." He moved toward the door, digging his keys out of his pocket as he was walking. "Yeah, whatever."

"Wyatt, where are you going?" Timothy walked after him. "Don't you even want to talk about it?"

"No." Wyatt almost slammed the door on his way out, and Timothy stared out the window, watching him cross the lawn to get in his truck and speed down the street.

WYATT WAS blinking back hot tears as he drove away from Timothy's place. He barely remembered to stop at the sign at the end of the block. Some guy with a round face scowled at him as he pulled around the corner heading home, and he was tempted to give the guy the finger, but he couldn't manage to muster enough anger, because he was too sad.

Chapter Eleven

When the doorbell rang, Timothy yanked it open expecting to see Wyatt. Instead he saw an older man, stocky and round, with thick arms and a thicker chest.

"Help you?" Timothy said, somewhat annoyed that he'd managed to end his relationship with Wyatt even before it had begun. He had his arms crossed in front of his chest, one of them holding on to his phone, hoping Wyatt would call or text.

The man's voice was deep, low, and almost musical even in the one word. He drew out the vowel sounds and raised and lowered his voice. Even as he spoke, his fist lashed out. "Sinner."

Wyatt was halfway home, and the entire drive he had something in the back of his mind. It wasn't only his being angry, though he was, or sad, though he was. He'd blown it with Timothy by being so needy. He wanted to be angry with Timothy. Instead he was angrier with himself.

Even with that thought, it wasn't the anger bothering him. It was something else nagging at the back of his brain. Something. Something bad. He was at a light, waiting for it to change when it struck him. The guy in the car, who was staring at him. He'd seen that face before. It was the guy who was staring at him when they stopped for coffee. Pastor Steve.

"Fuck!" He took a quick peek to make sure he wasn't going to crash into someone, and he stepped on the gas, turning the car around in the intersection, and grabbed for his phone as he stepped heavier on the gas, trying to pull it out of his pocket. Coming to a stoplight, he slammed on his brake, stopping halfway through the intersection because he was fumbling to get to Sheriff Mitchell's number. He put it on speaker and hit Call and then dropped the phone in the seat next to him as he stomped down on the gas again.

He screeched around the corner as Timothy's father picked up the call.

"Wyatt?"

"Get home, Sheriff. Now! I just saw Pastor Steve outside your house."

"On my way!"

The sheriff hung up the call, and Wyatt leaned on his horn, veering into the other lane, to get around someone in front of him.

Wyatt felt as if it took him five hours to get back to Timothy's house, and he slammed on the brakes and threw his truck into Park when he got to the street near the house. He ran up to the front door. It was closed, and he hoped he was wrong. Maybe it was some random guy in the car. He twisted the knob, but the front door was locked. Wyatt didn't waste time trying to knock or ring the bell. He lifted his big leg and slammed his boot right next to the lock. The wood splintered and the door flew open. He rushed inside and paused while his eyes processed what he saw. Timothy was on his back on the floor and the man Wyatt had seen in the car was on top of him with his hands around Timothy's throat.

"Get the hell away from my boyfriend!" Wyatt yelled and launched himself into Pastor Steve.

The breath rocketed out of the pastor, and they both hit the ground. They skidded a foot or so and slammed into the sheriff's recliner. Wyatt took the brunt of the impact, and he grunted, lashing out with a wild punch that missed Pastor Steve but made him duck. Timothy coughed and gulped air into his lungs.

Pastor Steve slammed a meaty fist into the side of Wyatt's head, which snapped to the side. The man scrambled to his feet and kicked Wyatt in the side. Wyatt felt an explosion of pain in his ribs and yelped. He pried his eyes open with sheer force of will and looked up as Pastor Steve was pulling his leg back to let another kick fly. He struggled to get to his feet, but his hurt ribs were making him move too slowly. Timothy lashed out with a punch into the pastor's side.

Pastor Steve grunted, and Timothy sent a roundhouse kick into the pastor's stomach. The man doubled over in pain.

"Not so tough when you don't ambush someone and take a cheap shot," Timothy spit out, his voice rough and still slightly hoarse from being choked. He threw two punches, and Wyatt flinched at the sound of the impact. Pastor Steve stumbled backward to the floor. He scooted himself toward the couch, and Timothy shifted so he was standing between Wyatt and the pastor.

Timothy didn't turn around, but he threw a glance over his shoulder. "You okay?"

Wyatt nodded, then realized Timothy couldn't see him. "Yeah. My ribs hurt."

Pastor Steve spit out his words. "You're both sinners. You're going to hell, sodomites."

"Like Bobby and Andrew?" Wyatt couldn't believe how calm Timothy sounded.

"I've saved disgusting souls." The pastor put his hands on the floor and struggled to his feet. Timothy shifted back to keep some distance between them. "I can save you too. Both of you. The Lord wants you to come back from your sinful ways." His voice became louder and more musical, as if he were preaching before thousands. He threw his head back and raved at the sky. "Let them see, Lord. Let them see if they use their faith in you and in your ways, I can save them from the eternal fires."

Wyatt struggled to his feet behind Timothy, and they spoke while the pastor continued his preaching.

"Lord, let me show them they can be saved. With your Word and the Bible and the belt, I can beat the evil out of them, Lord."

"Would you call my dad?" Timothy's whole body was tense.

"These sodomites, these disgusting creatures can be pulled back from the brink like the other children I shepherd."

"Already did on my way back. He's on his way." Wyatt rubbed his ribs. "Damn. Guy has a hard kick."

"They need to be bathed in your blood and fire and glory before they fall, Lord."

"We should get that checked out." Timothy kept his eyes on the pastor but backed up a few more steps. "You came back?"

"Yeah." Wyatt gestured at the pastor, who was pointing at them now. "I really want to hurt him."

"He's not worth it."

Sirens approached, and Timothy seemed to relax a little bit as a car screeched to a halt in front of the house, but kept his fists clenched and a fighting stance.

"Sinners! Sinners!"

A second screech came as Deputy Mike barreled into the house with his gun drawn. Wyatt automatically put his hands up, and Mike took in the scene at a glance.

"Y'all okay?" Mike's voice was tense, and he kept the gun trained on Pastor Steve.

"Yeah, we're okay, Deputy. Could probably use a look at his ribs and my throat. It still hurts."

Mike read the pastor his rights as he placed the cuffs on the man's wrists. He spoke loudly over the man's prayers and shouts at both Wyatt and Timothy. Sheriff Mitchell ran into the house, his gun also drawn, and he struggled to breathe normally after the scare.

The deputy managed to keep the pastor under control with one hand, while Wyatt carefully ran his fingers over the bruises on Timothy's neck. Mike hustled the pastor out of the house as he called EMS on his shoulder radio to come check on everyone. Another set of sirens came down the street, and Wyatt guessed the second the sheriff had called Mike for backup, Mike had put it out on the radio and every available officer was headed to their house.

The sheriff holstered his weapon and hugged Timothy tightly. He kissed the top of his son's head. "That's twice in one week you've scared the shit out of me, kiddo."

Timothy smiled at his dad and then burst into tears. He buried his face in his dad's chest, his shoulders shaking.

"Wyatt, would you—"

"Yeah, I'll head out." Wyatt took a step toward the door, but Timothy's dad grabbed his arm.

"No, would you close the door and then come back here?" He smiled at Wyatt, who gently closed the door and then stood awkwardly next to the sheriff, who pulled him into the hug with Timothy.

Timothy shook against Wyatt's arm, the shock of what happened obviously hitting him. It took a moment before the hot sting of tears came behind Wyatt's eyes, and both Timothy and his dad hugged him tighter.

Deputy Mike knocked, and the three men broke apart when the paramedics came in to check on them.

TIMOTHY'S MOTHER had caught a ride home when his dad left her at the store after receiving Wyatt's call. She'd been nervous, but he'd texted her, letting her know everyone was all right. Timothy had still been shaking when she'd gotten home, and she'd hugged both him and

Wyatt as hard and as long as she could. The family sat around the kitchen table drinking hot chocolate as Mike took Timothy's statement.

"And then Wyatt came in?"

"Why," his mother asked, cutting in, "can't Wyatt be in here now, so you can get all this information from the boys when they're together?"

Mike's lanky body shifted as he leaned on the counter. "We just need to make sure their statements line up. If Pastor Steve claims self-defense, then we need to make sure we follow all procedures. It's for the best, Janelle."

She sighed. "Fine. I'll go keep Wyatt company, so he's not all alone. And I'm not sure I want to hear more about my son being attacked." She walked into the living room with her cocoa, throwing his dad a look.

"Yes. He broke in the door and Pastor Steve was on top of me, choking me. Wyatt knocked him off me, and I think he and the pastor were punching each other. I was still on my back and trying to get my breath back. By the time I stood up, he was kicking Wyatt, and I punched him and then kicked him in the stomach and then punched him again."

"Where was Wyatt at this point?"

"Wyatt was on the ground. And the pastor was on the ground, and he started telling us we were sinners. Wyatt stood up and the pastor kept raving and then you came in and arrested him."

"Any other details?" Mike sipped from his coffee cup.

"Not really," Timothy responded. "It all happened pretty fast." He paused. "There was one thing, though. After he hit me and pushed into the house, he went on and on about my soul. Wyatt had to have been gone...." Timothy trailed off, thinking. "At least ten minutes. There was plenty of time if he really wanted to kill me. It was like he was genuinely interested in trying to convert me."

"Did he mention Bobby? Andrew? Anyone else?" his father asked, leaning forward in his chair.

"No." Timothy shook his head definitively. "He mentioned saving other souls. Lost boys. But no one by name."

"You're sure?"

"Positive, Dad."

"Okay, kid." Mike clicked his pen closed. "You did good. I'm going to go get Wyatt's statement." He turned to the sheriff. "You have someone on the way for the lock, sir?"

His father nodded and stood up, holding out his hand. "Mike, I can't—"

"I meant what I said last time, Ben," Mike interrupted. "The last time this one had us scared shitless. He is like my annoying little brother, who I hope like hell has learned his lesson this time. I would put myself in between him and a bullet, but I'm really hoping it won't come to that." Mike shook the sheriff's hand and then ruffled Timothy's hair. "Don't scare me like this again. I can't take it, Timothy. I'm not a young man anymore."

His father snorted, knowing Mike was barely a decade older than Timothy, and Mike left to get Wyatt's statement.

His father looked at Timothy when the two of them were alone in the kitchen. "You're sure you're okay?"

Timothy nodded. "I'm really, I don't know, tired, I guess."

"It happens." His dad sat back down and his whole body seemed to melt a little bit. "I'm tired too."

Timothy stood up and poured more milk into the pan to heat up. "I'm really sorry, Dad."

"Don't." He shook his head. "I'm so damn grateful you're all right. And Wyatt too. I'm going to have to do something nice for him. Maybe take him fishing or something."

"I bet he'd like that." Timothy stirred the milk, enjoying the repetition of movement, letting it soothe him. "I guess it's all over now, right? I mean with Pastor Steve."

"Most likely," his father replied cautiously. "We're booking him on attempted murder. We'll see if we can get any other information. We should have more than enough probable cause for a warrant. Maybe we'll find more answers."

"Good."

"How was it?"

Timothy turned away from the pot and stared at his dad. "What do you mean?"

"Your first taste of police work? Was it everything you wanted it to be?"

Timothy turned his back to his father and lowered the heat. "Is it always like that?"

"No," his father replied emphatically. "Not at all. Most of the time it's helping people out in simple ways. Making sure people aren't driving drunk. Making sure everyone is behaving respectfully and lawfully. But that's not the important thing." He stood up and went to the stove to turn off the heat. Both Timothy and his father looked at anything but each other. The moment seemed too private, too uncomfortable for them, so they spoke without any eye contact. "The important thing is the moments like today. They're few and far between and they don't last, but they're scary. It's what you do in those moments and after them that counts. It's those times that I really, really wanted to protect you from."

"I'm sorry, Dad."

"No. Don't be. I'm very, very proud of you. Of both of you." He finished pouring the milk into the mugs and passed Timothy's to him. "You kept your head. You didn't use any excessive force. You watched out for each other." They both kept quiet, and his father reached out, resting his hand on Timothy's shoulder. "Please understand that I don't doubt you. I never have."

"I know, Dad. I know that. And I know it's because you love me."

Mike walked into the kitchen with Wyatt and Timothy's mom behind him. "Sheriff, I think I got everything we'll need." He motioned with his head toward the front door. "Mind if we talk privately for a few minutes?"

His father nodded and followed Mike outside while Timothy's mom gently pushed Wyatt into the kitchen, closer to Timothy. She leaned on the doorframe. "If you're not up to school tomorrow, honey—"

"I'm okay, Mom." Timothy stood up straight and nodded. "I'll be fine."

"You can change your mind at any time."

"Thanks, Mom." He held out his hand for Wyatt's mug. "More?"

Wyatt shook his head slowly. "No. Thanks, though."

"Wyatt," she broke in. "Do you need me to call your mom? Let her know anything?"

"No, ma'am. Janelle. I don't want my mom to know anything about this. She'll ask way too many questions." He rubbed the back of his hand over his eyes. "You won't tell her anything, will you?"

"Wyatt," she sighed. "Never. I can tell you, however, as a mother, I'd want to know." She paused. "All of it. I know it may seem as if she wouldn't… react well, but never underestimate a mother's love for her child." She rested her hand on his forearm. "Think about it?"

He thought for a minute, letting the silence build, then finally nodded. "I will."

She smiled. "Good." She left her hand for a moment and then smiled at Timothy. "I'll be in the other room, if you need me."

When she left, Timothy put his mug down on the counter. "Thank you. For saving my life."

Wyatt shrugged. "You saved mine too."

"Not really."

Wyatt smiled at him. "You did. Son of a bitch has quite a kick." He rubbed his side. "I was in a bad position to fight back. That was quite a karate move."

"It was a roundhouse kick. Nothing special."

Wyatt reached out and grabbed Timothy's arm, pulling him into a hug. "It was. And I'm trying to thank you, so accept it and smile."

"You're welcome." His voice was muffled because his face was buried in Wyatt's chest. He inhaled and then pulled away. "You smell like cigarettes."

"You gonna ask me to quit?" Wyatt hugged Timothy tighter and then dropped his arms.

"I might, but we already had one fight today." Timothy pulled away and smiled. "I'm not up for another one."

"I don't want to fight, Timmy, and I don't want you to be mad at me."

"I know. Me either." He sighed. "Do you want to stay for dinner?"

"Can't. I've gotta check on my mom." He stepped away. "I left real early this morning, and I haven't checked on her all day."

"Is it really that bad?"

Wyatt shook his head and busted out laughing.

Timothy flushed bright red. "I didn't mean it quite like that. Sorry."

Wyatt was still laughing. "It's okay, besides I've got to check on Colonel." His laughter trailed off and the smile went away. Timothy missed the smile. "I don't want you around her. She's, I don't know. I don't want her to hurt you. I don't know any other way to put that. She's not a good person."

"She had you and you're a good person, so I don't think she's all bad." Timothy raised up on his feet and kissed Wyatt on the cheek. "Get home safe."

"You gonna be able to sleep tonight?" Wyatt ran his hand down Timothy's face. It was a sweet and intimate gesture, and it made Timothy a little uncomfortable.

"Probably not, but I have homework. I can read ahead in a couple of classes." Timothy moved carefully away from Wyatt. "You?"

"I'll be okay. Might skip tomorrow." He shook his head and smiled at Timothy as if he had a secret. "Call or text if you need anything, okay?"

"I will."

Wyatt walked slowly out of the kitchen and said goodbye to Timothy's mom. The front door opened and closed, and Timothy shivered, suddenly cold and very, very tired.

HE WAS right. He didn't get much sleep, and he was crabby even before the alarm went off. Both of his parents told him he could stay home, but he said he didn't want to fall behind. His father called him stubborn. He stuck out his tongue and filled a thermos with coffee.

Lacey was waiting for Timothy at the front door of the school. "Hey, stranger. Come here often?"

"You're funny. Seriously. Funny." He flipped the sunglasses to the top of his head and finished the rest of the coffee he'd started drinking in the car.

"Anything happen this weekend?" Lacey frowned and crossed her arms, staring intently at her best friend.

He hesitated for a minute. He didn't want to talk about what happened. It was bad enough that he was seeing Pastor Steve out of the corner of his eye. He certainly didn't want to relive those hands around his throat.

Timothy shook his head. "Nothing special."

"So, the rumors of your attempted demise are greatly exaggerated?"

"I don't think that's how the quote goes," he replied coolly as he walked up the steps.

Lacey grabbed his arm. "You. Me. After school. Food. No excuses. Either those are the most extreme hickeys I've ever seen or we have a lot to catch up on."

He nodded, and they ran to class as the bell rang. Whether his mom had called the school to let them know what was happening or his teachers heard through the grapevine, they cut him some slack, and he somehow managed to take legible notes. By the time the last bell rang, his eyes felt heavy, his throat hurt, and his whole body seemed about ready to give up.

Lacey was waiting at his car. "I'm driving. We'll get you carb loaded; you can tell me what the hell is going on; then I'll drive you home."

Timothy yawned and handed her the keys. "Fine. Just don't expect me to give you a ride. Once I'm home, I think I'll stay there forever."

"You should've stayed home today. Even the bags under your eyes have bags." She waited until he buckled his seat belt and then drove them to Daisy's Diner.

She ordered herself coffee, Timothy pancakes and bacon and water, and then stared at him. "Are you okay?"

He nodded in response, rubbing his neck, and then started to talk. He told her about looking for Bobby and finding the list of the other missing children. He told her about Pastor Steve breaking into the house, Wyatt coming in and rescuing him, Deputy Mike showing up and arresting him.

He left out that Wyatt had asked him to find Bobby in the first place. And he left out that before Pastor Steve tried to kill him, he and Wyatt had spent an hour making out on the couch. He wanted to keep that for himself. He needed to keep something between the two of them.

Timothy wasn't even sure how to describe what was going on between the two of them. He liked Wyatt. He was sweet and funny, and he was sure as hell attractive, but did Timothy want to do something long-term? He remembered his dad talking to him about not getting involved with Wyatt unless it was going to last. It'd seemed easy that day. No reason to walk away, no desire to run either, so why was he questioning everything now, especially after Wyatt wanted to talk about next year?

"Timothy?" Lacey studied his face, looking worried.

"Sorry," he said, shaking his head. "What was I saying?"

"It's not important. I'm glad you're all right." She smiled at him. "And Wyatt. I'm glad you're both good." She hesitated and spoke cautiously. "You're, well, the two of you are close?"

He slumped down in the seat. "Friends, Lacey. Just friends. Don't read into it."

"Friends." She smirked at Timothy. "Sure. C'mon. Let's get you home."

HIS MOM gave Lacey a ride home, while Timothy dragged himself upstairs. He checked his phone and saw four texts from Wyatt.

Did u sleep last night?

You ok?
Can u call me?
U mad?

He smiled at the phone and replied, his heart thumping more than it should have at a text.

I'm good. Just really, really tired. Sorry I didn't answer earlier. Lacey wanted to hang and wouldn't take no for an answer. She asked about you. Nothing bad and I didn't say anything. I swear. Are you ok? Going to school tomorrow?

He changed into his sleep shorts and a T-shirt, climbing under the covers as Wyatt texted back.

Maybe. Not sure yet. I'm ok. Got some sleep today. Call me later?

Timothy nodded tiredly at his phone and then realized Wyatt couldn't see him.

Sure. I'm going to take a little nap, okay? Call you later?

Anytime. Don't matter when. Doesn't matter when. Sorry. Sweet dreams.

Timothy clicked his phone off and fell back against his pillow. He had strange dreams.

TIMOTHY BOLTED awake when he felt a hand on his shoulder and he rolled away from it, breathing hard and batting it away.

"Son, it's me. It's only me." Timothy blinked at his father without recognition, but his heart was beating so fast, it took him a moment to pull himself together.

"I'm sorry, Dad. Did I hit you?" Heart hammering, Timothy rubbed his face as if trying to scrub it clean of something invisible.

"Don't apologize, Timothy. I should be the one saying sorry. I didn't mean to scare you." His dad's voice was steady, soothing, and calm.

"My fault. I guess it'll take me a few days to feel normal again."

"It'll take you as long as it takes you. Don't put a timetable on it. And if you want to talk to someone, I mean, a professional, I know someone who can help." His father reached out and gently cupped his son's chin. He moved Timothy's face carefully to the side. "Your neck looks better. You've been asleep for a few hours. Why don't you come downstairs and eat some dinner? I don't want you to wake up in the middle of the night and not get back to sleep."

"Yeah, sure. I'll be down in a minute, okay?"

The sheriff nodded and went downstairs. Timothy grabbed a pair of sweatpants and pulled them on while he turned on his phone. Nothing from Wyatt, so he sent a message.

Can you call me when you get this? Want to talk.

He shoved the phone in his pocket and went downstairs, where his parents were waiting.

"Did you get some sleep?" his mother asked, putting a plate of scrambled eggs, toast, and bacon in front of Timothy.

"A little, yeah."

"Any dreams?"

"Not that I remember, but I'm sure I've had better sleep." He yawned.

Hi mother kissed the top of his head. "Poor baby."

She sat down, and they ate until his father broke the silence. "We got a warrant today for Pastor Steve's property."

Timothy put his fork down. "Yeah? What are you looking for?"

"It's a pretty long list. He's being charged right now with attempted murder. His lawyer hasn't been able to keep him quiet."

"So he admitted to killing Bobby and Andrew?"

His mother cut them both off. "Maybe this is something we shouldn't talk about until there's a conclusion to the whole thing."

"I'd like to know, Mom."

She rolled her eyes at both of them. "Fine."

"His lawyer's seeking a deal. If he does get charged with murder, his lawyer wants capital punishment off the table in exchange for cooperation." His father shrugged. "We'll see what happens, but the DA isn't going to do any negotiating until we go through the property."

"Can I go?" Timothy leaned forward.

"No. That would be bad for the investigation and bad for you." His father's tone made it clear that at this moment he was a sheriff, not a dad. It was very clear to Timothy there was no room for negotiation. "Don't even ask again."

Timothy smiled. "Got it, Dad." It wasn't something he was going to argue about. He knew his dad was right. "But you'll let me know?"

"Of course. I will personally make sure that bastard never comes near you again." He picked up his plate and piled it on top of the others. As he walked to the sink, his father squeezed Timothy's shoulder. "And if I'm not around, your mother is much tougher than I am."

"It's true. I gave birth twice and still have sex with your father." She smiled serenely at their son, watching him turn red.

"Mom! Gross. As if I didn't have enough nightmares." He laughed and it felt good. Normal. "I'm going up to bed. I still feel like hell, and I'll make up the homework in study hall tomorrow." He stood up and kissed his mother's cheek, then his father's.

His mom stopped him on the way out the door. "I know you don't need it and probably don't want it, but I'll leave the hall light on tonight."

"And," his father added, "I'll try not to scare you when I wake you up tomorrow."

He nodded. "Thanks. Good night."

Timothy pulled off his sweatpants and checked his phone. Nothing from Wyatt. He tumbled into bed, thinking he'd get some sleep tonight and tomorrow would be just as good a day to catch up with Wyatt.

CHAPTER TWELVE

WYATT WENT back and forth between sitting in his truck and driving around town for almost an hour. He kept checking the time until it was after 4:00 p.m. He drove down Timothy's street and parked in front of the house. He saw Timothy's mother's car in the drive and figured she'd probably driven him to school.

Wyatt's stomach was rolling and he thought he might be sick, but he remembered how Timothy would take a deep, slow breath and he thought that might help. It didn't, but at least his stomach settled a bit.

He walked up the driveway and pressed the bell. He could hear it ring inside the house, and he waited, shifting his weight back and forth. Timothy's mom opened the door and smiled.

"Wyatt. So good to see you. Did you bring Timothy home early?"

Wyatt's hands were balled up into fists and shoved deep into his pockets. "Timmy's not home yet?" He tried to keep his voice steady, but knew he wasn't succeeding. "I, uh, I didn't go to school today."

"Are you all right?" Timothy's mom reached out a hand and placed it on his arm. "Would you like to come inside?"

He stood in the doorway and shuffled his feet, looking down at the ground and back at the street. When he saw her concerned, caring eyes, his entire face crumpled, and he started crying.

"My mom," he stammered, barely able to get any words out. "She kicked me out, and I don't have anywhere to go, and I slept in my truck last night, and I had to leave my dog, and…." More tears fell down his face.

She reached up and hugged him. His face went to her shoulder and his arms went around her waist, and he cried harder, knowing that everything had changed.

TIMOTHY KNOCKED on the window of his father's cruiser and waved. He waited for his dad to reach across and open the door. Once he was settled in, his father handed him coffee and he waved goodbye to a couple of kids he knew.

"Thanks, Dad." Timothy gulped some as his dad pulled out of the parking lot.

"Mom wants us home now."

Timothy's eyes narrowed. "Everything okay?"

"Yes. She wants us home." His father assured him everything was fine, but he stepped on the gas harder.

HIS MOTHER was waiting for them at the front door when they pulled up. Timothy noticed Wyatt's truck outside, the pickup bed half filled with boxes and bags. When he and his dad stepped up onto the porch, she put her finger to her lips and motioned them to follow her into the kitchen. Timothy dropped his backpack on the floor as he and his father sat down. His mother set her teacup down on the table.

"What's going on, Mom? Wyatt's truck is here."

She looked sad and her eyebrows drew together. "Wyatt's upstairs, sleeping. He, well, his mother kicked him out."

"What? Why?" His father sounded as confused as Timothy felt.

"He came out to her, and she kicked him out of the house. He ended up sleeping in his truck last night, and he didn't really have anywhere else to go. I had him go upstairs and shower and try to get some rest in Timothy's room." She stopped Timothy as he stood up, with a hand on his arm. "Let him sleep."

Timothy slumped back down in his chair. "This is my fault."

"No." His mother's voice was as stern as he'd ever heard. "You are not to blame. Neither is Wyatt. His mother is responsible for this and no one else."

His father ran his hand through his hair.

"And, yes, I told Wyatt he could stay here as long as he needed. This is not negotiable." She stood up and handed Timothy his backpack. "Start your homework. Ben, I'd like to speak with you in the other room, please."

She walked out of the kitchen, and his father sighed, stood up, and followed her.

Timothy moved slowly, trying to sort out everything his mother had told him. He knew he hadn't really pressed Wyatt about coming out, but he wondered why now? Why had Wyatt decided to...? No. He was not going to do this. His own feelings weren't going to fix the situation. Right now, he needed cold, hard facts.

He pushed all those thoughts aside and plowed through two days of homework. Trying not to eavesdrop on his parents' conversation.

"HEY." TIMOTHY sat down on the side of the bed. Wyatt's back was to him, and he had one pillow clutched to his chest, his face buried in it. The other one was under his head. "Wyatt."

"Hmmm." Wyatt stirred and turned over, still holding the pillow. He was wearing a sweatshirt a little too tight across his broad chest and belly, and the sweatpants Timothy's mother had found were too short and tight, but it was the first time Timothy had seen him in something other than jeans and a T-shirt. "Hey." He blinked and looked embarrassed when he glanced down and saw he was holding on to the pillow. "It smells like you."

"Oh, sorry." Timothy turned red and reached to pull the pillow from Wyatt. "I'll wash it."

"No," Wyatt said as he grabbed Timothy's hand. "I like it because it smells like you."

Timothy smiled. "Oh, okay." His expression turned sober. "I'm sorry. About your mom."

Wyatt nodded, and swiped a hand across his eyes. "I guess your mom told you."

"Yeah. It sucks." Timothy noticed they were still holding hands. "I'm sorry."

"It's not your fault."

"Are you sure?" Timothy squeezed Wyatt's hand tighter. "I feel like I might've pressured you—"

"No," Wyatt insisted. "You didn't. I thought she might be proud of what we did. What you did."

"We did."

"I didn't do too much."

"You saved my life," Timothy replied quietly.

Timothy's dad stuck his head in the door. "Dinner's in five minutes, guys."

Wyatt sat up in bed. "I'm not very hungry, Sheriff."

The sheriff tilted his head at Wyatt as if he didn't understand. "In this house, Wyatt, we all sit down together for dinner. Now wash up, and we'll see you at the table." Then he headed down the stairs.

Timothy shrugged and let go of Wyatt's hand. "There's lots of rules here." He laughed as he stood up. "Not really, but I'm sure they're making more."

In less than ten minutes, both Timothy and Wyatt were downstairs at the dinner table.

The meal passed peacefully. Wyatt ate everything on his plate and looked up sheepishly when he asked for seconds. "Guess I'm hungrier than I thought."

When Timothy had finished loading the dishwasher, his father called both teenagers to the kitchen table. "Now this is something we're going to make up as we go along, so any of these rules may change at any time, with no notice. Understood?"

Both boys nodded.

"We expect both of you to go to school and keep up your grades. No skipping without permission. You don't have to run home right after school, but we want to know where you are. And be home by five for dinner."

"Yes, sir." Wyatt nodded.

Timothy's mother spoke up, quiet but firm. "Wyatt, I know this might seem strange for you. I'm not sure what kind of rules you had at your house, and these aren't here so you feel overwhelmed. But we need structure here. And we want to make sure you're safe."

Wyatt nodded.

The sheriff cleared his throat. "We both feel that this is going to be an argument, and we'd like to get it out in the open. Wyatt, you'll stay in Isabelle's room for the time being. The couch is not good for sleeping so we'll have you in there for now. I know you're both teenagers, and I know there will be times that you're home alone, but I'm not comfortable with any type of sex happening in this house. The bedroom doors will remain open if you're both in the same room. If we find out there is anything *inappropriate* going on, Wyatt, you will be out on your ass in five minutes flat. Understood?" He nailed Timothy with his gaze. "You can be embarrassed all you want, but this is how it's going to be."

"I, um—" Wyatt stumbled over his words. "I have some money from work, and I'll keep working through—"

Timothy's mom cut him off with her hand in the air. "That's not something we're interested in, Wyatt. We're not charging you rent. If you want to buy some clothes or something else, that'll be your responsibility, but consider your room and board covered." Wyatt opened his mouth but she shook her head and he nodded and closed it.

"And we'll expect you to contribute to the chores around the house. Dishes, laundry, all of it."

"Yes, ma'am." Wyatt nodded at both of them carefully.

His father stared at the two of them. "Finish your homework and then get ready for bed. And, Wyatt," the sheriff said as he walked toward the door. "Take off your hat indoors."

TIMOTHY CAUGHT up on his homework, studying at the kitchen table, while Wyatt stood in the living room, explaining to Timothy's parents that, since he was in the vocational program, he didn't have as much homework as Timothy did. It wasn't quite late when Timothy went up to bed, and after he brushed his teeth and washed up, he went into Isabelle's bedroom to find his mom had given Wyatt an extra pillow. Wyatt was in his boxer shorts, lying on top of the covers, and his boxes of clothes were stuffed into the corner.

"You can get under the covers, you know," Timothy said, as he pulled the curtains closed. "It's not like you're going to get the sheets dirty."

Wyatt laughed and turned off his phone and set it on the bedside table. "Is it okay if I plug this in?"

"Wyatt," Timothy replied carefully, "you live here now. You don't have to ask me for permission."

"Yeah. I guess. That sounded weird, right?" Wyatt leaned over, plugging his phone into the socket behind the table, and the bed shifted when Timothy sat down. The two of them ended up sitting side by side, staring at the wall in the dim light of Isabelle's bedside lamp, trying hard not to touch each other. "Not exactly how I pictured us moving in together." Wyatt smiled at Timothy's laugh. "Thanks for letting me stay here." He lifted his arm and placed his hand carefully on Timothy's chest.

Wyatt's hand was warm, and he took it in his own. "Anytime. Good night, Wyatt."

"Night, Timmy." He leaned down to put a kiss on the top of Timothy's head, and Timothy went to his own room.

He could smell Wyatt on his pillow.

BENJAMIN WAS silent as he leaned against Timothy's doorframe, looking at his son. He almost didn't notice Janelle until she was next to him. They watched Timothy for a time and then quietly went across the hall to check on Wyatt. Janelle took her husband's hand and gently tugged him back to their own bedroom.

They settled into bed and he looked at the clock. 3:07 a.m.

Her eyes closed, and she whispered to him. "He had to grow up sometime."

He nodded, even though she couldn't see. "I didn't think it would be so fast."

"We did a good job." She started snoring in a minute, but Benjamin stayed wide-awake for another half hour.

WYATT WAS waiting for the coffee to brew, knowing he was going to have to mainline caffeine to get through the day. He was in the backyard, smoking, when the sheriff came out the backdoor with a cup for each of them.

"Morning, Wyatt."

"Sheriff. I hope I didn't wake you." Wyatt held out his hand as Timothy's dad passed him a mug.

"Not at all. I wasn't sure how you took your coffee. I hope black is okay."

Wyatt dropped his butt into the cigarette pail. "Black is great." Wyatt took a sip and pulled out another cigarette, then put it back in the pack. "Thanks again. For letting me stay. For everything."

"You're welcome, Wyatt. Seriously. As long as you follow the rules, you're welcome here. And I don't have to discuss underage drinking with you again, do I?"

"No, sir." Wyatt wet his lips unconsciously. "Can I ask a question?"

"Of course." He sipped his coffee and watched the sun as it was beginning to rise through the trees. "Ask away."

"How was it for you? I mean when Timothy came out."

Timothy's father inhaled deeply and seemed to consider the question. "It wasn't difficult." He shook his head. "No, that's not true. It was difficult, but not the way people think."

"Did you care?"

"That Timothy was gay? Sure. I didn't want him to have to deal with, well—even living in California, there were people who weren't—aren't accepting about it. I was worried. As a parent."

"Do you wish he wasn't?"

"Wasn't gay? I don't think in terms like that. He is who he is and he's my son." The sheriff took a large gulp of his coffee and Wyatt could see the bob of his Adam's apple. "He's my son and I love him. And as long as he's happy, no, I don't wish he were any different than he is."

"Do you think my mom might... might be like you one day?"

The sheriff yawned suddenly. "I don't know. Do you think she's told anyone?"

"Probably. Probably called all her friends and told them her son's on his way to hell."

"If you want to skip school today, if you're afraid—"

"No," Wyatt said. "No. I'm not afraid. I'm pissed."

"Good for you," the sheriff replied quickly. "Sometimes anger is what we need to survive. Go have yourself some breakfast and get ready for school." As Wyatt passed by, Sheriff Mitchell reached out and grabbed his arm. "You saved my son," he said, his voice thick with emotion. "I will always owe you for that. You'll always have a place here."

Wyatt wasn't sure what else to do except make a joke. "Unless I sleep with him?"

The sheriff laughed, only for a moment, but fully and heartily. "I didn't mean to come on so strong, Wyatt. I'm not a fool. Teenagers, especially boys, think about sex and I'd be lying if I said Janelle and I waited." His hand dropped from Wyatt's arm and he locked eyes with Wyatt. "I don't want you to think I'm afraid of your sexuality."

Silence.

"He's my son, Wyatt. I held him in my hands as soon as he was born, and I want him to be my little boy for a little bit longer. I know you have very strong feelings for him—"

"I love him, sir." That stopped the sheriff in his tracks and Wyatt kept talking. "How, um, how does he feel?"

He glanced down at the ground before raising his eyes to meet Wyatt's stare. "Timmy's not like other people. He doesn't talk about his feelings. He'd much rather show you. I can tell you this, Wyatt: if he does love you, you'll know it because he'll defend you."

Wyatt nodded. "I promise to do the same for him."

"Go on in. Get ready for school. It's going to be a bear of a day for everyone."

TIMOTHY'S MOM was working on breakfast and greeted him with a smile and more cheer than he was used to this early in the morning. His own mother would usually still be passed out and he'd be on his third or fourth cigarette. He went upstairs to his new bedroom and stopped in the doorway when he saw Timothy standing in the middle of the room wearing just his boxer briefs.

"Damn," he practically growled. "That's a good thing to wake up to."

Timothy turned around. He automatically moved to grab his towel and cover himself. "You scared me."

"Don't," Wyatt said quickly. "Don't cover yourself. You look too good."

"Yeah, right. Compared to Mr. Big Muscles you."

"I'm not into me. I'm into you. I mean, in case you didn't know."

Timothy smiled. "Hurry up in the shower. Breakfast's going to be ready in a few." He pulled on a pair of jeans and a loose-fitting Henley. "You want to take two cars into school?"

"Why?"

"Because if your mom didn't tell anyone, I don't want you to have to out yourself because of me. I meant it when I said I'd keep this private." He stuffed his phone in his pocket. "This, Wyatt, this is you and me."

"Not anymore, it's not."

"You mean my parents? They won't say anything."

"Are we taking two cars because you're embarrassed of me?"

Timothy walked toward the door, pausing to plant a kiss on Wyatt's lips. "If I was embarrassed, I wouldn't be talking to you, let alone making out with you. Go shower. You stink."

"You like my stink." Wyatt leered at Timothy, running a hand under the button of Timothy's shirt.

"Seriously? You're trying to turn me on with this?"

"Is it working?"

"Not so much. I haven't had coffee yet." Timothy was out the door when he turned around. "There's towels in the hall closet right outside the bathroom. And yeah, your stink is sort of sexy."

WYATT PULLED into the school parking lot, wishing they'd driven in together. His palms were sweaty and his throat was dry. He shut his car off and leaned forward, resting his forehead on the steering wheel. What was the worst that would happen? He was already pretty much a loner. Most everyone left him alone. No one ever really said shit to him or came after him physically. He was one of the biggest guys in school and had played football for a few years, so he had some cred. But he knew what the others said about him behind his back. Poor white trash. Drunk mom. Dead dad. Stupid as shit. Lucky if he graduates, but he probably wouldn't if he wasn't on the vocational track. End up a drunk. Dead by forty. Loser. Loser. Loser.

He used to think it was true, all of it, but maybe he could be more. He'd never get to college but maybe a trade school. He'd always liked woodworking. Maybe he could do something with that. Or welding. Building things. Timothy could make things right for people one way, but Wyatt could do it another. Wyatt could build houses. Maybe help out with one of those charities that did it for the poor. Maybe he'd finally found something to care about and look forward to, instead of seeing a slew of days ahead of him, strung together by nothing except the desire to get from one to the next without hurting so much inside.

The knock on his window startled him and he jerked his head up. Lacey was standing there. She was wearing a rainbow-patterned T-shirt and tights and a short black skirt. He nodded to her and opened the door, carefully shoving the bag lunch Janelle had made for him into his backpack.

"Hey, Lacey. What's up?"

She raised an eyebrow. "That's how we're going to play it?" She rolled her eyes. "Whatever. Thanks for saving Timothy's life."

He blushed and threw his backpack over one shoulder. "Sure."

They walked toward the front of the school. "I usually wait for Timothy, but I texted him and told him I was going to walk in with you."

"Why?"

Lacey straightened up, staring everyone in the eyes as they walked by. "Because you're out now, Wyatt," she said softly. "And I didn't want you to have to walk in alone. Which doesn't mean I'm not pissed at both of you for not telling me."

"So, you know?" He slowed down a little bit, and Lacey matched his steps.

"Yeah, but my mom works at the grocery store with your mom. She called out yesterday and told them, well, you know. I don't know how or if it's gotten around, but you know small towns."

"Great." Wyatt stopped at the bottom of the steps and looked up at the front door.

"Hey," Lacey said, placing her hand on his forearm. "I get it if you're nervous, but you don't need to be. First of all, you're a giant and no one is going to fuck with you. Second, I've got your back, and third, no matter what anyone says, you saved someone's life."

"Who knew you were a fag too?" Bo Watterley's voice was harsh and mean, but not loud. As if he was afraid to push Wyatt too far.

"Shut up, Bo," Lacey snapped back even more harshly. "You're an asshole."

"No one asked you, bitch."

"Hey," Wyatt said, stepping forward, and even with Bo on the first step, he was still taller. "Don't call her that."

"What are you gonna do about it, homo?" Bo's hands curled into fists. "Tell me how bad my clothes are?"

"Bo." Timothy's voice cut in from behind Bo. Relaxed and calm, he walked up to them and shifted his sunglasses to the top of his head. "Still running your mouth. I can't believe I haven't scared you enough yet. Do you really want me to kick your ass again?"

Bo snorted. "You like that, don't you, Tim?"

"Seeing you on your knees, begging me not to break your arm? Yeah," he said smoothly. "It's super fun actually."

Bo flushed red and glared.

"Come to think of it, didn't I tell you if you used the F-word again, I'd break your arm? You must really like goading me."

"Stay away from me," Bo spat out, turning his back on the three of them and heading into the school.

Wyatt exhaled. "How do you deal with that every day?"

"That?" Timothy smiled and took his glasses off his head. Shoving them into his messenger bag, he started up the steps. "That was nothing. Amateur hour at best."

Lacey followed Timothy up the stairs and motioned for Wyatt to follow. "The secret is that Timothy's so angry, everyone's afraid of him."

"Hey," Timothy said as he pulled the door open, "anger isn't a bad thing. Not all the time."

"The sheriff said the same thing." Wyatt waited for Lacey to go into the school and then followed her. He felt strange, like everyone was watching him, and he scratched his head.

"Relax, Wyatt," Timothy said. "I've got your back. You have any problems, let me know, and I'll be there."

"Yeah," Lacey said, heading to her locker. "Me too."

"Easy for you to say," Wyatt said, making a joke. "Your classes don't use saws."

"Yeah," Timothy shot back with a smile on his face, "but we have Bunsen burners."

Wyatt laughed and headed to his first class. It wasn't until he was sitting in his English class that he inhaled deeply and smiled, even as he kept his eyes on the book in front of him.

HIS PARENTS were sitting in the kitchen, a full pot of coffee freshly made and a plate of cookies and pastries waiting. Timothy was home first, worried when he saw what was waiting.

"Is everyone okay?"

"Yeah, son," his father said, waving him into a chair. "Sit down."

"You guys are freaking me out." He frowned as he poured himself a cup of coffee.

"We finished searching Pastor Steve's place today," his father said carefully as he folded his hands around his own coffee.

"That's good, right?"

The sheriff nodded slowly. "It is, actually. He's admitted to what he did to you. He's admitted to trying to 'beat the sin' out of six others, both young men and women."

"And?"

"We found some graves on his property."

"Graves?" Timothy felt his stomach drop, acid gathering in his belly and his throat.

"Three. So far. There may be some more digging on the other properties surrounding his. He's identified their names and pictures, but of course, we'll have to do some DNA testing, and it'll take a while."

"Bobby?"

The sheriff scratched his chin and then shook his head. "No. Pastor Steve said he didn't know anything about Bobby."

His mother passed Timothy the plate of cookies, but he shook his head. "He may be lying, honey."

Timothy shook his head, his eyes dark and wet. "He's not lying, Mom." His fists clenched and unclenched, the knuckles turning white. "He admitted he tried to kill me. He admitted to beating another six kids because of his beliefs. Kids, Mom. Kids. How many people did he hurt because he thought they were sinning? He's not lying. He doesn't know how. He's too convinced he's doing something righteous." He stood up and walked out the back door, slamming it open and closed.

AS SOON as Wyatt heard the news, he grabbed his cigarettes and sat out in the yard for close to half an hour, smoking and seeming as if he was about to punch something. Timothy knew his parents were watching them out the window as he and Wyatt didn't even speak to each other, both of them in their own worlds, Wyatt staring off into space, and Timothy working on his katas, stretching, throwing a few random strikes.

Dinner was an almost silent affair, except for an occasional attempt from the two adults. Eventually they gave up and had Wyatt take his turn to clean up, while Timothy did his homework.

When Timothy and Wyatt ran into each other in the hallway while getting ready for bed, they stared at each other for a minute in total silence.

"Timothy—"

"Can we not talk tonight, okay? Not tonight." Timothy turned his back to Wyatt and went into his bedroom, closing the door behind him.

THE REST of the week was neither quick nor enjoyable for anyone in the Mitchell household. The sheriff was waiting for the results of the

DNA tests being run on the found bones. Timothy was moody and barely spoke, spending as much as time as he could out of the house. He ran. He went to karate practice at the dojo three towns away. He studied. He went to the diner with Lacey. Wyatt sulked around the house.

Friday night, after they got home from school, Timothy's mother sent them into the living room to finish their homework for the weekend. Wyatt was doing some reading and Timothy was finishing up his calculus when his mother stuck her head in the living room.

"Boys, we're heading out to get some dinner, so you're on your own." She frowned as Timothy opened his mouth to protest. "There's a fridge full of food, so I'm sure you can make something. But I want you both to stay in tonight. No going out. I'm not comfortable with either of you being out tonight. I'd like to spend a night out with your father without worry, so turn the alarm on when we leave. Timothy, I'd like to speak with you in the kitchen, please."

He slammed his book shut and followed her into the kitchen. "What?"

She crossed her arms over her chest. "Hey. I'm your mother, not your punching bag, so drop the attitude from your voice."

He inhaled deeply. "Sorry, Mom."

"I know you're upset about… that piece of shit who broke into the house. And I know it's hard to deal with that kind of hatred. What I don't know is why you're so angry with Wyatt."

He opened his mouth, then closed it, then opened it again. "I'm not angry with Wyatt."

"Well, it certainly seems as if you are." She grabbed her keys off the counter and then stood in front of her son. Her hand went to the side of his face. "You know I always love and support you. Wyatt is very uncertain right now. He's lost the only family he's had since his father died, and he's nervous enough being here under the sheriff's roof without feeling like you hate him."

Timothy exhaled. "Yeah, I know."

"It might help to talk to him. He deserves that. And the two of you will be home alone so you can talk completely uninterrupted."

The sheriff honked the horn once, and she kissed him on the cheek.

"He's a good guy, honey." She stopped in the living room to kiss Wyatt's cheek and was out the door, leaving the two of them alone in the house. Timothy could hear the beeping as Wyatt set the alarm.

Timothy wandered around the small kitchen, avoiding Wyatt as best he could, before he finally pulled open the refrigerator and put his face into the cool air.

He yelled into the other room. "Omelets okay? I guess I could do sandwiches or something if you'd rather." He stood up and shut the door, letting out a small bark of air when he saw Wyatt standing next to him. "You scared me."

"Omelets?"

"Nothing fancy, only something standard. You want one?"

Wyatt nodded, and Timothy pulled the door back open. He grabbed some tomatoes, onions, and cheese.

Timothy handed Wyatt the vegetables and placed the cheese on top of the egg carton, putting them onto the counter. "Are you hungry? Two eggs or three?"

"Pretty hungry, I guess."

"Can you chop the tomatoes and the onions for me? You can use as much as you want." Timothy set a knife and cutting board on the kitchen table for Wyatt.

Wyatt started chopping slowly and carefully. He held on to the first tomato too tightly and Timothy heard the soft splat of seeds landing on the counter. They worked in silence for a few minutes. The quiet wasn't comforting or enjoyable. Timothy kept his back to Wyatt as he cracked eggs into a bowl. Wyatt finally placed the knife on the cutting board, the tomato half cut and somewhat mushed.

"Do you want me to go?"

Timothy stopped cracking eggs and turned around. "What?"

"Do you want me to go? I need a couple of days to find somewhere to crash. Maybe find a place I can take Colonel with me." Timothy heard a hard edge to Wyatt's voice and winced at the tone.

"No. I don't want you to go, and I'm sorry Mom's allergic. Otherwise we'd take Colonel here." His voice rose a little bit. "Where the hell did that come from?"

"You've barely said anything to me for a week. You don't even look at me."

Timothy shook his head and rubbed the flat of his hands over his eyes. "No, Wyatt." His voice softened, lowering in volume. "No. That's not what I want. It's just, I'm really angry."

"Tell me what I did." Wyatt stood up and walked toward Timothy, but he brought himself up short, stopping a few feet from Timothy. "What did I do wrong?"

"Wyatt," Timothy said, closing the distance between them. "It's nothing you did. I'm mad at me." He pushed the hair back from his forehead. "I'm sorry. I told you I'd figure out what happened to Bobby and I let you down." He sighed. "And then I took it out on you, and I made you feel bad because I'm a shit person."

Wyatt hugged Timothy, lifting him off his feet. "No, you're not!" He let go and then held Timothy at arm's length, leaning down slightly to stare into his eyes. "Do you know what you did? You stopped Pastor Steve from hurting anyone else. From hurting someone like me. If my mom had thought for one second I was gay, she would've sent me to him in a heartbeat. I might've died."

Timothy opened his mouth, but Wyatt cut him off before he could make a sound.

"Shut up. You saved people. That was a damn sight more than the cops did. No offense. Your dad and all. You saved me. And maybe it's time I, I don't know, let Bobby go."

"I don't know what you mean."

"I cared about Bobby, but maybe I need to move on."

"Bobby means a lot to you."

They both knew it wasn't a question and Wyatt sighed, choosing his next words carefully. "Bobby helped me at a time when I needed to know I was okay. He let me protect him, and he cared about me. But it's not like what I think about you. What I...." He shrugged. "What I feel about you. I love you, Timothy." He held a finger over Timothy's lips. "Don't say it back. Not until you really feel it. I don't expect you to say it back, and I don't want you to say it just because I did." He took his hand away. "You didn't let me down. You made me happy."

"I'm sorry. Not because I let you down. I'm sorry I took it out on you. I didn't mean to." Wyatt bent to kiss him. It was light and quick and Timothy smiled. "You suck at chopping food. You crack two more eggs in the bowl. I'll take care of the veggies."

"Go light on the onions," Wyatt said as his first egg hit the bowl. "I don't want bad breath."

Timothy smiled.

By the time his parents got home, Timothy was slouched down, feet propped up on the coffee table, his arm around Wyatt who was asleep on Timothy's chest. Timothy had his hand curled in Wyatt's hair and he looked up as his parents as they stood in the living room doorway.

His mom turned to his father, a slightly smug smile on her face. "Told you so."

TIMOTHY WASN'T sure how many times his parents had checked on him when he woke up, but his door was open slightly more than usual, so he knew it was at least twice. Probably more than that, knowing his dad, making sure they weren't doing anything like trying to sneak into each other's rooms. Timothy stretched and walked into Wyatt's room and stared for a minute, hoping he'd had good dreams.

Timothy ran his finger gently down Wyatt's arm and Wyatt stirred, cracking open an eye to look at Timothy. He smiled and rolled onto his side, wrapping his thick arm under his head. Timothy was kneeling beside Isabelle's bed, smiling gently at Wyatt's big frame in the smaller bed.

"Morning," Wyatt said, his voice was heavy with sleep. He rubbed the back of his hand over his eyes, making him seem more like a little boy than the grown man he was.

"Morning," Timothy whispered back.

Wyatt smiled quickly, yawned, and then held his hand over his mouth. "Sorry. Morning breath."

"S'okay." Timothy shrugged. "I have it too." Timothy's voice was even, but he knew his eyes would show more than he wanted to show at the moment, so he kept them on the wall.

"You okay?"

"Yeah, still tired."

"It's the weekend. Go back to sleep." Wyatt's gentle smile was at odds with his size. His voice dropped to a whisper. "Pretend I'm in bed with you, and I'll keep the bad dreams away."

Wyatt reached out and gently ran his hand through Timothy's hair. Timothy sighed, wanting to work a thought out on his own, but not wanting to hide anything from Wyatt. He opened his mouth to speak, then closed it again and shook his head at his own reluctance.

Timothy leaned forward until his forehead came to rest in Wyatt's hand. Wyatt stayed silent for a moment then another before he decided to talk.

"I need to ask you a favor."

Timothy shifted so he could stare up at Wyatt. "Sounds like I'm not going to like what you're asking me." He was grateful that Wyatt was talking so he didn't have to.

"Don't do that again."

Timothy pushed himself up on his elbows away from Wyatt's hand. "Do what again?"

"If you're pissed at me, that's fine. I can deal. But if you're upset about something, don't just cut me out. I can't handle it. It's what my mom would do." He inhaled and exhaled deeply. "Please don't shut me out, okay?"

"I'm sorry. I'm not always—I have trouble... sharing, I guess."

"I don't want you to hide stuff from me." Wyatt ran a hand down Timothy's neck.

"I have a favor to ask you too." Timothy kept his voice soft on purpose, but the hesitancy slipped in on its own. "What you said last night—"

"I didn't say it so you'd say it back. I said it because I felt it. That's the only reason. If you feel it, when you feel it, then say it. No pressure, I swear." He stroked his hand up and down Timothy's neck. "It's not something I just say, okay?"

"You're too good for me."

"Not hardly," Wyatt said quickly.

"It's not easy for me. This. Us." Timothy's voice trailed off because he didn't want to say anything that might break the fragile bond between them. Timothy pulled away from Wyatt, leaning back on his heels and taking a deep breath before staring Wyatt in the eyes. "Not because of you. I'm a jerk sometimes. I'll try to be better. For you. It's not because Bobby's gone, right? I mean, me. You and me." There it was, out in the universe for both of them to hear, and Timothy wanted to regret saying it but he didn't.

"What the fuck, Timmy?" Wyatt grabbed Timothy's hand. His was rough and calloused and contrasted with the smoothness of Timothy's. "You don't think that, do you? Did I make you feel like that?"

Timothy shook his head. "I'm sorry. I know it's a shitty thing to say, but I needed to know. Come here." Wyatt pulled Timothy closer. "C'mere. Maybe we should make out. It'll make us both feel better."

There was a knock on the door, and the two of them looked up as the sheriff stood in the doorway, arms folded across his chest. "C'mon, boys. Breakfast is in five minutes. And, Timothy, bring your notes, everything you have. We're going to start back at the beginning and figure this out."

THE SHERIFF and Wyatt sat at the kitchen table as Timothy and his mom cleared away the dishes. The sheriff had Timothy's computer files opened and was clicking back and forth between the Excel files Timothy had created.

"So, we have seven boys between the ages of twelve and sixteen. All white, all missing in the last six years."

"You want me to expand the search, Dad? Add in missing girls or different racial backgrounds?" Timothy dropped the silverware into the dishwasher.

"No. Not right now. I'd rather stick with a small group to focus on. Pastor Steve admitted to Andrew Madden, so we can eliminate him. That still leaves six."

"Until you get the DNA tests back, right?" Wyatt was both anxious and hopeful. "Might mean something."

"Yes, Wyatt. It might." Sheriff Mitchell looked over Wyatt's shoulder at Timothy. "You said you found the box originally at a house?"

"Over on Rural Route 38."

The sheriff nodded. "And Big Tommy owns the place?"

"Yep." Timothy leaned back in his chair. "I asked him who was renting it at the time, but then the whole Pastor Steve thing happened, and I never went back to ask if he'd gotten the information."

The sheriff shook his head, an eyebrow arching. "Should I ask where you ran into Big Tommy?"

"Probably, but it'd be better if you don't." Timothy scratched notes in the book he had in front of him, not looking at Wyatt or the sheriff.

"A rule of investigating: don't let anything go by the wayside."

Timothy blushed. "Sorry, Dad."

"I'm not saying anything bad, Timothy. I'm telling you where we need to go back and take a second look. Consider it a teachable moment."

Wyatt stood up to pour both himself and the sheriff a cup of coffee. "I'll go by Big Tommy's later this afternoon and see if he's got the information." He handed over the mug. "If that's okay."

"I think that's fine, provided you're asking and not doing anything else."

Timothy's mother closed the dishwasher and poured herself some coffee as well. Wyatt sounded guilty when he spoke. "I'm sorry, Mrs. Mitchell, I should have asked if you wanted some."

"It's fine, Wyatt. Please don't worry about it." She sipped daintily. "I may actually go with you this afternoon. We can stop at the grocery store afterward. We're shopping for two growing children and I can use the help."

"Yes, ma'am."

She raised an eyebrow. "I did say to call me Janelle, right?"

"Janelle, don't tease the boy." The sheriff smiled at his wife, and she smiled back. "Child abductions are generally someone who knows the child." He looked back and forth between Timothy and Wyatt. "You're sure Bobby's father didn't take him?"

"Miss Maddy thinks he's in jail."

"Bobby didn't even know his dad. Not really," Wyatt insisted, putting his coffee down. "Met him a few times. I remember when he was ten, he was out of school for a day, because his dad was supposed to come for a visit. He never showed up. Bobby waited all day. I doubt his dad'd even care enough."

"But Maddy said she'd seen a car?"

"Not her," Timothy replied. "Bobby. She said he'd seen it—" He paused while he flipped through his small notebook. "—three times."

"But he didn't get a license number? Make? Model?"

Wyatt shook his head. "Bobby wouldn't know the difference between a Ford and a Hyundai. The only thing he would've known is to say car or truck."

"Okay. Let's find out from Maddy if there are any more details about the car. Wyatt, you'll see if Big Tommy has any more information on whoever rented his house. I'm going to see if Mike's in-laws have any information on anyone else." The sheriff stood up. "From now on, you two let me know what you're working on with this. You don't need to ask my permission, but I do expect that you'll let me know what you're doing before you do it." He gulped down the last bit of coffee and handed the empty mug to Wyatt. "And be careful."

CHAPTER THIRTEEN

MRS. MITCHELL pulled into the parking lot of Big Tommy's bar and parked directly in front of the door. Wyatt noticed it was the same exact spot Timothy had used when they had their big blowout in the parking lot.

She tucked the keys in her purse and nodded when Wyatt opened the bar door for her. She ignored the glances a few of the regular, heavier drinkers shot her way and called out, "Tom. How are you?"

"Well," Big Tommy said with a genuine smile in his voice. "Nice of you to stop by, Mrs. Mitchell. How's the sheriff?"

"Oh, running around, saving the world, you know." She sat at the bar and motioned for Wyatt to join her as Big Tommy wiped his sweaty forehead with a red bandanna. "Same as always. I'd love to get a club soda if you would."

"Certainly. It's always a joy to have you here." Big Tommy poured her out a glass and dropped in a lime wedge. He wiped down the table before setting her glass down. "Wyatt, your usual? What is it? Cola, right?"

Wyatt shook his head. "I'm good, thanks, Big Tommy." He paused for a quick second and then leaned forward. "Hey, Tom, remember how me and Timothy were looking for whoever was in that house about four years ago? Did you have a chance to check those records yet? It's important."

"Jeez, Wyatt, I guess I plum forgot. Sorry about that." Big Tommy's eyes narrowed. "Seems like a lot of work to track down a diary."

Mrs. Mitchell smiled. "It may have a little more importance than the boys originally stated, Tom." She sipped gingerly and smiled. "How soon do you think you could let us know?"

Big Tommy pursed his lips, realizing he'd been slightly trapped. "Well, Mrs. Mitchell—"

"Please, Tom, call me Janelle." She kept a sweet expression on her face, knowing she'd pushed him into a corner. "We're really not interested in anything other than a name, Tom. It could help more than you realize."

"Oh?" He pulled out his bandanna and wiped the back of his neck. "Really?"

She leaned forward, lowering her voice so, even sitting next to her, Wyatt could barely hear her. "I wish I could tell you more, Tom, but we really need to get the name." Leaning back, Mrs. Mitchell kept her voice low but casual. "Do you think we could come by on Monday and get it?"

Big Tommy nodded, a strange grin spreading across his face. "Sure thing, Janelle. Why don't you stop by in the evening?"

She reached into her pocketbook and dropped a twenty on the bar. "I look forward to it. Come on, Wyatt." She waved to Big Tommy as Wyatt followed her silently out the door.

They were out of the parking lot before Wyatt said anything. "That was… impressive."

"Men like to do favors, Wyatt. Especially straight men for women. Remember that."

"Yes, ma'am."

THE GROCERY shopping went fine, at first. Wyatt pushed the cart for Timothy's mom and she taught him a little bit about how to shop and what to test for in the produce department.

"Timothy was such a fussy eater when he was younger. For a year, he'd only eat food that was white and red. About the only thing I could feed him were rice, tomatoes, red peppers, and chicken."

Wyatt laughed an actual laugh. "I like that story."

"Well, as his mother, I enjoy embarrassing him as much as possible."

"Do you think…?" Wyatt hesitated, walking down the aisle. "Do you think I could maybe make a special dinner on his birthday? Something he really likes."

"I didn't know you liked to cook, honey." She stopped next to the oatmeal and looked at the cannisters.

"I don't. I mean, I don't really know how." Wyatt held up a box of Frosted Flakes but put it back on the shelf when she shook her head. "I'd like to learn, but mostly I only made frozen dinners and mac and cheese. Simple stuff."

"No offense, Wyatt," Timothy's mom said, placing her choice inside the cart, "but heating up a frozen dinner is not cooking. Every man should know how to cook. And sew. If you don't know how to put a button on your shirt, we'll have to teach you that too."

"I'm not sure I own any shirts that have buttons." Wyatt's neck felt hot as he looked at another box of cereal.

"Oh, honey," she said quickly. "I'm sorry. Listen to me. I sound like a snob, and that's not what I mean at all. I truly think there are skills that everyone should have. Tell you what, I'll teach you cooking, if you teach me about football."

"Really?"

"Absolutely," she said. "Ben has no patience, and Timothy doesn't know anything about the game. He follows track and sometimes he'll watch basketball, if he thinks some player is cute, but that's about it."

"Sounds like Timothy."

She nodded cautiously, and they walked into the next aisle in silence. "If he really likes you, you don't need to worry, Wyatt. He's not the type to cheat. Not after Ethan."

"He said the name before, but he didn't really talk about it."

"If he wants to mention it, he will," she said blithely. "Would you grab that ten-pack of toilet paper, please." He reached up, and as he turned to place it in the cart, Timothy's mom started speaking again. "It must be difficult."

"Football? Not really."

She shook her head. "No. Not that." She wandered a few steps away, looking at the dish soap. "Being in the house. Being around Timothy."

"Why would it be hard? I like being around him."

She dropped some soap into the cart. "I suppose I should have said being around him but not with him."

"I-I…," Wyatt stammered, feeling like a fool. "I wouldn't. I mean, I've never. Him and me, we've never—"

"Wyatt." She cut him off and moved him past the spices, dropping pepper into the cart. "I realize I'm Timothy's mom, but I'm not so old I can't remember what it is to be a teenager or to be in love or to want to be…." She waved her hand while she searched for the word. "Intimate."

"I don't know what to say." He kept looking into the cart while he walked, almost taking out a display of crackers.

"I'm very glad you two are respecting the rules we've set down, but that doesn't mean I don't understand it might be difficult."

He pulled the cart up short and stared at her. "I like Timothy. I love him. And it's hard, because I want so bad to be with him, but...." He trailed off. "I don't know where I was going with that."

"It's more special when you wait." She sighed. "I suppose all parents say that, but I do speak from experience."

"Why are you still in this town? No one wants you here." The new voice was thick with an accent, deep from cigarette smoke, and filled with anger.

"Mom," Wyatt said softly as he looked up at her.

Timothy's mom moved between them and dug in her purse. She held out her keys to him. "Wyatt, why don't you go wait in the car. I'll be out soon."

"I...," he said, his voice soft and weak. "Yes, ma'am." He took the keys from her and walked away from his mother, not turning back, but he did hear the murmur of voices.

TIMOTHY AND his father had set up two corkboards in the dining room filled with notecards and names and timelines. Articles Timothy had printed out from online and pictures of everyone who had been on the list. Timothy had a half-drunk cup of coffee in front of him when the front door opened.

"You've been busy," Timothy's mom said, as she and Wyatt passed through the dining room.

Timothy's father stayed staring at the printouts and index cards mounted on the board. "It helps me focus. How was the grocery store?"

"I'm going to have a cigarette," Wyatt said, his voice quiet and flat.

She nodded. "Drop the groceries in the kitchen on your way outside and I'll make some lunch." Wyatt silently brought everything into the kitchen, and Timothy's mom lowered her voice. "We ran into Wyatt's mother at the store. He might be a little quiet and moody until he sorts it all out in his head." She waved at the board and kissed Timothy on the head before going into the kitchen. "Don't give yourself nightmares."

Timothy could hear cabinets open and close as she put away the food.

Timothy waited two minutes before he stood up. "I'll be right back."

His father nodded and kept his eyes on the papers in front of him. "About time," he muttered loud enough for his son to hear. Timothy ignored his father and went through the kitchen into the backyard where

Wyatt was sitting at the picnic table, facing away from the house. Timothy straddled the bench. Even with both of them sitting, he was too short to rest his chin on Wyatt's shoulder, so he settled for a kiss on Wyatt's biceps and wrapped his arm under Wyatt's.

Wyatt didn't look at him, but Timothy could see a small smile. "Thanks."

"You don't have to talk about it, but you can if you want."

"I want her to go away." Wyatt shook his head. "I hope she didn't say anything bad to your mom." He took a drag off his cigarette. "When I saw her, your mom sent me outside to wait in the car. You know, she actually stood right between me and my mom." He flicked ash from the end of his cigarette into the pail. "I figured out I'm never going to be able to pay your parents back for everything."

"You shouldn't even think about that." Timothy exhaled, and he watched the hairs on Wyatt's arm move as he did. "Seriously. If they didn't want to do it, they wouldn't."

"They're doing it because of you."

"They're doing it because they want to. Yeah, part of that is the fact you mean something to me, but it's not everything. They like you, Wyatt."

Wyatt turned to Timothy. "I hate her so much."

Timothy kissed Wyatt again. "She's not worth it." He sighed. "I'm not very good with words, Wyatt. To be honest, not so great with feelings either, but I want to tell you something. I like you because you're kind and sweet and gentle. Don't let hate turn you into something like her."

"I think…." Wyatt leaned down and kissed Timothy. "I think you're really good with words."

Timothy laughed softly. "See? Kind." He stood up and held out his hand. "C'mon. Let's go eat lunch and then help Dad. I have a Spanish test tomorrow, so I need to study tonight."

"Damn," Wyatt said. "I was kind of hoping we could make out for about a million hours."

"Down, boy." Timothy held the door open for him as they went in, where his mom and father were sitting at the kitchen table, eating sandwiches, waiting for them. Janelle wished them all luck and went into the living room to work on sorting the family pictures.

THE SHERIFF scratched the back of his head, frustrated at where they were. "Okay, we've got Bobby. He's been missing four years. Joey Travis, missing five years. Ryan Bolger's been missing two years." He pointed at each picture in turn. "Rob Lewis and Joe Freeman both missing six years. Where are they from again?"

"Um—" Timothy sifted through his notes. "—Rob went missing from Darlington and Joe from Hartsville." Timothy's eyes were tired from looking at his computer constantly, and he rubbed them gently.

Wyatt leaned his elbows on the table. "They're not far apart. Maybe a half hour at most."

"Far enough that the police departments might hear about the other kid, but not think they're related."

"Do you think it's another preacher? There can't be only one doing stuff like this, right?"

"I hope not," Timothy said. "I'd hate to think that many people believe God wants me dead."

His dad dropped his hand from the top of his head where he'd left it resting after the scratch. "God doesn't want that."

"I know, Dad. I wasn't making a religious point."

"Just as long as you know."

"Hey," Wyatt said, "look at this." He grabbed Timothy's computer and pulled up a map of the state. "If this is all one person, they're moving."

"What?" Timothy was confused, and the sheriff leaned over the two of them.

"Rob and Joe, six years ago, they were the most far east. Then everyone else goes farther west, like whoever's doing it is moving across the state. These are way too far apart for someone to be living in only one place. They're moving almost every year."

Timothy's dad nodded. "Someone transient?"

"A farm worker?" Timothy put his hand on Wyatt's arm. "Nice job." He left his hand there and gently stroked Wyatt's skin with his thumb. "Almost every job is transient today, isn't it? I mean how many people work from home on their computer?"

"A truck driver? Maybe a regular route?" Wyatt looked at both of them.

Timothy smiled at Wyatt. "Maybe once we're done with school, we could open up our own private investigator's office."

The sheriff arched an eyebrow. "Not funny."

"So, can we drive around in a fast car and wear cool suits?" Wyatt smiled at Timothy.

"Ooh," Timothy said, ignoring his father's exasperated face and focusing on the twinkle in Wyatt's eyes. "We could call it the Townsend Agency and use a speaker." He laughed and then trailed off when neither his dad nor Wyatt laughed as well. "Seriously? *Charlie's Angels*?" Timothy looked back and forth between the two of them. "Wyatt, if we're going to date, you really need to step up your gay pop culture references."

His father sighed loudly. "Can we please get back to this?" He pointed at the map on the computer. "We could eliminate most public professions. People do work from home, but it's not something most taxpayers would be happy with. And when this started, jobs were more structured."

"I guess not." Timothy smiled. "So, now we've got to find everyone who's moved over the last six years who might or might not be a truck driver and/or work from home. Fun." Timothy yawned and pressed the back of his hands to his eyes.

"Thanks, smartass," his dad said. "Very helpful."

Wyatt rested his hand on Timothy's. "Why don't you study for a while? You've got a test, and I've got to finish a book for English and do some math."

"Good idea, kiddo," Timothy's father agreed as he reached across Timothy and gathered some papers. "You're a good influence."

Timothy rolled his eyes. "Fine." He grabbed his computer and headed for the stairs. "I'll go study instead of hunting." He stopped with one foot on the bottom step and one on the floor.

Wyatt picked up his book from the dining room table and started to follow Timothy upstairs before Timothy's dad spoke up quietly. "Wyatt, why don't you read in the living room? That way the two of you aren't distracting one another." He threw a glance to Timothy, who'd been waiting for Wyatt at the bottom of the staircase.

Wyatt smiled carefully. "Yes, sir."

"And, Wyatt? Nice observation, son." Timothy's father nodded as Wyatt's face lit up from the compliment. "Good work." Timothy rolled his eyes at his dad as Wyatt went into the living room. He was up in his room before he realized his father had called Wyatt "son." He smiled for one quick second and then opened up his Spanish book.

SUNDAY MORNING was bright and warm, and Wyatt was still asleep while Timothy went for a run. There were a couple of things floating around his brain, and he was hoping the run might clear things out a bit. Timothy's mom had breakfast ready, and his father was already at the station when Timothy got back.

"Would you wake up Wyatt please?" His mother put a plate of pancakes down on the table. "Breakfast is ready."

"Can we let him sleep?" Timothy asked. "It took him forever to get to sleep last night. I heard him tossing and turning when I went to the bathroom at three."

She sighed. "I suppose this once. I do want him to get used to family meal time."

He laughed. "Believe me, Mom, he's never going to get used to this family. I'm still not used to this family."

"Very funny." She sat down at the table, and he put two pancakes onto her plate. "Think of it as our special bonding time."

"Sounds good to me." He passed her the butter and syrup and waited until she was done before he plopped a pat of butter on top of his own pancakes.

"Coffee?"

"I've got it." He shoved a forkful of pancake into his mouth and stood up to get them each a cup. "So, there's a couple of things I want to follow up on today. I should be gone for a couple of hours. I'll be home before dinner."

"I hope so. You have a Spanish test tomorrow, correct? And where are you going?"

"I'm heading over to Lockhart. I want to talk to Margaret Bolger about something."

"Do I know her?"

"No. Her brother's missing." He'd finished two pancakes and most of his coffee. Timothy grabbed his last pancake and rolled it up. "I'm going to run through the shower."

"Keep your cell phone on," she called out as he ran upstairs.

Timothy went into his bedroom to change his clothes and then went into the other room and kissed Wyatt's forehead for some reason. He wasn't sure why he felt the need to do that, but he shrugged and headed down the stairs. He poured the rest of the coffee from the pot into his insulated mug and headed to his car.

The ride to Lockhart was a bit strange. Except for his driving around Greenville while Lacey was at her aunt's house, he hadn't driven this far alone in a long time. He was listening to bad country music, wondering why the hell Wyatt always listened to this stuff. He couldn't figure it out, so he switched over to news radio.

He pulled up in front of the Bolgers' place and finished the rest of his coffee, trying to prepare himself for hurting these people by bringing up their lost son. He probably should have texted Margaret, but it wasn't a bad drive, and he needed a little bit of alone time.

He rang the doorbell, and Margaret opened the door after a few minutes. Her eyes narrowed a little bit. "Did you find anything else out?"

He smiled carefully at her. "It's been an interesting week. Do you have a few minutes?"

She nodded carefully and stepped out onto the porch, closing the door behind her, just as she'd done the last time. "My parents are out for a little while, so I have some time. I'd invite you in, but—"

"It's cool. I had a few follow-up questions, if that's okay."

"What'd you find out?"

He told her about Pastor Steve, about what had happened to Wyatt and him. He left out the personal parts and Wyatt's mom, figuring she wouldn't care, and it wasn't really relevant.

She was silent for a few minutes after he finished his story. "Wow. I'm glad you're all right."

"Thanks." He laughed. "Me too."

"Do you think he took Ryan?"

He shrugged. "I don't know. I guess it's possible. To be honest, this guy seems to me to be someone who knows exactly what he's doing and remembers everything. They asked him about all of the names I found. The cops would know way better than me, but I don't think so."

"I hope he didn't. I hope Ryan didn't have to go through all of that. This guy sounds like a bastard."

"Yeah." He sat down on the porch step. "I agree."

Margaret sat down next to him.

"I want to look in another direction, though. I found a lot of missing kids, and I need to follow up with you. My dad reminded me my follow-up sucks."

"Harsh dad." She laughed hard at her own joke.

"Heh." He joined in for a bit. "He didn't quite say it like that. But it was kind of close."

"What can I do?"

"Did you ever find that teacher's name?"

"Maybe. I found an old yearbook of Ryan's. It's not a real one, just a photocopied book the kids in his class made. I can show it to you."

"Please. That'd be really helpful."

"Wait here, okay?" She got up and brushed the back of her jeans as she went into the house. He stared out at the street. It was tree lined and pretty, and he saw flowers in every yard. He wondered what was going on behind the doors and windows. Was a child being abused? Was a wife being hit or an elder being ignored? What kind of sicko lived in that house? Who drove that minivan? Some lunatic who beat their little boy who wanted to be a little girl? He didn't like those thoughts running around in his head, and he hated this might be how he was always going to see the world. Maybe if he could save one person, one. Maybe it would be worth it.

The door creaked open behind him, and he stood up. Margaret handed him a stapled pile of papers. "This is it. It was something the kids put together. Ryan had a poem published."

Timothy flipped through until he came to a page toward the end. It was a short poem, sweet and lovely about sunshine and dreams. There were three other poems on the page and no pictures of any of the students or teachers. He smiled at the second poem. It was angsty and moody and whoever wrote it probably already regretted it, only four years later. The last poem was a sad love story. A breakup.

Margaret pointed to the bottom of the page. "I think that's him. The teacher. Tommy Mathis."

Timothy wondered what poems he'd rejected. "Do you mind if I hold on to this for a little bit? I'll get it back to you soon as I can."

Margaret shrugged. "Keep it. I'm not sure Mom or Dad would ever miss it. And I don't want it."

"Thanks. I'll give you a call soon." Timothy started down the walkway to his car, then turned around. "I'm sorry."

She looked puzzled for a second.

"About bringing this all back up. I didn't mean to open any old wounds."

She stared down the street for a second. "They're not old. They never healed. You didn't open anything back up again."

He nodded sadly and left before she said anything else.

TIMOTHY DROVE carefully toward home, turning everything over and over in his head. He felt like there was something he was missing, something simple. At first he thought it might be something about Wyatt. He was grateful his parents let Wyatt stay, but then Wyatt told him he loved him. He felt unsettled about hearing that. Then he felt guilty about it, about not responding. He should have said something. Wyatt had saved his life. He was sweet and kind and protective. And he was a hell of a lot smarter than anyone gave him credit for, even himself.

Timothy shut the music off, enjoying the silence... when it hit him. Something so simple he wondered if it was too easy. He pulled quickly off the highway and did a loop, getting back on in the opposite direction, cutting off another car while doing it. He waved an apology and pushed down on the gas, hoping he was wrong as he headed toward Greenville and the offices of the *Courier*. He drove as fast as he could and pulled up in front of the offices, almost dropping his phone as he grabbed at the door to yank it open.

"Dad," he said to his father's voicemail. "I had to come out to Greenville. I'll call as soon as I meet with Frank Carroll." He hung up and stopped short when someone called out to him.

"We're closed to the general public, kid." The guy behind the counter was in his early twenties, with mousey blond hair, flat around his face.

"Is Frank Carroll here?"

"Closed."

"I need five minutes. It's urgent. Seriously urgent."

"He's busy. You can come back tomorrow." His voice had the same tone of a bored cop who's pulled over a speeder for the fifth time in twenty minutes. He came from around the desk and stood between Timothy and the door.

Timothy reached into his pocket and pulled out his wallet. "Twenty bucks. It's all yours if you pretend you didn't see me."

The guy narrowed his eyes.

"It's all I have, and it's seriously something that can't wait."

The receptionist/bodyguard grabbed the cash and stuffed it in his pocket, turning away from the door. Timothy passed by and headed toward the office he went to the last time. Frank Carroll was bent over his computer screen, and Timothy knocked on the open door.

"Mr. Carroll?"

Carroll looked up, startled. "How the hell did you get in here?"

"I bribed the guy at the front door."

Carroll glared at him, completely taken aback for a moment, and then he barked a short laugh. "You have balls, kid. All that to drop off an internship application?"

"I need a favor, and I can't really explain it, but I need to know if you have a picture of Tom Matthews. The reporter."

"What? Why the hell did you interrupt me for this? I've got to get this to the printers in an hour." He smiled, which took some of the sting out of it, but his tone was clipped.

"Mr. Carroll, I can't give you the whole story, but I need you to believe me when I'm telling you this is a matter of life and death. I need to see a picture of this guy."

"Life and death?" Carroll leaned back in his chair. "Is this something I should hold the front page for?"

"If I promise to give you the full story once I figure out if I'm right, will you give me a picture?"

Carroll narrowed his eyes, but other than that he didn't move. "You're serious."

"More than you realize."

He stood up and gestured for Timothy to follow him. They walked to what seemed to be the office break room, neither of them saying anything. Timothy's heart was beating faster and his breathing was shallow, the way it was before starting a sparring match at the dojo.

There were various pictures along the wall, the office softball team, someone holding up an award at a dinner, a wedding, a newborn at the hospital, the everyday occurrences of an everyday life.

Frank Carroll stopped in front of a group shot at some fancy restaurant. "This was a fund-raising dinner for the local schools. That's him, in the back, with the red tie." He pointed at a tall, thin man with glasses, a receding hairline, and a goofy smile.

Timothy's voice was low and breathy. "Son of a bitch."

"What?"

Timothy ignored him and pulled out his phone. He snapped a picture of the picture and started dialing his dad. "Thanks, Mr. Carroll. I promise, as soon as I get this all settled, I'll call you." He backed out the door to run to his car. "And if you hear from him, call the sheriff's office and let them know. He's not a good man."

Before Frank Carroll could say anything, Timothy was out the door and running past the desk. He was already talking on the phone. "Dad, it's me."

"Where are you?" His dad sounded worried. "I got your message."

"I'm just leaving Greenville. Dad, we got him."

"Who? Are you okay?"

Timothy unlocked his car, yanked the door open, and tossed his bag inside. "I'm fine, Dad. I mean I'm pissed at myself but fine." He turned the car on and wrestled the seat belt into place. "Tom Matthews, Matt Thompson, probably Tommy Mathis—"

"Who's Tommy Mathis?" his father interrupted. "You're not driving while you're on the phone, are you?"

Timothy clicked over to the speaker and tossed the phone on the seat next to him. "You're on speaker, Dad." Timothy gunned the car and headed back to the highway as quickly as he could. "Tom Matthews, the reporter, the one who left the paper and went to teach? He's the same person as Matt Thompson, Bobby's favorite teacher. They're the same person, Dad. I can't find a picture of Tommy Mathis, but he was Ryan Bolger's teacher. The initials, Dad—*T.M.* The names are so close. I can't believe I didn't see this before. I'm such an idiot. This is it, right, Dad? I mean he changed his name. He's connected to Bobby. And he knew about Andrew. And Wyatt, he said Bobby was changing. I think he might have been being sexually abused. It has to be him, Dad."

"Timothy," his father said, using the cop voice. "I need you to take a deep breath. You can't drive when you're all over the map like this. Do you understand?"

"Sorry. Yes, Dad." He paused. "Deep breaths."

"How close are you to home?"

"About forty-five minutes, I guess."

The sheriff breathed deeply with his son and spoke calmly and clearly. "Do you have to get gas?"

"Nope. I have a full tank."

"Get home as soon as possible. Do not stop anywhere. You understand me?"

"I'm on my way, Dad."

"Be careful. Keep the phone close." He paused briefly. "And, Timothy? Damn good work, son."

"Thanks, Dad."

CHAPTER FOURTEEN

TIMOTHY HADN'T even shut the engine off before his father pulled the front door open.

"You're home."

"Safe and sound, Dad." Timothy wanted to be annoyed at what his brain thought of as his overprotective father, but his heart was grateful for a dad who watched over him so closely.

"Good. Get inside and get ready for dinner." His father waved him inside and shut the door behind them. "We'll talk after. I don't want your mother to overhear this type of thing."

Timothy dropped his bag next to the stairs and went slowly to his room, thinking about everything he'd learned today. He opened the door and kicked off his shoes as he walked into his bedroom. Wyatt was sitting up on the bed, with his math book in front of him. He stood up as soon as Timothy entered and grabbed him in a bearhug, lifting Timothy off the ground.

"You're okay."

"Yeah." Timothy hugged back, his face buried in Wyatt's neck. "I mean, I'm having a little trouble breathing right this second."

Wyatt dropped him. "Sorry."

"It's okay. Really." He went up on his tippy-toes, his arms around Wyatt. He brought his lips to Wyatt's and pressed them together gently. Timothy's kiss was achingly soft, but Wyatt kissed back hard. Timothy pulled back slightly, turning the kiss back into something light, and Wyatt moaned but didn't try for more. Timothy's tongue pushed out of his mouth and licked Wyatt's lips.

Footsteps sounded on the stairs and Wyatt pulled away, sitting on the edge of the bed. "When you turn eighteen, I'm gonna pay you back for being such a tease."

Timothy smirked at him. "Promises, promises." He ran into the bathroom and washed up for dinner, getting down to the table as his father was passing out the salad.

Wyatt gave the bowl in front of him a look.

"I take it you're not a fan of vegetables?" Timothy's dad questioned him. "I noticed them left on your plate the last week when you ate dinner."

"I like them on a burger, sir." Wyatt looked up from the plate and shrugged.

Timothy's dad sat down and passed Timothy's mom the dressing. "Wyatt, if you can call my wife Janelle, I think you can call me—" He paused for effect. "—Sheriff."

It took Wyatt a minute to catch on to the joke. "Yes, sir."

He nodded. "Better."

"Mean, Dad," Timothy said. "Mean."

"I can make a little fun if I want." The sheriff smiled and speared some lettuce with his fork. "After all, I can't be on my best behavior all the time. But vegetables are a must in this house."

Timothy's mother passed some grated cheese to Wyatt and then the pasta bowl. "Don't mind either of them, Wyatt. You'll get used to it. I certainly did."

"How long did it take?"

"Wow. Burn, Wyatt." Timothy laughed as he took the pasta bowl from Wyatt. He served himself and felt a strange little shiver. As he pushed the thought of what he'd learned today into the back of his mind, he wondered if this was what his future was going to be. His parents and his boyfriend around the dinner table, laughing with each other and enjoying each other's company. He smiled as he ate, deciding he liked the feeling.

TIMOTHY HAD finished his homework, studying more for his Spanish test. Wyatt had finished his math homework and was almost done with his book for English class. Timothy's dad had called Deputy Mike, who showed up with a six-pack of beer. He was halfway through his first one as Timothy passed around the pictures from the yearbook and the wall in the *Courier* office.

"That's him." Wyatt's voice was thick with emotion. "I remember him now. He was always joking with us. Trying to be our friend."

Timothy's father stood up. "I don't think you two should do any more work on this. You've been amazing and gotten the information we need, but—"

"Sheriff," Wyatt said, his voice rising slightly, "that's not fair."

The sheriff held up a hand, silencing Wyatt. "I think it's more than fair, given what happened last week." He came around the table and placed a hand gently on Wyatt's shoulder. "I understand what you're saying, Wyatt. I really do, especially given your... history with Bobby. But this is someone who's committing a series of crimes that are very serious and scary. Your safety, both of you, is my highest priority. I'll let you help where I can, but Mike and I will be taking charge."

Wyatt slumped against the back of the chair and crossed his arms. "Fine."

Deputy Mike turned to Timothy. "You're not arguing on this one?"

"About what?" Timothy gestured to the notes on the wall. "We can assume this guy is a murderer and a pedophile. As far as I'm concerned, you should shoot him as soon as you see him, and I don't want to be standing between him and the bullets."

"Weird," Mike said. "I'm not used to you being so reasonable."

"Thanks, Deputy." Timothy was shaking his head.

"Mike," the sheriff said, ending the conversation completely. "This will be only you and me. I don't want anyone else involved. This is all conjecture at this point. All we really have is someone who changed their name."

Mike was taking notes. "Got it, Sheriff."

"I'll call the departments in Darlington and Hartsville, see if I can get any information about the missing boys from there. I want you to get in touch with the state board of education. I want every teacher from the last ten years who has the initials TM or MT. Eliminate all the females, and we'll start from there."

Timothy leaned forward slightly. "You should start with English and journalism teachers. It might not hurt to check the local papers too. If he wrote for the *Courier,* he might have written for someone else."

Mike looked at the sheriff, who nodded.

Timothy's dad gestured at the stairs. "Okay, you two. Get ready for bed. You have a test tomorrow. And you've got a woodworking class."

Wyatt looked up at him. "Why do I need sleep?"

"Because you're working with power tools and I have no desire to have to visit you in the hospital." Timothy's father rubbed his eyes. "Speaking of which, we'll have to sit down this week and figure out your insurance and make sure that all the legal niceties are in order."

"Yes, sir."

He leaned down and gave Timothy a quick peck on the cheek. "Go on upstairs and get to bed."

"Night, Dad. Bye, Mike. Get home safely."

"Thanks, kiddo." Mike waved to both of them as they went up the stairs.

TIMOTHY AND Wyatt took separate cars the next day, because Wyatt had a study period first, so he could come into school later.

They sat with Lacey at lunch, and Timothy worried that he might have missed a couple of questions on the Spanish test.

"I'm sure," Lacey said through blue-tinted lips, "you'll be fine."

Timothy stared at her for a minute. "Does your lipstick make it easier or harder to eat food?"

She rolled her eyes at him. "Some gay dude you are. It's the same as any other lipstick. Just a different color."

Wyatt's eyebrows rose. "Hold on. Do I have to know about lipstick and makeup now?"

"Not really, Wyatt," Lacey said quickly. "Only one of you needs to know about makeup. Haven't you guys talked about that yet?"

"She's kidding," Timothy said as he finished his sandwich and tossed the napkin into his lunch bag. "Seriously, Lacey, don't say things like that."

"But it's fun." She laughed. "I'm messing with you, Wyatt, but damn, it's totally worth it."

"Nice friend there, Timmy."

"Timothy."

They stood up, the three of them tossing their garbage into the trash and headed into the hall toward their afternoon classes.

Wyatt grabbed Timothy's arm right before they went in different directions. "Are you going home right after school?"

"Sure. You?"

Wyatt shook his head. "I've got to stay late and fix something in woodshop. My spice rack didn't come out right."

"A spice rack?"

"It was either that or a bookshelf, and my mom doesn't read." Wyatt's gaze dropped to the floor before he raised it quickly. "I started it before everything. I guess I could give it to your mom."

Timothy smiled and reached out to put his hand on Wyatt's arm, then pulled back, remembering they were in the middle of school. "See you later."

"Yeah. Later."

AFTER SCHOOL Timothy sat in his car until the parking lot had only the teachers' cars and the few students' on late detention. He turned the ignition and drove out to the house on RR 38. He wanted to see it. To see where it all started. Where Wyatt pulled him into a case; where he first heard Wyatt was gay. He pulled into the gravel driveway and texted his father to see if he'd found out who rented the house four years ago. The house itself was nothing but a few beams and walls. Barren and empty.

He walked around the house, wandering his way in and out of the frame, into the weeds covering the ground. He was lost in thought, wondering about Bobby. And Wyatt. It wasn't until branches cracked behind him that he turned around, expecting to see Wyatt or his dad. Instead there was a tall, thin man with a receding hairline and a sweaty forehead. He wasn't smiling a goofy smile, but Timothy knew immediately who he was. Matt Thompson. Tom Matthews. Timothy swore and turned around to run into the woods when a click he knew well sounded. He'd first heard it when his dad took him to the shooting range.

"Don't move. I don't want to shoot you here, but I will." The voice was thin, reedy, and almost childlike. "Sheriff Mitchell's son. The one who started all this."

Timothy swallowed the lump in his throat, trying hard to remember everything his dad had ever taught him. *Don't do something stupid because you're panicking, Timothy. You can't do both at the same time.* That's what his father had said. Timothy forced himself to breathe slowly, not to show any panic. He stood up straighter.

"What should I call you? Matt? Tom?"

The man laughed. "You can call me Matt, I guess. It's what Bobby used to call me." He stopped laughing abruptly. "Why did you even start? Why didn't you leave it alone?"

"I... I'm not sure what you mean."

"Like hell!" The force behind the voice startled Timothy, and he almost stumbled back. "You know what I mean. Why?"

"Because it mattered. What happened to Bobby. How did you even find out? Who I am and what I was doing? How'd you find out?"

"Stupid Frank Carroll."

Timothy blinked, trying to understand. "He called you? He said he didn't know where you were."

"He didn't. He put a story in the paper about the police looking for me." Timothy could see Matt was sweating more and more and his voice was rising and falling in volume and pitch. "It only took a few calls to some old coworkers, letting them talk about the town gossip, who was asking for what. Are you actually writing a story for the school paper?"

Timothy shook his head, keeping the rest of his body as still as he could. He could see the panic in Matt's manner, and he didn't want any sudden moves to set him off. Not more than he was now, anyway.

"No. It was an easy way to explain asking questions." He briefly thought about how he was going to punch Frank Carroll in the face. "What happened to Bobby?"

"Your little buddy happened."

"What? I don't understand." Timothy was sweating, and he realized the sun was at his back, which meant it was in Matt's eyes. If he was fast enough...

"Wyatt happened. If he hadn't come along, then Bobby and I would have stayed in love." His hand shook slightly. "Bobby was the first one I ever loved. There were a few before him. Rob and Joe. Joey. Joey was very sweet, but I never loved them the way I did Bobby. He was so lovely." Matt's eyes were squinting, and Timothy shifted slightly forward. Matt noticed and waved the gun at Timothy, motioning for him to circle, shifting their places so Timothy lost his advantage. "But sweet Bobby decided he wanted to be with Wyatt. He told me to leave him alone or he'd tell. I couldn't let him do that, could I?"

Timothy didn't answer, so Matt barked at him.

"Could I?"

Timothy's mind was swearing and trying to figure out something. The woods were now behind Matt and his car was too far away.

His voice might waver, and he hated sounding scared, so he decided not to answer the question and ask his own. "He's here, isn't he? You buried Bobby here."

Matt threw back his head and laughed. "You're dumber than I thought." Matt gestured with his gun again. "Get out your phone." Timothy reached into his pocket and slowly pulled it out. "Call him. Wyatt. Tell him to meet you at the school. I'm going to put the two of you with Bobby and no one will even think about looking for you there."

"You kill a cop's son and you'll never have a second of peaceful sleep for the rest of your life."

"The cops are too stupid. Not that you're much smarter, but they haven't caught me yet." He laughed again. "Unlock it and pass it to me." Timothy opened the phone and passed it slowly to Matt, staring at the gun barrel. Matt took a couple of steps back, out of range even if Timothy tried to kick at him. Matt flipped through the contacts until he got to Wyatt. He pressed the Call button and passed the phone back to Timothy. "If you even try warn him, I'll shoot you right here."

Timothy swallowed hard and listened to the phone. Wyatt picked up on the fourth ring. "Wyatt? It's Tim."

"Huh? Where are you?"

"Wyatt, can you hear me? It's Tim."

Matt gestured at him to hurry up.

"Wyatt, I need you to meet me at the school, as soon as you can. Can you meet me there?"

"Um, yeah, sure. I left, but… are you okay?"

"Yeah. Fine. Just meet me at the school."

Matt grabbed the phone out of his hand and hung it up. He shoved the phone into his pocket and gestured to Timothy's car. The phone buzzed in his pocket. Timothy opened his mouth, but Matt shouted at him.

"Open the rear door, right behind the driver's side. Then get in the driver's seat and keep your hands on the wheel."

Timothy was starting to panic now, but he kept his voice and hands steady. They were headed toward the main street, and Timothy's foot pushed gradually on the gas, picking up speed. He felt a sharp slap to the side of his head.

"Slow down. I don't want your cop buddies stopping us. If you even try to pull something, I'll shoot right through the seat. Maybe even shoot whatever dumbass deputy stops us. Thanks to you and that redneck shit, I've got nothing left to lose."

Timothy didn't respond except to slow down. He wasn't in a position where he could fight back or run. Even if he crashed the car, he might be worse off than if he played along. There'd be another chance. There had to be. *Stay smart, stay calm, and stay alive.* That's what his dad would say.

"Why'd you write the article?" Timothy asked. His voice shook more than he wanted it to.

"I knew I'd never met that other kid—"

"Andrew," Timothy interrupted. "His name was Andrew."

"I was hoping the cops would try to link the two and make any investigation even more convoluted." Matt pressed harder on the back of Timothy's seat. "Not that they had any clue then anyway. I was gone from the school by that time."

There was the school. He couldn't see Wyatt's truck, but he pulled into the lot, preparing to park close to the street, and Matt laughed at him. "Closer. Closer." His voice had gained back some of the childish singsong quality. Maybe he was relaxing more, Timothy thought. Hoped. "Roll down the window. Then shut the car off. Then drop your keys on the ground outside the window."

Timothy followed the orders. His heart sank when Matt kicked the keys under the car. Matt moved back and gestured for Timothy to step out of the car. Timothy could feel himself losing what control he had, his breath quickening, his hands shaking.

Matt kept his back to the street, but he turned slightly whenever a car passed by. When Wyatt's truck pulled into the lot Timothy's shoulders tightened, and his eyes darted back and forth. Wyatt's truck pulled close and shut off. Timothy's feet started bouncing as the door closed.

"Hey. You okay?" Wyatt's voice was concerned, thick with worry. "Timothy?" he asked when Timothy didn't respond. "Who's your friend?"

Matt stepped back, keeping his body angled so the gun couldn't be seen from the road. "Wyatt. Good to see you came."

"What the hell are you—Mr. Thomas?" Wyatt took a quick step forward, then stopped when the gun shifted toward Timothy.

"Move slowly and carefully," Matt barked. He waved the gun at the school. "Move toward the side door. The one that leads into the gym."

"Timmy—"

"No talking." They walked toward the door, with Matt following and Timothy hoping that someone, anyone would come by. Timothy glanced at Wyatt, who looked back. The brim of his baseball cap was pushed slightly back and Timothy could see his eyes, wide and worried.

The door was unlocked. "So much for school security," Timothy said, not even realizing he'd spoken out loud.

Matt snorted. His voice and mannerisms were getting angry again, and Timothy clamped his mouth shut.

"I'm not sure the school actually knows about it. We told them for a year, but there was a new principal who came the year I did. He was so overwhelmed he could barely wipe his ass."

Timothy was tempted to slam the door on this guy. He was tall but slim, and if it was a fistfight, either Wyatt or he could take Mr. Thomas in a heartbeat. But there was a gun. And Wyatt. There was Wyatt to worry about.

Matt Thompson ushered them through the hallway until they came to the basement door. He reached into his pocket and tossed a ring of keys at Timothy. They fell short and landed at his feet. "The one with the red mark is for the basement. I'm going to say goodbye to Bobby and then the two of you will be joining him."

"Bobby?" Wyatt's voice got loud. The sun was almost down and the light coming through the school windows was fading quickly, throwing gray shadows on the floor. "Bobby's down there? He's been... he's been down there the whole time?"

Wyatt looked like he might throw up. He backed away from the door and moved to the side, causing Matt to shift his view for a moment. Timothy grabbed the keys and threw them hard at Matt, who instinctively held up his hands, aiming the gun at the ceiling. Timothy moved forward and threw a front kick into Matt's chest, and he went down, landing hard on his back. The gun clattered to the ground, and he grabbed hold of Wyatt's hand, tugging him away.

"Wyatt, let's go! Run!"

Wyatt hesitated for a second, then took off after Timothy and they headed away from Matt. He was between them and the gym they entered through, so the two of them headed away from him, deeper into the school. Timothy thought for one brief second about scrambling for the gun, but the gun was gray, the floor was gray, and the light coming in through the window was gray as well. He wasn't willing to bet he'd find the gun before Matt did. Wyatt was falling behind, damn cigarettes, and Timothy barreled through the door to the second floor a minute before Wyatt did. He grabbed Wyatt and pulled him up the stairs as fast as he could. Their breathing was loud and ragged, echoing off the walls.

Timothy pulled Wyatt as fast as he could toward Mr. Ridley's classroom. The science teacher always kept his door unlocked, knowing the students might arrive at school before he would, and he didn't want them to have to wait outside. He yanked the door open and pulled Wyatt to the floor, sitting with their backs on the door, bracing it in case Matt tried to break in.

Timothy was breathing heavily, and Wyatt was gulping in air. "Wyatt, do you have your phone?"

Wyatt nodded, still sucking air into his lungs.

"Call Dad. You didn't call him already, did you?"

Wyatt shook his head. "I texted him. You called yourself Tim, but I wasn't sure why."

Timothy nodded. "Try again. If you can't get in touch with him right away, call 911 and tell them there's an active shooter at the school. That'll get them here quick." He got to his knees but pushed Wyatt down when he started to do the same thing. "Stay here."

Wyatt opened his mouth, and Timothy put his hand over it.

"Don't argue with me. I don't want this guy leaving and escaping when he can't find us. I don't have any intention of looking over my shoulder for the rest of my life. It's harder for him to chase us if we split up. He's got to search for two people instead of finding both of us together." He stood up and carefully listened at the door. "I'm going to lead him away as best I can. You call Dad, okay? Call him now." Timothy opened the door and Wyatt grabbed his hand. "Don't argue."

"I wasn't going to," Wyatt responded, his voice shaking as he was still getting his wind back. "I was just going to say—I know you said you didn't want to rescue anyone." Wyatt started speaking quickly. "I want you to know, you saved me. I didn't have much, shit, I didn't have anything. Not till you. Not till your family. I need you to—"

Timothy knelt down and kissed Wyatt quickly, stopping his rambling. "I love you. I want you to know that. You know, in case."

"Really?"

"Yeah." Timothy stood up. "Call Dad."

TIMOTHY WAS almost to the back staircase when footsteps sounded behind him. He turned around as Matt Thompson raised the gun. Timothy pushed the door open and ran through as a shot rang out. He said a silent prayer that Wyatt would keep his mouth shut. He ran down the stairs, taking them two at a time, stumbling as he hit the bottom step. The door above him opened, and someone came after him.

"I'm going to kill you both. You know that, right?" Matt said, his voice whispered and harsh. "Might as well get it over with. I'd hate to see the cops show up and have to kill your dad."

"Fuck you, asshole!" Timothy shouted and then ran. He was ahead of Matt but needed to get that gun away or the distance wouldn't mean anything. He pushed the door open and hesitated, wondering if he should take the chance running through his head. He pushed himself into the corner, shifted his weight to his left leg, and waited until the door pushed halfway open. He slammed the door as hard as he could with his right leg and Matt grunted in pain. The stairwell was too enclosed and cramped for Timothy to have any advantage in a hand-to-hand fight, so he ran again, heading back toward the gym as fast as he could. Timothy needed to stop this guy quickly. He didn't want Matt Thompson going after Wyatt, and he didn't want him to be able to hurt his dad in any way. The stairway door slammed open, and he ran around the corner. Timothy pushed himself against the wall, putting himself in a crouching position, making sure he could get as much power as possible in a tackle.

He slowed his breathing as much as he could and strained to hear soft footsteps coming toward him. They kept stopping and starting, and random doors rattled as doorknobs were tested, making sure they were locked. Timothy shut his eyes, clenching them tight, and then opened them as the footsteps got closer. Matt stopped shy of the corner and then took one step. One more. It seemed he was about to turn the corner when police sirens rang out, getting closer. It sounded as though every cop car in town and a couple from the neighboring district were headed toward the school. Matt swore, and Timothy knew he was distracted. He knew there wouldn't be a better chance, so he pushed up and launched himself around the corner. He lucked out that he only had to adjust his direction by about an inch as he landed shoulder-first into Matt's midsection. Matt grunted in pain, and Timothy took him off his feet, then slammed him as hard as he could into the ground. Timothy didn't stop to think as the gun clattered a few feet away. His attention never left the face in front of him. He punched and punched and punched. His knuckles ached as he impacted flesh and bone. Doors bashed open and what sounded like twenty people ran down hallways.

"Stop," Matt said weakly as he held his hands up, trying to block the fists. "Stop!"

"Timothy! Timothy!"

He knew that voice. It wasn't his dad, but he knew it. Where did he know that voice? A hand grabbed his shoulder.

"Sheriff, east hall! East hall! All officers, east hall!"

Strong hands pulled him off Matt Thompson or whatever the hell his name was.

"Timothy, it's me. It's Mike. Are you okay? Are you okay? Are you okay?"

Timothy's breath was coming short and sharp and shallow, high up in his chest. He felt himself being moved as Mike shifted so he stood between Timothy and the man on the floor.

More footsteps sounded as the entire department came down the hallway. There was shouting and someone yelling at the man on the floor, and Mike pushed him farther away.

"Timothy? It's Dad. Are you okay?"

Timothy nodded twice and then looked up at his dad's face. When he saw his father's eyes filled with worry, Timothy started sobbing and buried himself in his father's arms.

His dad rocked him back and forth, whispering in his ear, then kissing the top of his head. "You're okay. I've got you. Dad's got you."

AN HOUR later Timothy was sitting in the back seat of his car with a blanket from the police wrapped around his shoulders and a cup of coffee in his hands. Wyatt was chaining one cigarette after another, standing next to the car. Neither of them spoke.

The principal had opened the basement door, and Deputy Mike went down with Matt Thompson, checking the evidence of his story. Mike came out of the building, and Timothy saw Matt's swollen face. Mike's expression was grimmer than Timothy had ever seen him, and Timothy looked away quickly. Mike placed Matt into the back of a squad car and spoke quietly with the sheriff for a few minutes.

His father came over to Timothy and Wyatt and leaned down. "I'm going to get you boys home now." He opened the door to let Wyatt sit in the front and waited for Timothy to close the car door. When they got back to the house, Timothy's mother fussed over them, made sure they ate, and fussed some more. Timothy took a shower and Wyatt went in after he was done.

Afterward they stood in Timothy's room, looking at each other. Timothy walked into Wyatt's arms.

Wyatt hugged him carefully. "Thank you."

"Hmm?" Timothy had lost all the adrenaline from his system hours ago, and as keyed up as his mind was, his body was exhausted.

"You saved my life. Thank you."

"I love you," Wyatt mumbled, squeezing Timothy tighter.

"You too." Timothy closed his eyes and felt Wyatt's breathing slow down until neither could figure out where one ended and the other began.

CHAPTER FIFTEEN

TIMOTHY AND Wyatt stumbled downstairs a little after 8:00, scrambling to get to school on time until Timothy's mother stopped them.

She'd been up since 6:30 a.m., only after, she told them, she'd dragged his father back from watching over the two of them.

Timothy and Wyatt both sat down at the table, and she handed them coffee. There was a knock on the front door, and his mom led Mike into the kitchen. Mike smiled tightly at Timothy.

"He killed Bobby, didn't he?" Wyatt's voice was quiet, determined.

Mike shook his head. "Seems like. We found bones in the basement of the school. They're checking the teeth against dental records. I put a call into Darlington and Hartsville police departments, asking them to check out their own school basements, and Ryan Bolger's school district too." He stood up and poured himself some more coffee. "Smart of him, actually. There's generally no need to go into the basements at schools unless something goes really wrong. It doesn't happen so much as you'd think."

"So we got him?"

Mike was careful not to say anything too revealing. "He's meeting with his lawyer."

"Is the DA going to let him plead out?" Timothy pressed, anxious. "He tried to kill us. He took a shot at me."

"What?" Wyatt's sounded shocked. "You didn't tell me that. I thought the shot was to scare us."

"It's not important."

"Yeah," Wyatt said, "it is."

Mike cut them off. "We have him on attempted murder. If we can get him on three murders, we won't have to worry about Matt Thomas, which is his real name, ever again."

"Hope he rots," Timothy's father said as he entered the room, his eyes still puffy and his hair askew.

His mom put more bread into the toaster as his father poured himself some coffee. "Maybe this is a discussion we shouldn't have in front of the children," she said.

"We're not children, Mom."

"You're *my* children," she answered, planting a kiss on first Timothy's head and then on Wyatt's.

"I came by to make sure you're all okay," Mike said as he pulled his keys out of his pocket. "By the way, Tim," he continued with a smile, "here's your phone back. And we'll get your car and Wyatt's truck back here this afternoon." He put Timothy's phone down on the table. "You'll need to charge it."

"Thanks again, Mike." Timothy stood up.

Mike smiled at him, nodded, and opened up his arms. Timothy hugged him, and Mike squeezed back.

"You're a good fake big brother."

Mike grinned and then walked up to Wyatt. Wyatt stood up and Mike hugged him too, then headed out the door. When Timothy looked over at Wyatt, he noticed Wyatt staring after Mike, a strange look on his face.

Timothy's mom stood up and smiled. "Why don't you two clean up, and I'll make something a little more substantial for breakfast."

WYATT HEADED outside for a morning cigarette, and Timothy followed. They looked at each other carefully and in silence as Wyatt lit up and smoked for a few minutes.

"Want to tell me," Timothy said with a careful tone, "what that glare was about?"

"What glare?"

"Wyatt." Timothy's arched eyebrow made Wyatt roll his eyes.

"It's just… you seem to find it easy. Hugging Mike and all that."

"Are you jealous?" Timothy's grin was shit-eating.

"No!"

"You are." He reached in and grabbed Wyatt's hand, kissing the palm. "It's easy, with Mike or Lacey. Mom and Dad." He dropped Wyatt's hand but stayed close to him. "It's not so easy with you, Wyatt. What I feel for you, it's different. With you I'm a little lost because I'm not used to it.

I meant it, though. Yesterday. When I said I love you, I meant it. It's not easy for me to say it when it's… romantic."

"How about I'll say it and you can say 'you too'? Then I'll know what you mean. Anytime you want to say it but you can't, just say 'you too.'"

Timothy smiled. "Yeah, I think I can do that."

WYATT KNOCKED on Maddy LaFleur's door and stepped back, waiting for her to answer.

"Wyatt," she said with a small smile. "It's nice to see you."

"I wanted to let you know we got him, Miss Maddy. The guy who… who killed Bobby. We found him."

"Did you? Bobby." She leaned against the doorframe and looked down at the ground, her eyes wet with unshed tears.

"I'm sorry."

"No," she said quickly. Miss Maddy reached out and grabbed on to his arm. "Thank you. Will I get to bury him?"

He nodded slowly. "Yes, ma'am. It'll be a little bit longer, because the sheriff has to take care of some things."

"Did he suffer? My baby?"

Wyatt shook his head. "No, ma'am. I don't believe he did." Wyatt had thought about it long and hard. He wondered if Bobby had hurt. If he hadn't met Bobby, would he still be alive? He'd thought about that too, even spoke with Mrs. Mitchell and the sheriff about it. They made sure to say Wyatt had nothing to feel guilty about. But still….

"I'm grateful."

"I have some things for you." Wyatt held up the papers he'd found in the wall at Big Tommy's place. He'd taken out the articles about Bobby's disappearance. Miss Maddy didn't need to see them. "They're old papers of Bobby's, things from school. I thought you might like them." Wyatt handed her everything and smiled weakly.

"Really? Thank you."

"I've got to go, but I'll stop by and see you real soon, Miss Maddy." He'd backed up and stepped down off the porch when she called out to him.

"Wyatt?"

He stopped and turned around.

"You loved him, right? I heard about you from your mom. You loved Bobby."

"I did, Miss Maddy."

She smiled. "Good. I'm sure glad Bobby knew what it was to be in love. And I'm glad it was someone sweet as you."

He nodded at her, afraid of what his voice might sound like if he answered. He went to his car and drove back to the Mitchells' house. Wyatt parked out front and went into the backyard from the gate, sat down at the picnic table, and reached into his pocket. There was one thing he kept. Wyatt cut the writing off the top, leaving just Bobby's careful penmanship.

He keeps me safe at night and day
He keeps the cruel, cruel world at bay
He is strong and gentle and lovely and kind
He is always on my mind
But he hides
From himself
From me
From the world both here
And the world to be
Will he ever
Just be here?

"You know it's about you, right?" Timothy had said to him when Wyatt suggested giving the papers from the box to Miss Maddy.

"You think?" Wyatt went back and forth between the paper and Timothy.

Timothy ran his hand down Wyatt's face gently. "Definitely."

"You think she'd mind if I kept it?"

Timothy shook his head. "Nope. I don't think she'd mind at all."

"And…." Wyatt looked guilty, almost blushing. "And you don't mind if I keep it?"

"No, Wyatt. I think it'd be real nice for you to keep it."

Wyatt had taken Timothy's hand in his own. "Thanks."

WHEN WYATT rang the bell on Christmas Eve, Timothy's mother answered the door wearing a bright red sweater and black skirt. The Mitchell household was different than it had been three months before.

Wyatt had moved into Deputy Mike's house right before Thanksgiving. As much as both Timothy's parents protested, when Mike mentioned he needed to find a new roommate, Wyatt thought it might be best if he moved in with the deputy. He could pay his own way and not feel like he was leeching off the Mitchells. Plus, he could finally get his dog away from his mom's house. He went to get Colonel when she was at work. He didn't leave her a note, just took the dog, who seemed thinner and more nervous than before, but Colonel was thrilled to be back with Wyatt and had latched on to Mike quickly. Colonel seemed to understand that Wyatt had him for good now and was slowly getting used to watching Wyatt and Timothy make out.

Pastor Steve was already serving his time, and the DA had linked Matt Thomas to three murders, plus the attempted murders of Timothy and Wyatt. Thomas was pushing his lawyer to take the case to court, and his attorney was pushing for him to take a plea deal.

"Wyatt!" Timothy's mother hugged him as he came in the door. "Don't you look handsome." She smiled at his button-up shirt and striped tie and dress pants. She'd bought them for him to wear tonight. "Mike, you look handsome too." She kissed Mike's cheek and waved them into the living room where Isabelle had stood up the second she heard the doorbell. She held out her hand to Wyatt.

"So, you're the guy who's making out with my brother?"

The sheriff shook his head. "Isabelle, don't say things like that to the boy. It's good to see you again, son." He was wearing a crisp white shirt and a red and green tie with reindeer all over it.

"Good to see you, too, sir." Wyatt's face and neck felt hot, but he held on to Isabelle's hand. "It's nice to meet you."

She smirked. "It won't be so nice over dinner. I intend to ask you a ton of embarrassing questions." She leaned over as her father got Mike a beer. "Timothy's upstairs, getting all fancied up for you. Why don't you go up and say hello?"

Wyatt smiled at her and practically ran up the stairs. Even though they saw each other at school every day, it wasn't the same.

Wyatt knocked on the door lightly and opened it, hoping to catch Timothy in his underwear. "Hey," he said quietly as Timothy was straightening his tie.

"Hey. I didn't want you to see me until I was all put together."

"You look good." Wyatt stepped inside the bedroom.

"You too." Timothy pointed at him. "You have a shirt with buttons. Is it your first?"

"Ha. Ha. You're so funny."

"You can close the door, you know. I'm pretty sure now that you're not living here, we can keep the door closed."

"Nice." Wyatt closed it quietly and perched on the edge of the bed, and Timothy sat down next to him. They kissed for a few minutes before Wyatt pulled away. He looked at the floor. "That was good. It's been a while."

"Well, we can spend all of winter break making out. And it's nice. You not smelling like cigarettes."

"Almost a whole month now."

"How's it feel?" Timothy brought one leg under the other as he shifted on the bed.

"It sucks." Wyatt laughed. "But I'm glad it makes you happy."

"You make me happy. And if you tell Isabelle I said something so sappy, I'll break your leg."

"It'll be our secret." Wyatt exhaled a laugh. "I was thinking, and no pressure here. Since your birthday is next month. And you'll be eighteen... maybe we could? Sorry. I shouldn't ask that. I was thinking.... I think I'm ready. I mean I've wanted to be with you for a long time. But I think I'm ready now. I think we're ready. Don't you?" He felt foolish and spoke so fast his words strung together. "Sorry. I shouldn't say that. I shouldn't think just because I want it means you do too." He cleared his throat. "Hey, I got some information about the trade school over in Greenville. I could take some classes there come the fall, woodworking. Get some real fancy education."

"That's great," Timothy said, smiling. "And Wyatt, it's okay. I do understand, you know. I'd be lying if I said I didn't think about it." Timothy rested a hand on Wyatt's arm. "I think we're ready too. Really. I'd like that."

"Yeah?" Wyatt stood up and held out his hand. "C'mon, we should go downstairs before your dad comes up here and yells."

"Has Dad ever yelled at you?" Timothy took his hand, and they started down the steps.

"Not yet," Wyatt said, "but why give him a reason?"

Timothy tugged on Wyatt's hand, bringing him to a halt at the bottom of the stairs. "Hey, Wyatt?"

"Yeah?"

"You too."

They smiled at each other.

JOHN R. PETRIE grew up in Boston and now lives in the Bronx, NY. Almost his entire working career has been spent around books, from his first job in the town library to more than twenty years bookselling in one of the biggest bookstores in the US. He's also worked for the Housing Works thrift stores in NYC, Valiant Entertainment Comics, and is now a bookstore manager, which gives him too much access to books and not enough time to read them.

He's had stories published in *True Romance* magazine, had a play he wrote produced at his college, acted, danced, and was nominated for a Barrymore award playing Belize in *Angels in America*.

He stays up too late, eats too much junk food, and has been reading *Wonder Woman* comics for over forty years.

He is very, very happy to be published by Harmony Ink Press. He hopes to continue writing stories which make people smile.

He can be reached at johnrpetriewrites@gmail.com and can be found on twitter at johnpetriewrite. He likes to hear from people, so say hello.

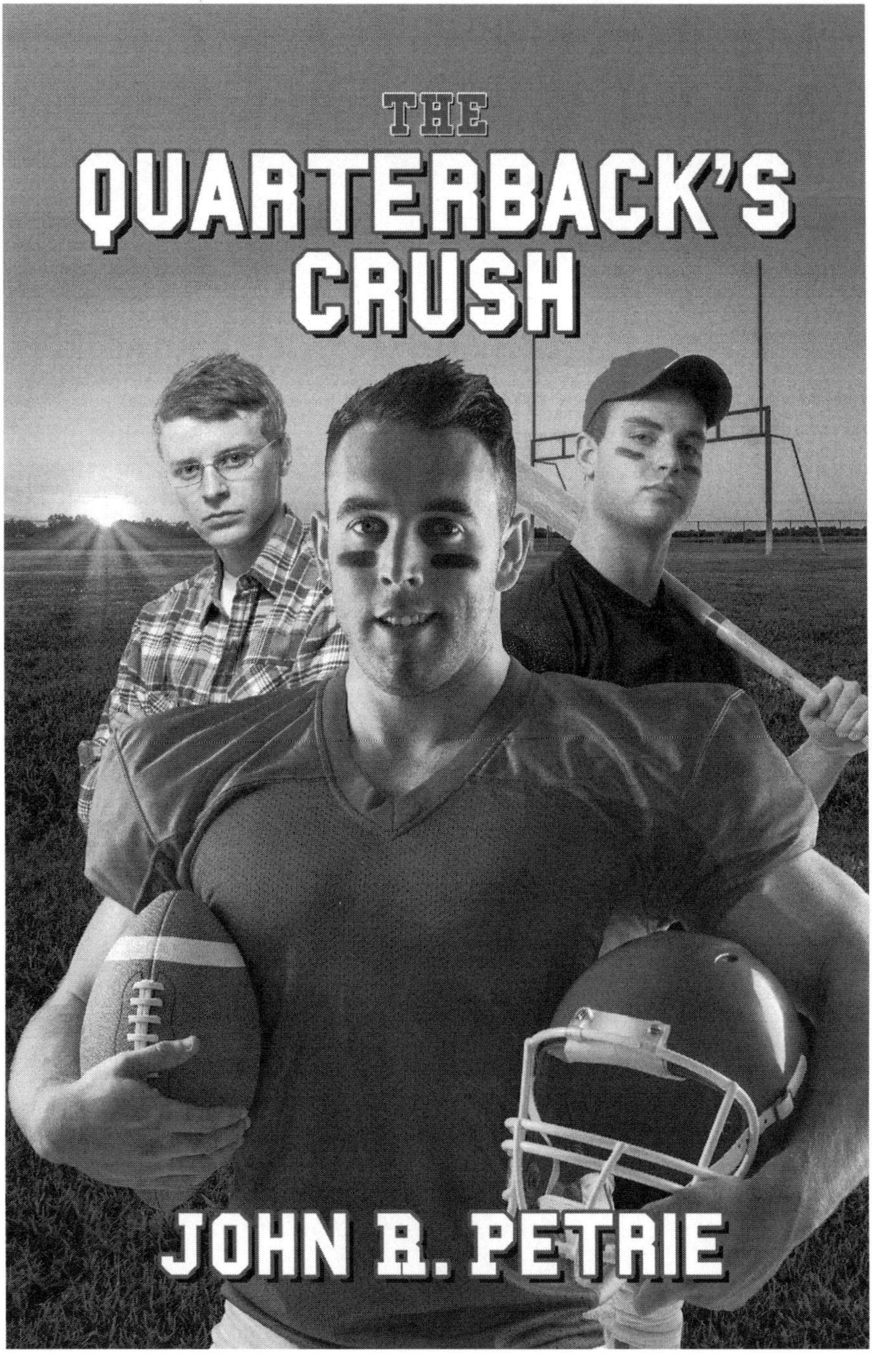
THE
QUARTERBACK'S
CRUSH
JOHN R. PETRIE

Dylan Porter needs a Hail Mary....

Because it'll take a miracle for him to pass English and trig so he can stay on the football team, get a scholarship, and go away to college—where the distance from his friends and family will give him the confidence to finally tell them he's gay. But flunking his classes will put a stop to all of his dreams.

Luckily there's Tommy Peterson to help him. In Dylan's eyes, Tommy's perfect. Short, smart, and sexy, he checks every one of Dylan's boxes, so it's no surprise when Dylan falls head over heels. Too bad Tommy doesn't seem to feel the same, and a pining Dylan accidentally outs himself to the team. Now Dylan has to deal with the fallout of his coming out to the team, his dad, and his coach while trying to score the ultimate touchdown—the love of Tommy Peterson.

www.harmonyinkpress.com